MAESTRO'S MOVE

MAESTRO'S MOVE

a Bradley Whitman novel

CHRISTINE NOYES

Haley's

Athol, Massachusetts

Haley's
488 South Main Street
Athol, MA 01331
marcia2gagliardi@gmail.com • 978.249.9400

Copy edited by Debra Ellis.

Cover designed by Christine Noyes.
Cover image courtesy of Adobe Stock Photos.

International Standard Book Number, trade paperback: 978-1-956055-37-5

International Standard Book Number, eBook, Kindle: 978-1-956055-38-2

International Standard Book Number, audiobook: 978-1-956055-39-9

Library of Congress Control Number: 2025924453

For my devoted readers who inspire me every day.
And for Al, forever in my heart.

CONTENTS

DUST TO DUST

He placed his dinner dish in the kitchen sink, kissed his wife on the cheek, and shuffled out the door. A red paisley handkerchief hung from the back pocket of his worn overalls, and the soles of his boots were as thin as cloth.

The sun had just begun to set as the elderly farmer reached his fields. While walking among his crops, he held his hand over the top of the wheat stalks as if willing them to reach for his palm. With bones creaking, the farmer expelled an involuntary grunt as he knelt. He dug into the cracked earth with his wrinkled and calloused hand, then watched the arid dirt slip back to the ground through his thick fingers. With much effort, he stood, then wiped the dirt onto his chambray shirt.

He continued his walk among the rows and inspected the stalks. With scarce rain the previous fall, crops were well behind schedule in growing tillers critical to the yield of the plants. However, he knew better than to worry. It took too much energy and never provided a solution. Instead, as always, he chose to have faith.

"Be nice to me now," he spoke to his stunted crops. "I don't know how much time we have left together."

He reached for his cap, pulled it off his head, and revealed a thick crop of bright white hair. Wiping sweat from his brow, he dragged his sleeve across his forehead, then glanced at the setting sun. With its final rays, the sun seemed to concentrate all its energy on the old man. Had anyone been there to witness the moment, the sparkle from the farmer's brilliant blue eyes would have been a sight to see.

A thin smile creased his lips as he once again wiped sweat from his brow, an increasingly common occurrence. Perspiration had accompanied a slight headache, and he'd been having difficulty swallowing. Not wishing to worry her, he hadn't mentioned to his wife the discomfort he had felt the previous twenty-four hours, but something told him he was beginning his final countdown. He just hadn't expected it so quickly.

He scuffed his worn leather boots in the dirt before turning toward the farmhouse. He took only five more steps before his throat swelled and drastically reduced his air flow. Pus-filled blisters formed where perspiration had been, and his royal blue eyes turned black.

Staring toward the heavens but seeing only darkness, he collapsed to the ground with his arms by his side. He once again dug his hands into the scorched earth, clinging to his lifelong mistress, one of the few components of his grueling life on whom he could always depend and with whom he would soon be reunited.

THE DEVIL'S CURSE

Bradley Whitman slumped in his wheelchair as the gravity of his thoughts sunk his chin to his chest. The computer screen he studied displayed an archived Hopkinton Engineering Institute's newsletter dated ten years earlier. The headline read, Diabolus Pestis Strikes Again.

Diabolus Pestis, the devil's curse, Bradley translated. He remembered the mysterious string of events chronicled in the newsletter from the nearby institute. At the time, he had been with the Chelsea, Massachusetts, division of the Federal Bureau of Investigation for only two years. Bradley's old friend, then Supervisory Special Agent Derek Richards, had hired him fresh from graduation from Massachusetts Institute of Technology, as an analyst.

It was no surprise that Bradley went to work for Derek. Each had done his best to make it happen. But life, as usual, is ever changing. Derek accepted a promotion to executive assistant director of FBI Criminal, Cyber, Response, and Services that moved him to headquarters in Washington, DC. Nearly nineteen months later, Bradley's new position with the FBI National Security Branch brought him there as well. Although Bradley no longer worked directly for Derek, they occasionally worked the same cases.

Bradley tried to recall circumstances around the unsolved, life-threatening incidents attributed to the satanic spell that occurred at the prestigious Hopkinton Engineering Institute but remembered little. As he read through old issues of HEI Weekly, he could remember only the underlying feeling of helplessness he refused to show in those days.

In everything other than his physical being, Bradley had always had the confidence of a mountain lion doing battle with a mouse. But as a young man, the inability to use his legs caused him to feel inadequate. The one-in-a-million enterovirus he contracted at the age of six had cost him his original dream of following in his father's footsteps and becoming a marine.

At twelve, after a chance encounter with Derek during an FBI investigation, he made up his mind to join the FBI. He had hoped to be a field agent, but disappointment struck him once again as his physical limitations held him to an analyst position with the bureau. He had worked hard over the years to accept his fate and to conquer what he called his psychological flaws, the most prominent of which was his savior complex.

Sitting shirtless in his wheelchair in front of his computer, Bradley delved into the actions of the man who had since been identified as responsible for the atrocities at HEI. The same man he had grossly underestimated just eight months earlier remained a threat. And with that thought, Bradley felt the scrutiny of a sword-wielding mouse slash at his lion's confidence.

"You said you were going to the bathroom," a voice said from behind.

Bradley straightened in his chair, then turned it around to face her.

Wearing nothing but his blue oxford shirt, Cassie rigidly stood with hands on hips. Her short black hair sprouted in every direction, and her five-foot, five-inch frame loomed larger than it was due to the menacing glare from her deep brown eyes. With that gaze, Bradley knew she could instill fear into most everyone with whom she came in contact. She had an unpredictable aura about her. The only evident softness to Cassie Papadakis was her smooth, caramel skin. Bradley allowed his eyes to travel from her accusing glare down to her bare feet.

Her defiant stance made him grin.

"What are you smiling about?" she barked.

"Am I smiling? Sorry. I know how you hate it when people seem happy," Bradley said.

"What the hell, Bradley. You're out here working again? It's Sunday. I've got to leave today. It's hardly worth me coming all this way if you're not going to pay attention to me."

Rusty, Bradley's black-and-rust-colored Doberman Pinscher, pranced into the room and sat next to Cassie.

Cassie continued, "I get more attention from Rusty than from you."

"I couldn't sleep," Bradley replied.

"I hadn't planned on going back to sleep, numbnuts. I thought you were coming right back to bed."

"That was two hours ago, Cassie."

"Yeah, well, I fell back to sleep. But that's not the point. I thought we could go another round, but if you'd rather sit in front of your computer, then fine, I'll just pack and go home." She finished with a deep huff.

"Are you done?" Bradley asked.

Cassie began to open her mouth, but Bradley held up his hands in defeat.

"I'm sorry. You're right. I've been preoccupied, and that's not fair to you. Look," Bradley said as he turned back around, "I'm shutting down the computer."

For a moment, neither said a word.

"I'm really sorry," Bradley told her as he inched his way toward her.

"No, I'm sorry. That was stupid. It's just that . . . "

"What?" he asked as he reached for her hands.

"Sometimes I wonder if this is a bad idea."

"Why would you think that?"

"Because I live in Boston, and you live in DC. And it's not like we're a couple or anything. I mean, don't you think our relationship is a little weird?"

"Maybe unconventional, but not weird. I like you, Cassie. I enjoy spending time together without having to worry about the whole relationship thing." Bradley paused, then continued. "Unless you're changing your mind about that."

"No. I'm still not ready for a relationship. I'm not sure I ever will be."

"I told you before. I think you're more than ready. And you don't need to worry about hurting my feelings. I'd be happy for you if you found someone special. I want that for you."

Cassie moved to the couch. Bradley followed and parked his chair in front of her. Rusty jumped on the couch and cuddled beside her.

She sighed, then said, "I'm going on a date."

He didn't expect it. A boot to the gut. A totally irrational response to Cassie's news. But he wouldn't let it show.

"That's great! Who is he?"

"A guy I met in court."

"A petty thief?" Bradley teased.

"A lawyer. He was assigned to a case that I investigated for Damien. He's been after me for a month to go to dinner with him. He finally caught me at a weak moment."

"A weak moment? What does one of those look like on you?"

"Stop, Bradley. I'm serious. What am I going to do?"

"Is he a good guy?" Bradley asked.

"Damien says he is."

One of the best lawyers in Boston, Damien Sullivan, had helped Bradley prove his friend Zayt, a Navy Seal who served three tours in Afghanistan, innocent when he was framed for murder. Bradley and Cassie met when Damien hired her as the private investigator on Zayt's case. She was largely responsible for Zayt being exonerated. Bradley and Cassie had worked on the case together but not without personal clashes. They eventually found mutual ground and ultimately a mutual bed.

"Well, I trust Damien's judgement, don't you?" Bradley asked.

"Yes, that's not the problem."

"Then what is?"

She flashed him the "You-know-what-the-problem-is" glare.

Bradley knew the look. Before they met, Cassie was in a long-term abusive relationship. After she extricated herself from it, she found it nearly impossible to trust men. Bradley understood that brandishing an intimidating personality was Cassie's way of protecting herself.

Bradley grasped her hand and said, "You trust me, right?"

"Most of the time."

"Come on, Cassie."

"Yes, I trust you. But you're you! An FBI nerd in a . . ."

"Wheelchair?" Bradley interrupted.

"I was going to say a dorky oxford shirt, but now that you mention it, if I'm being brutally honest, the wheelchair did make it easier. Sorry."

"Really? You didn't seem to cut me any slack when we met," Bradley laughed, hoping to lighten the mood.

"Seriously. What am I going to do about Tom?"

"Tom?" Bradley felt a twinge of jealousy, a useless emotion since he decided he would never again allow himself to fall in love. "You're going to dress in your best baggy cargo pants, do something with that electromagnetic mop on your head, and go have a nice dinner with Tom."

"I don't know if I can."

"You can. You're ready."

Rusty lay his head on Cassie's lap and gazed into her eyes.

"See? Rusty agrees. Now, are you going to pack? Or are we going to . . . . How did you so eloquently put it? Go another round?"

The corners of Cassie's mouth curled, but only slightly. "Lead on, Maestro."

Bradley laughed at the use of the nickname his college chemistry professor had given him. "I never should have told you about that. I don't know why I did. I never even told Derek about it, and he's my best friend."

"But the name fits you so well," Cassie smiled. With Bradley's hand still in hers, she stood, and they made their way to the bedroom.

Three hours later, Bradley booted his computer. While the desktop updated, he thought of Cassie on her way to the airport. The simple, uncomplicated relationship they had had seemed anything but at that moment.

He felt uneasy about his involuntary reaction to her news of dating. Not because he was in love with her. He knew he would never fall in love again. And he knew she didn't love him. They were two broken people who each used the other to try to make themselves feel whole. And it had worked until that morning. Bradley knew he had no right to feel betrayed, but illogically, he did.

"You're a selfish bastard, Bradley Whitman."

Lying by his feet, Rusty looked up.

"What are you looking at?"

Bradley reached down to pet him, and Rusty gladly accepted the affection.

Once the desktop came to life, his research captured his full attention. He didn't take his eyes off the screen for the next four and a half hours.

The focus of his research was a man named Ali al-Haqani.

After the sudden death of his fiancée, Laney Weaver, Bradley was at the lowest point of his life. When he found himself considering suicide, he knew he needed to take drastic measures. He left his job with the FBI and his home, his family, and his friends. He and Rusty spent the following year traveling through Italy, Spain, Bhutan, Tibet, and India. It was in India that he received a message from his old friend Derek Richards. A national threat was imminent, and he needed Bradley's help. The threat was Ali al-Haqani.

Bradley flew to DC to help with the case. More like brothers than friends, or boss and subordinate, Bradley and Derek were always there for one another. No one knew him better. With Bradley's help, and working with the National Security Branch, they were able to thwart Ali al-Haqani's attack. But there was unfinished business. Al-Haqani remained at large. And the unresolved matter gnawed at Bradley.

Al-Haqani had struck several US targets, killing hundreds, before the FBI averted his final attempt in Cambridge, Massachusetts. But Ali al-Haqani was never apprehended. And not until the smoke cleared did Bradley realize that he had been duped.

Haqani had outmaneuvered him. He had used the attacks to gain intelligence of the workings of the FBI. He studied their tactics and responses to his strikes. It seemed that al-Haqani had a much larger plan in mind, and Bradley had no idea what it might be. He found himself in unfamiliar territory. He questioned the one thing he could always count on—his analytical and profiling skills.

Ali al-Haqani had not been heard from since his last plot eight months prior, but Bradley and the FBI knew it was just a matter of time. And Bradley wanted to be armed with as much information as possible.

If it weren't for his cell phone ringing, Bradley would have spent the rest of his day off trying to get inside al-Haqani's head.

"Yeah?" Bradley brusquely answered.

"Well, I don't know how I feel about that greeting, Bradley."

"Cate?"

"It's bad enough you live so close and I never get to see you," Derek's wife said.

"I'm sorry. I didn't realize it was you calling. I'm a little preoccupied. How is the most wonderful woman in the world?" Bradley asked.

"I'm on to your adulation tactics. But," Cate hesitated, "it doesn't mean you should stop."

"The luckiest day of Derek's life was the day he met you on that cruise ship. If he hadn't scooped you up, I would have."

"Bradley, you were twelve years old."

"Yes, but not so young as not to know a good woman when I saw her."

"And you haven't changed a bit since then," Cate giggled.

As much as Bradley would have liked to believe that, too many things had happened in his life to sour the young Bradley's enthusiasm. Not only had his personal dreams been shattered, but his professional life had developed a chink in its armor. He had begun to second-guess his instincts. And his instincts, Bradley thought, were what made him who he was.

As always, he hid his doubts and replied, "That's why you are my number one girl. You still see me as that overconfident, cocky kid. So, what's up?" Bradley asked.

"I'm calling to remind you that dinner is at six o'clock and I will not accept any excuses. You've backed out the last two times. I'm starting to think you really don't like me at all." Cate feigned a whine.

"Cate, I . . ."

"Nope."

"I really . . ."

"Unh-unh!"

"Would you believe . . ."

"Six o'clock. Bring wine." Cate hung up the phone.

He had forgotten he had committed to dinner at Derek and Cate's that evening and wished that he hadn't. His reluctance wasn't because he didn't enjoy their company but because Cate would inevitably bring up the subject of dating, and it made him uncomfortable.

It had been more than two years since he lost Laney from a sudden brain aneurism. She was the one person who made him feel truly whole. The idea of giving himself completely to anyone else was unthinkable. Not only did he believe there was no one else in the world who could take her place, he was also exceptionally loyal. And even though he knew Laney would want him to be happy and find someone with whom to share his life, he just couldn't reconcile that option within his heart.

Cate didn't understand that. Or, if she did, she was unwilling to accept it. Cate only wanted Bradley to be happy, and he loved her for that. Besides, how could she know what he felt. He never told her, or anyone.

It was 5:30 when Bradley packed a bottle of red wine, a bottle of white, and one Doberman Pinscher to head to Derek and Cate's. Once Rusty realized where they were headed, his back end jiggled like gelatin in the bed of a pickup truck traveling a winding dirt road at ninety miles per hour.

Rusty went almost everywhere with Bradley. He was a registered service dog complete with red vest and collar. The two had found each other during an FBI investigation back when Bradley worked in Chelsea. Bradley had placed himself in a dangerous situation, and Rusty—whose owner had recently passed away—was there to save Bradley's life. The two had been inseparable ever since. On the occasion Bradley needed to be out of town or couldn't take Rusty to work, Cate looked after him. Cate and Rusty were best friends, so it wasn't unusual for Rusty to join them whenever they got together.

Derek and Cate had purchased their home in DC with Bradley in mind. They constructed a ramp to the front door and, when Bradley first arrived in Washington, he and Rusty lived in their first-floor bedroom. The house provided an open floor plan, making it easy for Bradley to maneuver his wheelchair from room to room.

When he and Rusty arrived for dinner, they showed themselves into the house. The no-knock protocol had been established long before. He found Derek mixing drinks in the living room.

"Dammit, I lost the bet."

"Funny," Bradley said glibly.

Rusty ran into the kitchen to find Cate.

"Drink?"

"Absolutely."

Derek handed Bradley a Manhattan and poured one for himself. Bradley took a sip and let slip a moan of approval.

Bradley raised his glass to Derek. "You missed your calling. You should have been a bartender."

"I was. Back at Northeastern, my junior and senior year. But I worked near campus, so most of the drinks I served came out of the tap. Didn't I ever tell you about that?"

"No. You never mentioned it. I never pictured you working for a living. I mean, other than the bureau."

"I had to eat," Derek chuckled as he sat on the couch.

"Why is that?"

"Why did I have to eat?"

"No. Why haven't you ever mentioned bartending before?"

Derek paused. "I don't know. I guess it just never came up."

Bradley's eyebrows pinched, and he turned to stare at the wall. Then he said, "You know everything about me. Everything. The good, the bad, the ugly, and the very ugly. Ever since I was a kid."

"That's because you were a kid when we met."

Bradley processed Derek's reasoning, then contemplatively replied, "But we're like brothers. It seems to me I should have known that about you."

Derek moved to the edge of the couch and placed his elbows on his knees, drink still in hand.

"What's this about? What's going on in that head of yours?"

Having fallen deep into thought, Bradley snapped back to the conversation. "Huh? Nothing. It's just odd, that's all."

Derek wasn't convinced that it was nothing. He knew Bradley too well. Something was bothering him, and it had nothing to do with not knowing Derek had bartended in his younger days. But he also knew that, whatever it was, Bradley would be unwilling to share it.

Derek knew the best way to uncover Bradley's innermost thoughts was to outflank him. If he used the direct approach, Bradley would deflect. If he circled around the subject, then caught him off guard, he might reveal a clue. Derek had been using the tactic for years.

"Bradley. You finally made it!" Cate said as, followed by Rusty, she came into the room. She leaned down and kissed Bradley on the cheek.

Bradley reached for the bag that he had stuck by his side and handed it to Cate.

"I didn't know what you were serving, so I brought one of each," he said.

"Perfect. Red with dinner, white with dessert," she said as she took the bag. "Dinner will be a few more minutes."

Bradley inhaled the scent drifting from the kitchen. "Is that Osso Bucco I smell?"

Thrilled to see Bradley's smile, Cate replied, "It is. Your favorite, as I recall."

"Wow, what's the occasion?" Bradley asked.

Cate replied, "Anytime we can get you here for dinner is an occasion. I've become an expert at this dish. It's just too bad you missed it the last two times I made it." Cate sent Bradley a gibing glance.

"His loss was my gain," Derek said. "And I don't think berating Bradley is going to keep him coming back, Cate."

"I'm sorry. I don't mean to berate. I just miss you, Bradley. I see Rusty more than I see you." Rusty looked up from the floor at Cate. She reached and stroked his head.

"I know. I miss you, too. I'll try to be better. This is nice, Cate. Thank you."

"I'm glad you're here," Cate said as she reached for Bradley's hand. "Oh, and Sheila made me promise to say hello and give you a hug."

"How are your sister and David. And the twins?"

"The boys are doing amazing things. Max just got another promotion, and Alex is working on his second novel. He's in India or Bhutan or someplace like that. Sheila was going off her rocker because she hadn't gotten his postcard yet. Apparently, he writes to her like clockwork, once a week. And, you know that David is planning to make Alex's first novel into a movie, right?" Cate asked excitedly.

"Yes, I know," Bradley sunk his head.

Derek shot Cate a warning glare. Cate's eyes widened as she realized her foible.

Alex Carson's first published novel was based on the real-life account of the Pathside Predator, a case Bradley and Derek had worked together. There were several reasons that the subject triggered bad memories for Bradley, foremost being that was the case he was working when Laney died. It was after the Predator case that Bradley decided to leave the bureau—and everyone else—behind.

"Anyway, Sheila sends her love," Cate said.

"Be sure to send her my love when you speak to her next," Bradley replied.

For several minutes, they ate in silence until Derek asked Bradley, "So, what have you been doing with your weekend?"

Bradley hadn't told Derek or Cate about Cassie's visit. In fact, he wasn't sure if they even knew that he and Cassie were still in contact with one another. He never discussed it. Not that he was ashamed, but he just didn't want to answer questions about their intermittent encounters. And he thought Cate would get the wrong idea. It was because of a visit from Cassie that Bradley had backed out of the previous dinner.

"Not much. I caught up on some reading," Bradley said, neglecting to mention the reading came in the form of archived HEI newsletters. "How about you two?"

"Yes, Derek. Tell Bradley how you spent your morning."

Derek rolled his eyes.

"I had to go into the office," he said as Cate let go a huff. "But only for a couple of hours. Then I came home and offered to help with dinner but was told my services were not required."

Bradley chuckled.

"What are you laughing at?" Cate asked.

"I love it when you two pretend to be mad at each other. It's like a vintage fifties television show."

Derek and Cate stared waveringly at each other, then laughed.

After dinner, Cate placed angel food cake on the table while Derek opened the Riesling. Along with cake, Cate brought an individually wrapped Twinkie. Rusty jumped from the floor and sat in front of her. He raised first one paw, then the other. Cate giggled.

"You really need to stop spoiling him," Bradley said.

"But he loves these. Why do you think he came running to me the minute you got here?"

"Because he loves you?"

"Well, yes. But mostly because he smelled the Twinkies."

"Yes, Rusty's sense of tracking the smell of sweets is well documented. Just go easy on them. I can't imagine they're part of his veterinarian's recommended diet."

"Don't worry. He only gets one on special occasions."

Cate opened the cream-filled yellow sponge cake treat and fed it to Rusty. Bradley would swear he saw him smile.

Knowing he had to drive home, Bradley declined a glass of Riesling.

When he did, Cate said, "I'll go make some coffee," and went to the far side of the kitchen. That time, Rusty stayed lying on the floor next to Bradley.

"Why didn't you tell Cate about Cassie?" Derek quietly asked.

Surprised, Bradley cocked his head toward Derek. "Are you spying on me?"

Derek chuckled. "No. I talked to Damien yesterday, and he said Cassie was in DC for the weekend. I put two and two together."

With his elbows resting on his wheelchair's arms, Bradley linked his fingers together, then rested his chin on them and whispered, "I don't want Cate to get the wrong idea."

"And me?"

"I didn't want you to think I was a heel."

"Why would I think that?"

"I don't know."

"That's a copout. Why would you think that I would think you're a heel?"

Bradley paused before answering. "Because you're perfect, Derek. The perfect gentleman. The perfect husband. You've got the perfect wife, house, job, and . . . "

"Everything you've ever wanted," Derek said.

Rather than allow his emotions to get the better of him, Bradley did what he always did. He attacked himself. "Because I am a heel. I'm using Cassie."

"For what?"

Bradley glared at Derek.

"Besides sex," Derek clarified.

"Isn't that enough?"

"For some men, maybe. Not for you."

"She thinks I'm a brilliant analyst. She won't say it, but I know she thinks it."

"You are a brilliant analyst," Derek said matter-of-factly.

But the apprehensive look on Bradley's face showed Derek what he had been fishing for. He had just outflanked Bradley. And if he was correct in his assumptions about what was bothering Bradley, Derek would need to watch him closely.

"It will only be a few more minutes for coffee," Cate said as she returned to her chair and lifted her wine glass.

"Guess what, Cate. Bradley thinks I'm a perfect husband," Derek said with a wide grin.

Cate nearly spit her wine onto the table. "Excuse me?" she asked.

"Seriously. He just said so."

"Derek!" Bradley snapped.

Cate laughed. "Are you trying to make me choke?"

"I didn't . . ." Bradley started to say, but Derek interrupted him.

"I suppose he's right. I am tall, dashingly handsome, and a very gener . . ."

Cate cut in. "And full of shit!" Mockingly she added, "You're a mildly good-looking fifty-three-year-old who nearly always puts his work before his wife. You leave your dirty socks in the living room, all your home projects remain undone, and you never take me dancing. And another thing. When you shave in the morning, you leave little bits of hair all over the place. It's disgusting."

Bradley couldn't contain his laughter. His lips slightly parted in contrived wonder, Derek looked at Bradley and raised his brows.

Cate continued. "You're just lucky you married the perfect wife!"

Derek raised his wine glass toward Cate and replied, "Now that's something on which we can all agree."

The remainder of the evening was pleasant, and Cate only skimmed the idea that Bradley should begin dating again. Bradley handled it well, saying he was getting everything he needed out of life and was perfectly happy.

On the ride home, Bradley replayed the brief conversation he had with Derek about Cassie. He thought it odd that Derek seemed offended about him keeping Cassie's visit a secret. It wasn't like him at all. It didn't fit his profile. But, Bradley thought, maybe that's just another example of something I missed.

WE'RE ALL HIDING SOMETHING

Monday morning, Bradley and Rusty drove to the FBI Academy in Quantico, Virginia. Bradley was scheduled to give a presentation on profiling for a class of recruits. The hour-and-a-half drive had given Bradley time to practice his foundational seminar with Rusty as his audience. Although he had always been comfortable in front of a classroom, the past eight months had him wondering if he was an imposter—a man posing as an expert on the art of profiling.

With Rusty by his side, Bradley rolled his chair into the full lecture hall. The eager recruits immediately went quiet. They saw what most people saw—a youthful looking, broad-shouldered man with thick arms and chest sitting with thin, weakened legs perched on the wheelchair footrest.

Bradley had long since gotten used to initial reactions from strangers. And he either used it to put people at ease or to keep them off guard, whichever proved more advantageous.

"One of you is hiding something!" Bradley stated as he turned off his cell phone to prevent interruption.

Each of the 250 people in the room looked puzzled and began to scan the class for the culprit.

Bradley waited until the group was sufficiently ill-at-ease.

"In a group of people this size, it's inevitable that someone is hiding something. Maybe it's a propensity for footie pajamas or a fear of dandelions."

The group laughed at the thought.

"Or maybe it's a desire to decapitate a small animal," Bradley said.

The mood in the room darkened.

"Look around you again. What do you know about each other? Is anyone in this room confident that you're not sitting next to a serial killer or rapist? Come on. Raise your hand if you're sure."

No one raised their hand. Then Bradley raised his hand and glanced down at Rusty sitting by his side. He received another laugh.

"My name is Agent Bradley Whitman, and I'm here to talk about criminal profiling. And this is Rusty. Before this class is over, Rusty will reveal the culprit concealing the secret."

More sideways glances ensued.

"We'll only touch on a few aspects of profiling, so please understand there's much more to the subject than what we discuss today. This is merely a simplistic overview of the process. Feel free to ask questions along the way."

A young man in the third row raised his hand.

Bradley laughed. "Wow, that was quick. Go ahead with your question."

The man stood. "Hello, Agent Whitman. My name is Gary Hart. I was just wondering if you're the same Agent Whitman who tracked down the Pathside Predator in Massachusetts."

Bradley cleared his throat. "Yes, Gary. I worked on the Lessing case with my fellow agents in the Chelsea department. It was a team effort, as it always is, and we received a lot of support from law enforcement agencies from every affected state. Communication is essential in this job."

"But you were the one who shot her, right?" Gary asked.

Bradley lowered his head. Silence filled the room.

After a moment, Bradley lifted his head and looked directly at Gary. "Yes. It was one of my greatest failures."

"I don't understand," Gary said.

"I know."

Gary sat.

"Look. It's not like television or movies when you're out there. There's nothing glamorous about this job. Often, we deal with broken people. But they're still human beings. They have mothers, fathers, sisters, and brothers. Many have families of their own. You must get to know your unknown subject, and I mean really know them—the whys and the hows. That will lead you to the who."

Bradley took a deep breath.

"Write this down. It is the most important thing I'll say today. Why plus how equals who! Why did the unsub do what they did? Did the unsub come prepared? Or was the crime unplanned? Maybe it was planned but poorly executed. Delving into these questions will give you a decent profile of the perpetrator. Behavior reflects personality. It's also imperative to examine victimology and demographics to understand your unsub."

Bradley gave the class a moment to catch up. The sound of tapping laptop keys made him grin.

He continued.

"When profiling criminals, whether murderers, rapists, or thieves, you need to examine the condition of the crime scenes, the victims, and the suspect's or suspects' behavior. The perpetrator will fall into one of three categories—organized, disorganized, or mixed. We're going to talk about the first two today, organized and disorganized, as these are the two most common."

For nearly an hour, Bradley explained the difference in traits between organized and disorganized criminals. He told how an organized suspect pre-plans their crime and covers their tracks, how they tend to have stable lives, a good job, and are most likely in a relationship. He then spoke of how the lack of planning of a disorganized suspect's crime scene would look chaotic. The disorganized perpetrator would be socially awkward, have an inconsistent work history in a menial job, and commit their crimes close to home. They're often confused or distressed, possibly with a drug problem or mental health issue.

The class listened intently until, from a side door, a woman entered the room holding a sheet of paper. She approached Bradley and handed it to him.

Bradley read it to himself. It read, "Wrap it up. Need you back now. Sam"

Bradley tucked the note from his boss into his pocket and thanked the woman, then said, "I'm afraid we'll have to cut this session short. Thank you for your attention and good luck to you."

"Wait!" A woman from the back of the class stood. "You said one of us was hiding something!"

"That's right. I did."

Bradley leaned down to Rusty and whispered in his ear.

Rusty jumped up, lifted his nose in the air, and trotted up the middle aisle. He stopped three-quarters of the way and ducked into a row on the left. Then he sat in front of a man who quickly became nervous.

"Would you stand up, please?" Bradley asked.

Tentatively, the man stood.

"Please look under your seat," Bradley said.

In its wrapper and taped to the bottom of the chair was a Twinkie. Laughter generated from the crowd when the man held it up for everyone to see.

"We're all hiding something," Bradley said. "Some just do it better than others. Go ahead and give Rusty his reward."

The recruits clapped as Rusty chomped his Twinkie and returned to Bradley's side.

Bradley pushed the throttle on his PW-4x4Q all-terrain power wheelchair. The electric motor quietly whirred as he made his way out of the academy building with Rusty keeping pace.

"Good job, buddy. But no more Twinkies for you for a while." Bradley thought he saw Rusty frown.

He didn't have a good feeling about the message his boss, Sam, had sent. Sam Houghton, executive assistant director of the FBI National Security Branch, had hired Bradley not long after he returned from his yearlong absence from the bureau to help Derek with the Ali al-Haqani case. Sam recognized Bradley's rare abilities and offered him a full-time position. After much deliberation, Bradley accepted. By then, Bradley had made peace with his tumultuous past and was ready to put all his time and effort into his work. At least that's what he had told himself.

Although Derek was not happy losing his best analytical mind to the National Security Branch, he knew it offered a great opportunity for Bradley. And since Derek and Sam's cases often overlapped, Derek and Bradley continued to work together on occasion.

Once in his truck, Bradley called Sam. "What's going on, Sam?"

"We got a communication from Ali al-Haqani."

Bradley's stomach twisted. "We knew it would come."

"Yeah, we did. But I'd hoped we would have had more intelligence on him by the time it did."

"Yeah. I'm leaving now."

"Come directly to my office. We're gathering the task force. I've scheduled a meeting in the situation room in three hours.

I'm redirecting all your current cases to other agents. As of now, you'll concentrate your efforts on al-Haqani."

Bradley shifted his customized truck into gear. He thought back to when he first arrived in Washington to work on the case. He had been instrumental in preventing Ali al-Haqani's attack at Haqani's alma mater, Hopkinton Engineering Institute. Through his research, Bradley learned a lot about the man. After analyzing the information from the prior year's bombing attempts, Bradley concluded that the terrorist's ultimate goal was not only to kill Americans but to annihilate them.

Nearly two hours later, Bradley and Rusty entered Sam's office. Derek sat on the leather couch to the right of Sam's desk, one leg crossed over the other. Rusty went and lay at Derek's feet, prompting Derek to pat his head. Because Derek oversaw CIRG—Critical Incident Response Group, it was not surprising that he was there.

Sam sat behind his desk with a sour expression and handed Bradley a sheet of paper.

They sat silently as Bradley read.

Who laid the foundations of the earth, that it should not be removed forever. Thou coveredst it with the deep as with a garment: the waters stood above the mountains. At thy rebuke they fled; at the voice of thy thunder they hasted away. They go up by the mountains; they go down by the valleys unto the place which thou hast founded for them. Thou hast set a bound that they may not pass over; that they turn not again to cover the earth.

Something is lost, and it cannot be found. Let me rather lose all things than lose God, my supreme good. Let me never suffer the loss of my greatest treasure, eternal life with God.

When Bradley looked up, Sam asked, "What are your initial thoughts?"

"We know from previous communications that he likes to manipulate the intended meaning of bible verses. To me, it seems his use of the word thy corresponds to himself. He's claiming to possess God's ability to create and destroy."

"That's the general consensus," Sam replied.

"But there's a lot more here," Bradley stated. "He quotes, 'That it should not be removed forever.' This is his endgame. Not all of the earth. Just the portions he wishes to eliminate. He's telling us that our time is up and his has arrived. 'Thou hast set a bound that they may not pass over; that they turn not again to cover the earth.' He's got a plan. And he's ready to implement it. It's possible he already has. And that last paragraph seems to say he's willing to die to achieve his goal—'Let me rather lose all things than lose God, my supreme good.'"

"What about that last paragraph? The analysts say it doesn't come from the bible. They say it's the prayer of Saint Anthony, the patron saint of lost things."

"That's new. Al-Haqani has never quoted a saint before. Interesting."

Sam turned to Derek.

"What do you think?"

Derek shifted to the edge of the couch, his elbows resting on his knees, his hands cupped between them.

"I think Bradley's right. I get the feeling we're behind the eightball already. He's spent years studying how we responded to his attacks. He knows our strengths and weaknesses. We know he favors chemical weapons—it's his specialty. Now it looks like he may have chosen his delivery method. I'm going to put the CIRG team on standby."

"If you're right and he's already implemented his plan, we're playing catchup." Contemplating, Sam paused, then picked up the telephone and dialed the extension for Jonathan Williams, the task force leader. Into the phone he said, "Send an alert to every field office. Tell them to monitor hospitals for suspicious illnesses and unusually large numbers of hospitalizations or deaths."

When he hung up, he turned to Derek. "I think you and I need to speak to Deputy Director Mendez. We're going to need open lines of communication with every state and local law enforcement agency."

Derek nodded.

"One hour from now, we meet in the SIT room," Sam said to Bradley. "Bring everything you've got on al-Haqani."

Back at his desk, Bradley coordinated with Agent Naila Noor. The two had previously worked together on the case. Naila spoke fluent Arabic and had a great analytical mind.

"I'll gather our case files and analysis," Naila said.

"Yeah, good. I'll print out my research," Bradley said.

"What research?" she asked.

"On al-Haqani."

"Why isn't your research in the files?" Naila asked with pinched brows.

"It's just background stuff I've been working on at home. Nothing official."

"At home? We've been working sixty-five hours a week. When do you find time to work at home?"

"It's not work. I just do it in my down time."

"What kind of research?"

"School records, thesis analysis, class papers, things like that. I've also been gathering Boston newspapers from the time he was at HEI and Al Jazeera news reports from when he was a child in the Kunar Province of Afghanistan, everything I could find on his hometown of Asadabad, oh, and newspaper articles from everyplace he visited in the United States during the time he was there."

"This is what you do in your downtime?"

"I knew we hadn't heard the last of him. I wanted to be ready when we did."

"Well, what have you found out?" Naila asked impatiently.

"I've found out a lot, but I don't know if any of it will help us. I haven't gone through all the newspapers yet, either."

"What do you think you'll find in those?"

"You never know. All it takes is one small thread to unravel the cloak."

Naila chuckled. "Cloak? You've been reading those corny mystery novels again, haven't you?"

"My friend Holly's publishing company just released a new one, Cloak and Badger. It's quite entertaining," Bradley said with a grin.

Naila stood from her desk. "I'm going to get the files. I'll see you in the SIT room."

Rusty lifted his head and watched Naila walk away, then glanced at Bradley before plopping his head back down on his bed.

When Bradley read aloud Ali al-Haqani's note in the presence of Sam and Derek, he hoped he'd successfully hidden the feeling of dread that consumed his entire body. He wasn't accustomed to questioning his analytical and profiling abilities, but he'd been duped by Ali before, and he worried it would happen again. This time with catastrophic consequences.

Al-Haqani was smart—a genius some might say. According to Bradley's research, he lived his teenage years in the thick of the United States war on Afghanistan and vowed retribution on the western world. Al-Haqani knew he couldn't achieve that from outside, so he enrolled at HEI and received a master's degree in chemical engineering with a minor in biology.

Many times, Bradley imagined himself in al-Haqani's shoes, plotting his revenge on the people he held responsible for the devastation of his country—the bulk of his rage centered on Americans. Bradley envisioned what it must have been like for him to live in Hopkinton surrounded by his perceived enemies while attending one of the United States's foremost academic institutions. Bradley assumed the experience exacerbated al-Haqani's hatred toward the US enough for him to envision multiple ways to destroy the country.

During the previous year's investigation, the FBI concluded that, in his senior year, Ali al-Haqani had used toxic paint to kill a fellow student. They also uncovered that al-Haqani caused other classmates' and school neighbors' incidents of chemical burns, asphyxiation, tissue deterioration, and respiratory maladies—all of which had previously been designated as unsolved. Diabolus Pestis.

The recent thwarted attempt to detonate a chemical bomb at HEI seemed an effort to kill students and teachers, but, Bradley thought, not the ultimate reason for his attack. Al-Haqani had been testing the waters, Bradley imagined, by placing traps in the fertile currents of American freedom and consumerism. And it seemed to Bradley that al-Haqani was ready to slay the lion.

The situation room bustled with activity as people hauled in boxes of files and folders. Bradley found Derek sitting at the end of the front row of the stadium-style seating. In front of the room was a large screen that displayed the FBI emblem. Derek read from a file. Bradley parked his chair next to him.

"Anything new?" Bradley asked.

"Yes, I think so. Sam has been busy with something."

"What?"

"I don't know," Derek replied, still looking at his file. "I'm just refreshing my memory. Every other communication we got from al-Haqani had to be translated from Arabic. This one came written in English. Why do you suppose that is?"

"I didn't know that."

"Yeah, things are happening fast. Any idea why he would change now?"

"If I had to guess, I might think this is his final communication. When we got the other letters, we assumed he just wanted to kill Americans on American soil. That was exactly what he wanted us to think. He used his own form of riddles and codes to play with us. Now, he doesn't care that we know what his endgame is. To eliminate all Americans."

Derek nodded.

Sam hurried through the door with Jonathan on his heels. He quickly walked to the front of the room and faced the agents. The room fell silent.

Sam began. "Incoming communication from multiple states indicates the presence of an unknown, quick spreading, highly toxic and lethal substance."

Bradley straightened in his chair as his chest tightened.

"So far Nebraska, Texas, Kansas, Oklahoma, and Colorado have reported an estimate of 3,000 hospitalizations and 460 deaths," Sam continued. "Those same states are also dealing with suspicious cattle and other livestock deaths. We've got specialists on the way to those locations to investigate. We received a communication earlier today from the terrorist

Ali al-Haqani and are working under the assumption that he orchestrated this deliberate attack."

A wave of whispers rolled through the room.

Sam nodded to Jonathan, who stood by a laptop computer. Jonathan tapped a key, and al-Haqani's letter appeared in place of the FBI logo on the large screen.

"This is exactly how we received the letter, written in English and directly from the King James Bible—Psalms 104, verses five through nine. The last part comes from a prayer to Saint Anthony, the patron saint of lost things."

Jonathan's phone pinged. Bradley noticed him glancing at a message and watched his eyes grow wide.

"Where are we on locating al-Haqani?" Sam asked the group.

Agent Chavez stood to address the question. "My contact at Langley says he's back home in Asadabad, but we don't have an exact location on him. He continues to move around with a very small contingent of security. He's careful and doesn't draw attention to himself. And, we're told, he doesn't trust easily."

Sam glanced at Derek, and the two made eye contact. With that look, Bradley realized he hadn't been privy to all of the available information. Derek and Sam knew something that they were not willing or allowed to share.

Jonathan's phone pinged again. Annoyed, Sam glared at him. Jonathan walked his phone over to Sam and showed him his screen. Sam turned pale. After composing himself, Sam said, "The Centers for Disease Control is reporting six more states have recorded hospitalizations and deaths. At this point, we'll have to assume that every state has been affected.

"We don't have much information to go on," he continued. "We know it's a poison, but we don't know if it's contracted from a food source or contaminated water or if it's airborne. What we can conclude is that it's widespread, moving quickly, and extremely deadly."

Once again, Jonathan's phone blared.

"What is it?" Sam barked.

"The World Health Organization is monitoring the outbreak and hasn't received any reports of incidents outside of the United States."

Bradley turned to Derek. "Now we know why Ali wrote the note in English. He didn't want there to be any doubt that he was responsible for what was about to happen. His timing was precise."

Sam coordinated assignments, then quickly wrapped up the meeting. He finished with, "If this is a deliberate attack on US citizens, we could be looking at the worst case of genocide in history." Done with his comments, Sam joined Bradley and Derek.

Bradley took advantage of having the two together and asked, "What is it you're not telling us?"

"What do you mean?" Sam asked.

"You and Derek know something about al-Haqani that you're not sharing. It seems to me we're in crisis mode here. What could possibly be the point of holding back information?"

Sam looked at Derek. Their facial expressions indicated a silent conversation.

"Let's go to my office," Sam said.

As soon as the office door closed, Sam said, "This is sensitive information. Understood?"

"Absolutely," Bradley replied.

Sam nodded to Derek.

Derek began. "Ali al-Haqani isn't in Asadabad. We received word that he crossed into the US a few days ago. We were lucky enough to catch him on camera. A fluke, really. A guard at the Canadian/North Dakota border randomly picked his vehicle for inspection.

"As al-Haqani stood outside the SUV, a gust of wind knocked the hat he was wearing off his head. We got a good picture of him, and we have his vehicle information. Unfortunately, they didn't catch his phony identification. Or, if they did, he has inside help. That's why we need to keep this quiet—need to know only. We've got every law enforcement agency in the country looking for the vehicle."

"When did you find this out?"

"Routine offsite monitoring of the border cameras picked it up this morning," Derek replied.

"You stressed not to try to pick him up if sighted, right?" Bradley asked, shifting his gaze from Derek to Sam.

"Not unless absolutely necessary. There's no telling what he might do if he's cornered," Sam said.

"Any sightings yet?"

"None."

After a moment of reflection, Bradley said, "It makes sense. He would want to make sure everything fell into place. He wouldn't trust anyone else with his plan."

"There's more," Sam said. "We checked the activity of the passport he used. He's been here twice since the HEI attack. The first time was only twenty-five days after the incident. The second time was four months ago."

"Four months. Just ahead of spring. Planting and fertilizing season," Bradley murmured.

"What was that?" Derek asked.

"All my research has shown that al-Haqani doesn't take chances. He wouldn't take the risk of using an airborne substance. It's too susceptible to weather conditions. And to contaminate our water source, well, it would take a lot of chemicals or bacteria to achieve this kind of result. Everything I know about him tells me he wants to disrupt our food source."

"How can you be sure?" Sam asked.

"He experimented with paint and upholstery toxins when he studied at HEI. If he were going to use that kind of method, he would concentrate on cities, not the scattered population in the middle of the country. The same would apply if he tampered with a drug, like the acetaminophen poisoning in 1982.

"And cattle are dying. That's not a coincidence. He hit the areas where the bulk of our food supply comes from. That's got to be his plan. I'd bet my life on it. He used something that spreads quickly and easily."

Bradley paused, shifted his gaze to the ceiling, then continued. "What was it he wrote? 'Who laid the foundations of the earth, that it should not be removed forever. Thou coveredst it with the deep as with a garment.' Also, 'Thou hast set a bound that they may not pass over; that they turn not again to cover the earth.'

"'Coveredst the earth,'" Bradley repeated.

"In his senior year at HEI," he continued, "there were unexplained instances of asphyxiation, tissue deterioration, and multiple respiratory maladies. It was discovered later that the only explainable cause found was bacteria-contaminated soil."

Sam moved behind his desk and reached for his phone. "Bradley, get over to the CDC right away. I'll let them know you're on the way. Bring your research with you," Sam said.

Not sure how long he would be there, he left Rusty back at the office with Derek. If needed, Cate could pick Rusty up and take him home with her.

The drive from the J. Edgar Hoover Building to the DC office of the Centers for Disease Control and Prevention took him twelve minutes. Twelve minutes for him to consider that his instincts in the case were suspect. Twelve minutes to remind himself that if he led the investigation in the wrong direction, it could cost thousands of lives.

The District of Columbia office of the CDC was housed in Patriot Plaza at 395 E Street SW. Sam texted Bradley and told him to find Dr. Howe on the third floor.

The sign over the door read, Dr. A. Howe, Environmental Health. Bradley steered his chair to the open doorway and tapped on the door.

Dr. Audrey Howe jumped in her seat.

"I'm sorry," Bradley said. "I didn't mean to startle you."

Holding her hand to her chest, she stood from her seat and sighed.

"No apology necessary. I tend to get tunnel vision when I'm at my computer. Come right in." She walked from her desk and met Bradley with a handshake. "Audrey Howe."

"Bradley Whitman. I suffer the same malady," he grinned.

"You're with the Federal Bureau of Investigation?" She asked.

"Yes. I'm an analyst with the bureau."

Getting right to the point, she asked, "How much do you know about this case?"

"I believe we may be dealing with a soil or fertilizer contaminant. The suspect has a master's degree in chemical engineering with a minor in biology. He's been developing his plan for decades and is extremely thorough. How much do you know?"

"Not much yet. As soon as we got word of an outbreak, we started collecting the available information. It's always best to assume the worst until we can rule out a crop problem. There wasn't much coming in at first, but things are developing quickly now."

She paused before adding, "If what you're saying is true, it would make sense that the individual would target these states first. We have confirmation that eleven states have experienced death of both humans and animals so far. These states are best known for raising cattle and other livestock, but they're also the countries' largest producers of wheat, corn, and soybeans."

Bradley scowled. "In other words, our entire food chain will be affected."

"Again, if your suspicions are correct . . . not will be, has been," Dr. Howe corrected.

"Right!" Bradley winced. "Dr. Howe, what is the first step in containing a situation like this?"

"I don't know to what extent it can be contained. Almost every food product made in this country uses these grains, meats, and by-products."

"What about importing food. As of yet, there haven't been any instances outside the country."

"Yes, but you just said it. As of yet, there haven't been. The United States exports over a million metric tons of grains per year. It's just a matter of time."

Bradley found himself speechless.

It was moments before he found his voice. "What is the procedure from here?"

"We start at the beginning. The first reported case. I arranged to have samples of soil, water, fertilizer, and pesticides sent from the Kansas farm where the first victims, an elderly farmer and his wife, were reported. I was getting ready to head to the lab when Director Houghton called. You're welcome to join me if you'd like."

"Yes, I would appreciate that. Thank you, Dr. Howe."

"It's going to be a long night, Agent Whitman. Call me Audrey."

"Bradley," he replied.

WHAT YOU DON'T KNOW

The text from Bradley raised the hair on Derek's arms.

Could you ask Cate to care for Rusty? I don't think we'll be coming up for air any time soon!

As he waited for Cate, Derek's anxiety grew. Rusty could sense his uneasiness and stayed by his side.

Knowing there was nothing he could do about the rising loss of life, he felt sick to his stomach. He examined the interactive map of the United States displayed on his computer screen. Red blotches concentrated heavily in the center of the country, but as time had progressed, the dots spread outward, covering more area. He could almost feel the cancerous growth eating his own organs.

Derek glanced at his shaking hands resting on the keyboard, and a rancid feeling welled inside him. He jumped from his chair, hurried to his private office bathroom, knelt in front of the toilet, and promptly expelled his lunch.

Wiping his face with a damp cloth, he readied himself for the possibility of another round of vomit.

"Derek, are you alright?"

His face ashen and eyes glazed, Derek peered at Cate standing at the bathroom door with Rusty by her side.

Cate rushed to him and held his head in her hands.

"My God, Derek. What's going on?"

Not wishing to scare Cate, Derek answered, "Must've been something I ate."

Just as he said it, the enormity of the statement hit him. What if Bradley is right about the nation's food chain?

Cate helped him off the floor and steered him to the leather couch. She rinsed the cloth in cool water and wiped his forehead, face, and neck. Rusty stayed by Derek's side.

Color began to return to his complexion, and he showed a hint of a smile.

"I'm taking you home," Cate said.

Derek placed his hand on her arm.

"I'm fine, Cate. It was nothing. Something wasn't sitting right in my stomach, that's all. I feel much better now," he said.

And, to his relief, he did. For a moment, Derek had wondered if that was what it felt like for all those people represented by red blotches on his computer. But he consoled himself with the fact that he had been struck by that kind of anxiety in the past. He just never told Cate about it. He had, however, talked about it with Sahani Kumar, an FBI psychologist with whom he had sessions some years before. He began seeing her after someone planted a bomb in the limousine where he, Cate, and others were passengers.

The thought of getting in touch with Sahani crossed his mind while also preventing him from hearing Cate's concern.

"I'm sorry. What did you say?" Derek asked.

"That's it! You're going home. Pack up your things," Cate demanded.

Derek smiled at her assertiveness.

"Cate, sit down." He patted the couch.

"You're not well. Your face is pale, your eyes are cloudy, and you just lost your breakfast," she said as she sat beside him.

"I'm just a little tired, that's all."

Derek took Cate's hand in his. "I have to tell you something important. In an hour or so, the CDC is going to announce a warning regarding a very serious situation. I'm not sure what they'll recommend, but please listen carefully."

"What's happened?"

"I don't have all the facts. The best thing to do is to leave the radio or television on to get the latest news. I may not have time to keep you informed. Things are going to get hectic around here."

As if he understood, Rusty looked up at Derek with dark eyes.

"You're scaring me, Derek," Cate said.

"Honey, there's nothing to be afraid of. The CDC is on top of the situation and will keep the public informed."

"You keep saying situation like you don't know what's happening. Tell me what's happening."

"I don't know exactly. All I know is that people are getting sick."

Cate's eyes opened wide. "Sick? Like you? Is there something wrong with . . . "

"No, Cate, no! Not me!" Derek wrapped his arms around her, and Rusty jumped to Cate's side. "I'm fine, really. It was just a bout of anxiety, that's all. I'm sorry. I didn't mean to scare you. I should have chosen my words better."

Cate placed her hands on Derek's chest and pushed away slightly to look into his eyes. "What do you mean, anxiety?"

That time, Derek tried to choose his words carefully.

"It's been a difficult morning. As you might have noticed, occasionally this job can cause anxiety." Derek tried to hold a smile but watched Cate unravel what he said and knew he had made things worse.

"Has this happened to you before? Do you spend your days retching in this office?"

"Of course not. That's not what I meant."

Without a word, Cate stood and walked out the office door. Derek heard her ask Madelyn, his executive assistant, for a cup of hot tea with honey. When she returned, she held a bottle of water.

"Here, drink this. Take small sips. Madelyn is making you some tea."

"Really, I'm fine."

"Drink!"

Derek did as he was told. Madelyn arrived with the tea.

"Is there anything else I can get for you, Cate?"

"No, thank you, Madelyn. He's being a little difficult," Cate said.

"I'll be right outside if you need assistance keeping him in line," she smiled.

Derek turned on the office television and tuned to a news network. He knew to expect a statement from the CDC shortly. With the volume low, he kept his eyes on the screen and sipped his tea.

"You don't have to stay, Cate. I feel great! You and Rusty should head home."

"We're not going anywhere. It's obvious you don't feel great."

Derek's intercom buzzed.

"Yes, Madelyn," he answered.

"Director Houghton asked that you meet him in Deputy Director Mendez's office," Madelyn said.

"Tell him I'll be right there."

"Really, Cate. You should go. I'm going to be extremely busy."

"Go to your meeting, Derek," Cate said, without getting up.

Derek reached for a folder on his desk, looked at Cate and shook his head, then left the room.

Cate invited Rusty up on the couch with her, then turned up the volume on the television.

After several minutes, the news anchor said, "And now for this special bulletin. After reports of serious illnesses resulting in hospitalization of heartland residents, the Centers for Disease Control and Prevention has issued the following warning.

A severe outbreak of listeria infection has hit the middle of the country and is spreading. Listeria, otherwise known as listeriosis, can result in hospitalization and, in severe cases, death. Symptoms may include fever, chills, nausea, and muscle aches. Currently, the cause of the outbreak is unknown. The CDC recommends avoiding all fresh vegetables, grain products, and dairy until the source of the outbreak is determined. Watch for updates to this warning on the CDC website. And now, back to your network news.

Cate turned the volume down on the television. She picked up her phone and googled listeria poisoning. Even though the CDC reported it as an infection, from her days working as a restaurant manager, Cate knew that listeria was considered food poisoning. She wondered why Derek would get so worked up about a food poisoning occurrence. She didn't think it was too unusual as it happened frequently.

She read that listeria presents itself like a bad case of the flu and is particularly dangerous for the elderly. She made a mental note to inform her parents.

She glanced back at the TV set and watched video from a helicopter. The bottom of the screen read, KSAS-TV Kansas. The setting looked like a cattle ranch, but as the camera panned in for a close-up of the cattle, it showed them lying still on the grass.

She turned up the volume.

"... unexplained. For more on this story, we go to Alexa Rose reporting on the ground in Wichita, Kansas."

Thank you, Stan. I'm here outside the Triple T Ranch in Wichita where the property is cordoned off preventing us from getting any closer to the scene. Many plain white vans can be seen on the property . . . let's go ahead and pan the camera to that area.

The cameraman shifted focus of the camera to the vehicles.

The Triple T Ranch raises Angus steer and, as you can see here, everyone on the property is wearing a hazmat suit. We can assume they're examining the animals using an abundance of caution until they determine the cause of these mysterious deaths.

The camera panned back to show Alexa with the ranch in the background.

Tim Anderson, secretary of the Kansas Department of Agriculture, has declined to comment on the situation at this time. We'll provide updates as information becomes available. Until then, I'm Alexa Rose reporting for KSAS. Back to you, Stan.

Huh, Cate thought. They're having a bad day in the heartland.

"That's it?" Derek asked, shifting his gaze from the television to Deputy Director Michael Mendez. "That's the entire report?"

"It's what Director Rhoades and CDC Director Ashad thought best," Mendez replied.

Sam said, "With all due respect, Mike, the news report made it sound like every other food poisoning incident we've ever had. Nobody's going to pay attention to that."

"The CDC is going to bombard the airwaves with warnings. If we need to ramp up the intensity, we will. We can't have people panicking, Sam," Mendez replied.

"But how many people will die because we made it sound like they could get the flu if they ate the wrong thing. You saw the map! The numbers of deaths are staggering and getting worse by the minute," Derek argued.

Mendez took a deep breath. "I agree, but my hands are tied. And so are yours. The best thing to do is concentrate on your job. Apprehend this son-of-a-bitch. Let the CDC and other responsible agencies do theirs. Keep me posted on any updates."

Outside Deputy Director Mendez's door, Derek and Sam stood stunned. Neither had words to express their frustration.

As they walked toward the elevator, Sam said, "I'm sending Jonathan's team to the border. Ali al-Haqani would want to monitor his work firsthand to make sure he was successful, but he won't linger forever. Now that things are set in motion, he's going to want to get to a safe place, if he hasn't already."

"Do you really think he'll leave the same way he came in?" Derek asked.

"I don't think it's luck that's gotten him across that border without detection five times. He had help. Jonathan's people will pose as crossing agents. Hopefully we're not too late."

"The border guards have instructions not to let him leave the country. Unless he left before the BOLO, we may still have a chance."

When Derek returned to his office, he wasn't surprised to see Cate and Rusty still sitting on his couch.

"You must have better things to do than hang around here," Derek said as he walked to his desk.

"Can't think of a thing." Cate stared him down.

When Derek sat and noticed the glare, he asked, "What?"

"I want you to tell me what's really going on with you."

"There's nothing going on with me."

"Do you really think I know you so little? Every muscle in your body has seized, and you're heaving your guts into the toilet. You're a ticking time bomb, Derek. I thought it might have something to do with this CDC announcement, but that can't be it."

Derek's eyes closed as he lowered his chin to his chest. His fears were confirmed that no one would take the report seriously. Cate had been looking for a reason why he might be uneasy, and even she didn't think it important.

He stood and went to sit beside her on the couch.

He sighed before he began.

"I can't talk about what's going on. But promise me you'll take the CDC's recommendations seriously."

"But I . . ."

"Promise me, Cate."

"Alright, of course. I won't eat any fresh vegetables or dairy."

"Or grains. No baked goods or cereals. And no meat. No beef, chicken, or any meat." Derek searched his brain for suggestions. "Fish and seafood should be alright. But make sure any canned, dried, or frozen goods you eat have been around for a while."

"I . . . what . . . you're scaring me, now. This doesn't sound like a typical listeria outbreak."

It killed him not to be able to tell her how dangerous the situation had become. His only hope was that she could feel the desperation in his warning.

They gazed at each other without speaking. The gravity of Derek's glare hit Cate.

"I've got to make some phone calls," Cate said, sounding panicked.

"Not here," Derek said. "Go home. Take Rusty with you. I think we have some canned dog food in the hallway closet that we bought last year. Feed him that. Not anything newer."

Cate's eyes widened.

"It'll be alright," Derek said. "Just be careful."

Cate stood from the couch and headed to the door. She stopped, turned, and asked, "What about water?"

"I don't know," Derek somberly replied.

"Are you going to be okay?" Cate asked.

"Yes. I'm fine. I'll call you later." He tried to smile.

POSSIBILITIES

After shadowing Audrey Howe, Bradley discovered she was not only head of the District of Columbia's National Center for Environmental Health, but she was also at the top of her field in soil science.

Although the main CDC laboratory was located in Atlanta, the state-of-the-art lab in the DC facility impressed him. As many as twenty scientists occupied the room, each examining different samples sent from Kansas.

Audrey placed a fertilizer sample into a machine Bradley thought resembled an inkjet printer with a cylinder sticking out of the top. She typed something into the connected keyboard, and then Bradley noted a faint whirring sound from the apparatus.

"What are the odds you'll find something in these samples?" Bradley asked.

"If the cause is here, we'll find it. We've got crops, soil, fertilizer, and water samples. The animals are being tested in Atlanta."

"What about pesticides? Wouldn't that be the most logical place to start?" Bradley asked, curiously.

"Yes, it would. But I'm told this farm didn't use chemical pesticides. That's not unusual. The trend has been veering away from conventional chemicals and moving toward organic and eco-friendly sprays and biofertilizers. It's been a long time coming, but we've made great strides in the science," Audrey replied.

"I've read a little about that," Bradley said. "Organic matter in the fertilizer increases the retention of water, which reduces the impact of drought."

Audrey flashed him a smile.

"You read about soil retention? Was it for a case you were working?"

"No," Bradley chuckled. "Just some light Sunday reading."

Audrey laughed before continuing.

"The retention of water also allows the soil to absorb and store carbon and other nutrients. Studies have shown that organically managed fields reduce nitrate leaching by fifty percent as opposed to conventional management practices. This leads to healthier crops that are better able to resist insects and diseases."

"So the biofertilizers contain microorganisms meant to enhance the nutrients of the plants, correct?" Bradley asked.

"Exactly."

"I'm sorry I'm asking so many questions. Please let me know if I'm disturbing you or keeping you from your work," Bradley said.

"You're not bothering me at all. I could talk about dirt and fertilizers all day," she chuckled.

She has an engaging laugh, Bradley thought. And her face lights up when she smiles. For the first time since he arrived, Bradley took a moment to notice Audrey Howe. Her eyes were the color of soft caramel, and her silky pale skin seemed to shimmer. He guessed she didn't see the light of day very often. Her auburn hair would have reached her lab-coat covered shoulders had it not been tied in a ponytail. She had a natural beauty, and she didn't try to enhance it with cosmetics.

Realizing he had been staring, he dropped his head and cleared his throat before speaking. "Well, I do have another question, but I'm hesitant to sound ignorant," he said.

"You consider the subject of soil retention as light reading. I doubt any question you ask will come off as ignorant."

"You're analyzing the soil with added biofertilizer. How many microorganisms will you have to wade through? It's like a needle in a haystack, isn't it?"

"It's worse. The soil alone generally contains somewhere between a hundred million and a billion bacteria. And we can only identify about ten percent of them."

"Wow. That's a bit discouraging."

"Yes, but the good news is we can usually recognize if something doesn't belong. If something's in the soil that shouldn't be there, we should be able to isolate it."

"How long does the process usually take?"

"There's no way to say. Hopefully, you're correct with your assumption of a soil-based contaminate because that's where we're starting. Otherwise, we may be looking at a protracted process of elimination."

"Uh huh!" Bradley murmured. Doubts resurfaced and caused a nauseous feeling in his stomach. "I think I'll go wait in the corner over there and review my notes."

"Feel free to use the desk up front," Audrey said, turning her attention back to the whirring machine.

Bradley knew the only way he could be of any help was to review everything he knew about Ali al-Haqani. He felt a desperate need to find conclusive evidence telling him that his instincts were correct. He thought about going back to the office but didn't want to waste time. Something Audrey said had tickled the back of his brain, so he removed the briefcase sitting on the footrest between his legs and opened it to retrieve the thick file folder he'd brought with him.

While attending HEI, al-Haqani had written many reports about chemically altering compounds and elements. In his files, Bradley vaguely remembered reading something about the antagonistic relationship between certain elements and the resulting effects. When Audrey mentioned that biofertilizers augmented the ability of crops to absorb and store nutrients, Bradley thought of al-Haqani's research papers.

After an hour of sifting through the stack, Bradley happened upon the scratch to his itch. The paper was titled "Antagonistic Effect of Copper and Zinc." The bulk of the report focused on the need for balancing the two elements for human metabolism. But, as an addendum, Ali included a section on soil imbalance and the effects it could have on vegetation.

While Bradley reread the report, the overhead light in the office directed its rays on the paper and revealed ink on the back of one of the typewritten pages. Bradley turned the page over, read the two written words, and froze. Written in blue ink, it said, "maestro move."

Bradley's arms swelled with goosebumps. He recalled his chemistry class at MIT when Professor Forsythe compared his research papers to a symphony. He had told Bradley that he was adept at turning chaos into cohesion. That was when the professor gave him the nickname Maestro. From then on, the professor complimented Bradley's best work by designating it a maestro move. And here he was, seeing his nickname on one of Ali al-Haqani's research papers.

It certainly couldn't have been a coincidence, Bradley told himself. Although his professor taught at both MIT and HEI, he had assumed he was the only student of Andrew Forsythe's to acquire the moniker. But after seeing the scrawl on the back of that page, he thought otherwise. Not only did it sadden him, finding the name on one of Ali al-Haqani's school reports sent chills through him.

Bradley's thoughts were interrupted by a flash of white passing in front of him. When he looked up, he saw Audrey scurrying around the room, sometimes stopping to speak in low whispers with three other scientists.

Bradley set the report on the desk and directed his wheelchair toward Audrey.

"What is it?" He asked.

"I don't know." She looked perplexed. "It isn't right. Both the soil and fertilizer readings are way off."

"How so?"

"The nutrient levels are way out of balance. It's very odd."

"I don't understand," Bradley said. "Did you find something that doesn't belong there?"

"No, not yet anyway. The nutrient levels are all over the place, though. Nitrogen, phosphorus, zinc, potassium, copper. All of it!"

"What does that mean?" Bradley asked.

"It doesn't make sense. This kind of nutrient imbalance doesn't happen naturally. It could be that our equipment needs calibration," Audrey said, pensively.

"You don't sound too convinced."

"No, I'm not. But we're running the soil and fertilizer analysis again to make sure."

"May I see the report?" Bradley asked.

"Of course," Audrey said as she walked back to her lab station, picked up the printout, and handed it to Bradley. "This is for the fertilizer. The numbers on the left indicate the manufacturers' specifications. The numbers on the right show the reading. You can see that nitrogen, phosphorus, and zinc are at extremely elevated levels. So it does make sense that the copper level is that low. But look at those percentages!"

Bradley studied the readout.

"What about the copper? Why would that . . . ?" Bradley stopped mid sentence. "Zinc and copper work against each other, correct?"

"Yes! And one of the reasons for using fertilizer in the first place is to add copper to the soil to help prevent disease. Much like in humans, it assists in plant metabolizing of carbohydrates and proteins."

"Excuse me," Bradley said as he turned his chair and rode back to the desk. He returned with the report about zinc and copper that al-Haqani had written and handed it to Audrey.

She began to read.

"Skip to the addendum," Bradley said.

She shuffled the pages and began to read.

"Yes, this is all very detailed and accurate. But I don't understand."

"If someone wanted to disrupt—no—destroy the growth of grains in a certain region, what would be the best way to do that?"

"If someone were to manipulate the chemical balance of the soil, it would make it difficult to grow grains in that soil. But it wouldn't explain why people and animals are dying."

"Unless that's only part of the plan. Once you weaken the soil and the crops' ability to stem disease, you could introduce a bacterial infection or insect that could run rampant. And without proper bio-nutrients, the plants no longer have resistance. Also, they won't retain water but will leach it, spreading the disease quickly and efficiently."

"And unseen?" Audrey asked. "Any farmer would notice the effect of bacterial disease on their crops. And they would certainly see insects."

"I don't believe we're looking for an infestation of insects. But he may have found a way to disguise the effects of disease," Bradley was thinking out loud.

"So, you think we're looking for a grain disease poisonous to both humans and animals."

"Maybe not just grains. Al-Haqani wouldn't limit himself. And it would be nearly impossible to infect the soil of so many growing areas unless they all use the same fertilizer. I need to make a phone call."

Bradley lifted his phone and speed dialed Sam's number.

"Bradley, what have you found?" Sam asked.

"I think it's got to be the fertilizer. The tests show a huge discrepancy from technical specifications with the actual composition. We need to send people to the manufacturing plant as soon as possible. Either they're behind this, or someone has tampered with their product."

"Who's the manufacturer?" Sam asked.

Bradley glanced at the report that Audrey had given him.

"Genetic Eco Corporation. Cedar Falls, Iowa."

"I'll get Cessy ready. Get to the airport. Agent Noor will meet you there with a team."

Cessy was the pet name the agency used for the Cessna Citation jet at their disposal for emergencies. Bradley had flown on Cessy once before when he returned to assist in the original al-Haqani case.

"What's the latest, Sam?" Bradley asked.

"Not good. The number of reported deaths has more than doubled, and hospitals are filling up. We've got confirmed cases in nineteen states."

"I'm leaving now! And Sam?" Bradley said.

"Yeah?"

"If Naila and I are working this case together, I can't keep the news about al-Haqani's movements from her."

Sam paused, then said, "Okay."

Bradley exchanged telephone numbers with Dr. Audrey Howe and apologized for his quick departure.

The sun hung low in the sky. Once comfortably on the plane, Bradley called Cate.

"Bradley, hi. Are you with Derek?" Cate asked.

"No. I'm on a plane to Iowa. I hate to do this to you, Cate, but could you keep Rusty for a few days?" Bradley asked.

"Of course. You know I love having him. Have you talked to Derek?"

Bradley noted concern in Cate's voice. "Not lately, why? Is everything alright?"

"I'm worried about him, Bradley. Whatever this thing is that's going on, it's getting to him. When I saw him earlier, well, it wasn't good."

"I'll give him a call and check in. I'm sure he was just feeling a little stress."

"Nice try, but I know it's more than a little stress. He told me about the CDC warning."

"He did?"

"Well, he didn't really tell me anything except that I should take the CDC warnings seriously. But I'm guessing the situation is more dire than the reporters made it out to be. I've already warned Sheila and my parents. Am I wrong?"

Bradley paused, then said, "Derek never could get anything by you, Cate. I'll call him when I hang up with you, alright?"

"Thank you. Be careful, Bradley."

"I will, I promise."

He dialed Derek. "I'm on my way to Iowa," Bradley said when Derek answered his phone.

"What's in Iowa?" Derek asked.

"Genetic Eco Corporation. They manufacture fertilizer. I think it might be our link."

"We need a lead fast. Things are progressing too quickly."

"Yeah, I talked to Sam. How are you doing? How's your stress level?"

Derek paused. "You talked to Cate."

"She's very perceptive."

"That she is. I'll be fine once we have a handle on this thing."

"That could take a while. I've been thinking. This might be a good time to call in reinforcements."

"Who did you have in mind?"

"What about Sahani Kumar? She helped everyone during the Predator case."

"Except you, you mean."

"No, that wasn't her fault. I just wasn't in a good place to recognize it. But I understand now. I think you should call her, Derek."

"I'll think about it."

"In the meantime, I'm here if you need to vent."

Derek chuckled. "Right! Keep me posted on Iowa." And with that, Derek hung up.

FAMILY MATTERS

Sheila's conversation with her sister Cate had her on edge. She enlisted the help of her housekeeper and cook, Daisy, to empty the cabinets and shelves of all fresh vegetables, fruits, and grains, then placed an order with a local seafood company to restock.

Sheila and her husband, David, lived outside of Los Angeles in Hollywood Hills in the celebrity laden neighborhood of Whitley Heights. Protected from view by towering arborvitae, their sizeable home sat back from the winding road. During the mid 1980s, the area went through periods of high crime and vandalism and eventually got divided between single-family homes and an apartment complex. The property with homes were later designated as an historic preservation overlay zone. Many of the beautiful estates, including Sheila and David's, snuggled into the steep hillside and featured beautifully manicured lawns and flower gardens.

David's work as a Hollywood producer had catapulted him into the limelight after the release of the highest grossing film to date, Maker's Mark. Since then, he had been hounded with producing proposals prompting the need to hire additional staff to wade through the material. His current project, based on their son Alex's book of the true story of the serial killer known as the Pathside Predator, had just begun filming.

Successful herself, Sheila had created one of the most popular fashion salons on Rodeo Drive in Hollywood—Elegance by Sheila. She took pride in her accomplishment in

Hollywood, but her success on the outskirts of Los Angeles filled her passion. Her shop Fashion Cents sold new and used clothing and catered to those whose income did not stretch to accommodate name-brand wedding gowns, business suits, office wear, and school clothes.

She found that most of her Fashion Cents customers came to her because they needed an outfit for an important job interview, and it filled her with the greatest pleasure when she could help. Her customers paid only what they could afford, and most eventually became donors to the shop. So successful was her business, she had recently opened her third location in the South Bay region of LA.

Mid-afternoon in California, Sheila knew her son Max would be at work, but she wanted to make sure he had heard about the listeria outbreak. She tapped his picture on her cell phone and waited.

"Hi, Mom."

"Hello, Max. I'm sorry to bother you while you're working, but I know how busy you are, and I wanted to make sure you heard the news."

"What news?"

"Aunt Cate called. There's been an outbreak of listeria poisoning that's affected fresh fruits, vegetables, and grains. She said it's extremely dangerous. And, you know Aunt Cate isn't an alarmist, so please take this seriously. I just emptied my shelves. So should you."

"Okay, thanks, Mom. I'll do that when I get home, I promise. It shouldn't be too hard. I haven't grocery shopped in a while," Max chuckled.

"Good. Have you heard from your brother?"

"Ahh, no. I haven't talked to him for a week or so."

"We didn't get his postcard this week. Alex is usually very good about sending them."

"He's probably too busy traveling. I imagine India is full of remote areas for him to wander."

"That's what I'm afraid of." Sheila winced.

"Relax. I'm sure he's fine. He's probably sleeping right now. I'll call him later tonight. It'll be morning there."

"You're right, of course."

"I've got to get back to work. Love you."

"Okay. I love you, honey."

Sheila always felt better after talking to Max. He was so grounded and confident. And as twins, the two brothers seemed to have a connection that defied logic. No matter where in the world they were, one could sense the other. She tried to reassure herself that Max would have felt something if Alex were in trouble, but the reassurance wasn't sticking.

Max set down his cell phone and returned his attention to his laptop computer. The screen displayed a map of India.

He hadn't talked to Alex in two weeks. That was unusual. They made a habit of talking at least once a week, usually on Saturdays, although it wasn't unheard of that Alex would miss a week. It had happened before. But Max had been feeling strange the past few days. He had that uneasy feeling when you think you've left something behind but aren't sure what.

He hadn't wanted to worry his mother. He knew she did that well enough on her own. But he found it even more unnerving that she had asked about Alex just as he opened a map program on his laptop to locate the capital of the state of West Bengal—Kolkata.

During their most recent conversation, Alex mentioned that, while in Kolkata—formerly known as Calcutta, he planned on visiting Mother Theresa's tomb at Mother House, the headquarters of the Missionaries of Charity.

When Max found it on the map, he sensed nothing. That was his first warning that something wasn't right.

WASTE NOT WANT NOT

En route to Iowa, Bradley reached out by phone to Audrey Howe to see if she had the results of the second fertilizer and soil tests.

"Yes, they're identical to the original findings. It's highly unikely we're having an equipment problem," Audrey said.

"Is there anything in particular I should ask the manufacturer? Other than why their product isn't as advertised?"

"I'd be interested to know if their inventory is out of whack."

"Is that the scientific term? Out of whack?" Bradley smiled as he asked.

Audrey chuckled, then replied, "Yes, absolutely." Then her manner turned serious. "These facilities keep strict inventory of their products. It wouldn't make sense that something like this could happen without them noticing."

Bradley thought the statement through. If they were to tell him they haven't noticed an inventory discrepancy, either the company is hiding the fact that they deliberately altered their product or someone sabotaged it.

"Okay, I'll ask them if their inventory is out of whack," Bradley said.

"Please let me know if you find anything," Audrey said.

"I'll pass on everything that I am able to."

Bradley hung up and glanced around the cabin of the jetliner at the team Sam had assembled. He only knew one.

Naila looked up from the report she was reading and asked, "Well?"

"It's the fertilizer. I'm sure of it." Bradley paused. "I mean, I think so." He pointed to the others on the plane and asked, "Do you know any of these other agents? I've never seen them before."

"That's because they aren't all agents." Naila pointed to a man and woman a few seats away. "That's Mufti and Loukanis. They're with us. They work under Director Richards in the criminal division. The other three are CDC hitching a ride."

Bradley wondered if Audrey knew CDC was on board. Why that mattered to him, he wasn't sure.

Settling back, Bradley opened his laptop and typed Genetic Eco Corporation into the computer's search engine. He came up with multiple hits. He clicked the link to the website home page, and the screen filled with a beautiful, lush field planted half with cornstalks and half with what appeared to be soy. A large well-used red tractor sat parked on a dirt road beside the field. Next to the tractor, a white-bearded old man dressed in farmer jeans stood staring out over his crops.

Across the blue, sparsely clouded sky in a Kelly green bold font arced the name, Genetic Eco Corporation. The tag line presented in a smaller type under the name stated, Eco-friendly, Eco-sound! Chopin sounded from the laptop speaker. A soft-rolling piano etude gave the impression of a slight breeze tickling the tops of the cornstalks.

He then clicked the tab titled About Us on the website header. The screen displayed a boy playing with his dog in front of a large white farmhouse with a wraparound porch. The music became whimsical. Flutes and clarinets clashed with the sound of the jet's engine. He turned off the speakers of his laptop.

The webpage told of the Rawlins family of Iowa. Six generations before, in the year 1877, Jedidiah Rawlins scraped up enough money to buy a small plot of land where he built a tiny house for his family. With the help of his growing boys, he worked tirelessly to clear the land and plant the first of many crops. With each harvested crop, Jedidiah socked away profits for future land acquisition.

After Jedidiah's death at the age of forty-eight, his sons continued his legacy. Every generation of Rawlinses managed to grow the family farm, some more than others. The largest growth happened during the Rawlins third generation amid the Great Depression. William Jedidiah Rawlins bought thousands of acres of surrounding property from struggling farm owners, "paying the owners more money than the land was worth," according to the story.

Sixth generation Sarah Lee Rawlins-Barkley and her husband, Meyers, owned the farm and business as Bradley read on. At the age of twenty-eight, Sarah's father, Douglas William Rawlins, incorporated Genetic Eco Corporation in 1974 with the idea of creating an environmentally sound farming process from fertilizing and insect control to harvesting and processing.

On the surface, Genetic Eco Corporation sounded like the American dream. Each generation of Rawlins had done its part to make the family farm a better place to live and work. "Work hard, be responsible, and prosper," the website stated.

Bradley clicked on the header "Our Mission" and read "Our goal is to create a non-toxic, environmentally safe, and profitable solution to the growing process, from planting to harvesting and processing, to distribution."

The page went on to describe the dangers of conventional procedures and products and the wasteful nature of the traditional agricultural system. It cited unsustainability of traditional processes due to dependence on petroleum-based pesticides.

Bradley wanted to believe everything the website told him, but his years in the bureau had made him more cynical than he liked. After searching online, however, he couldn't find any bad publicity or comments about the company other than complaints about the high cost of their products.

Sam had arranged transportation from the airport to the GEC plant for the four FBI agents.

By the time airline personnel lowered Bradley and his wheelchair to the tarmac, the CDC contingent were getting into a plain white van.

"Where are they going?" Bradley asked Naila.

"I don't know."

Lit at night and from a distance, the plant might have been mistaken for a small town. A tiny blonde woman wearing jeans, baseball cap, heavy red and black plaid flannel jacket, and work boots met them at the main entrance.

"Sarah Lee Rawlins-Barkley," she said, holding her hand out to each. "But Sarah is fine. This is my husband, Meyers."

He looked the bookish type—not overly tall, with wire-rimmed glasses that perched on a thin, protruding nose. Bradley thought he looked a bit like the Pink Panther actor Peter Sellers, who played the character Inspector Clouseau.

Meyers stood by quietly while his wife did the talking.

"The director said someone accused us of corporate espionage. That's a complete fabrication. Our records are available for your inspection, and the facility is at your disposal. All I ask is that, for safety and insurance purposes, you always be accompanied by a GEC employee. I'm here to answer any questions you may have about the business. Meyers can answer any financial questions you have. We're eager to dispel all accusations about our business and products."

Sarah seemed confident that they would not find any discrepancies. However, she didn't know the real reason for their visit.

"Sarah, thank you for opening your facility to us. We appreciate your cooperation. I'm Agent Bradley Whitman, and this is Agent Naila Noor of the FBI. We have a lot of questions and very little time, so I hope you don't mind if we split our resources."

"Whatever you need, Agent Whitman."

"These are Agents Mufti and Loukanis. Meyers, if you could walk them through the inventory control system from delivery to distribution and provide copies of your vendor list and such, we can try to get through this as quickly and efficiently as possible. Agent Noor and I will need a tour of the manufacturing process from raw materials to finished product," Bradley said.

"I'll be happy to walk you through the entire process," Sarah replied.

Bradley and Naila exchanged a quick glance. They'd assumed Sarah would delegate the tour to the plant manager.

Sarah Lee Rawlins-Barkley is either concerned about the possibility of a problem with her plant or she wants to control what we see, Bradley thought. He decided to watch her closely.

Sarah led Bradley and Naila to the back of the large plant where they took delivery of raw materials such as food, animal, fishery, and forestry waste. At that late hour, employees still went about their business moving composting materials and running machinery.

"Here," Sarah explained over the noisy machine, "the waste is shredded to uniform size to hasten the composting process. Then it's mixed to the desired carbon/nitrogen ratio."

"Which is what?" Bradley asked.

"The finished product is 24 to 1, but the raw can vary, depending on the mixture. We then take that mixture and place it in piles, turning the piles periodically to supply oxygen to the bacteria and to ensure temperatures of 55 degrees centigrade to destroy pathogens. The complete process takes roughly four to six weeks. Let's move inside, shall we?"

She then walked them through grinding, drying, and screening procedures. After that came the horizontal mixer.

"It looks like a large bathtub," Naila chuckled.

"I suppose it does," Sarah smiled. "This is where we mix in our proprietary combination of organic nutrients and mineral fertilizers."

"I assume Meyers will provide a list of all the products you use and the vendors who provide them?" Bradley asked.

"Yes, of course." Sarah moved to the next room. A muscular man with thick biceps and broad chest shoveled organic matter into a funnel-like object on top of a machine. "This is the fertilizer granulator. As you can see, it's fed from the top and moves through the tube. The product is expelled as granules."

"Why is this needed?" Bradley asked. "Why not leave it as is?"

"Granulation aids in time release or slow-acting properties. It's also easier to use and store. And it helps to avoid nitrogen starvation."

"At this stage, how do you know if your carbon, nitrogen, and proprietary nutrients are where you want them to be?" Bradley asked.

"The product is tested between each stage. If needed, adjustments are made before moving to the next step. Let me introduce you to Ed." Sarah waved to a man wearing a denim apron and hovering over a machine that looked similar to the one Bradley had seen in the CDC laboratory.

Ed removed his protective eyewear and walked toward them.

"Ed, this is Agent Whitman and Agent Noor. Would you explain the product-testing process to them, please. Then show them the drying, cooling, and screening areas. I'll meet you in packaging. There's something I need to take care of. If you'll excuse me."

"Of course," Bradley and Naila said.

While Ed described the company's commitment to quality control, Bradley watched as Sarah disappeared through a doorway on the opposite side of the room.

Before moving on to drying and cooling and after Ed finished his complimentary account of Genetic Eco Corporation's safety and quality record, Bradley asked, "Ed, hypothetically, if someone wanted to tamper with your product, how would they do it?"

"Impossible."

"Really? Why do you say that?" Bradley asked.

"Because of the testing. And because the products are always under our control."

"Always? Even at night?" Naila asked.

"We have a security system."

"Okay. But let's say someone managed to get into the facility undetected. How would you know if your product was tampered with?" Bradley smiled, trying to ease Ed off his defensive stand.

"Again. We test it at every stage. Right up to the final screening."

"What happens at the final screening." Bradley asked.

"I'll show you," Ed said.

They nodded at the people operating the drying and cooling machines as they walked by them and toward the door Sarah had exited. As they passed by, Ed gave them an abbreviated version of the processes.

When they entered the next room, they saw Sarah on the far side in a heated discussion with a woman. When Sarah saw them, she took the woman by her arm and led her through another doorway and out of sight.

"See," Ed said, pointing to a machine that was identical to the one he had been using when they met. "The final testing is done here. Then it's screened and sent to packaging in the adjoining building. We have security cameras covering every inch of both warehouses, each one with a motion sensor connected to the alarm system. If a mouse ran through here at night, we would know about it. Not that we have mice here," Ed quickly added.

Bradley focused on the fifteen rotary drum screening machines and the enormous bins of granulated fertilizer that sat beside each.

"Is all of this product waiting to be screened?" Bradley asked.

"Yes. The machine will sort it in three sizes. Whatever remains goes back to the grinder and is recycled."

"How much fertilizer does each bin hold?"

"About three hundred tons," Ed replied.

"And how long will it take to screen that much?"

"Each machine can screen roughly twenty tons per hour, so fifteen hours."

"So, is it safe to say you process about forty-five hundred tons of organic fertilizer per day?"

"Yes, give or take," Ed replied. "But we're getting ready to expand again. The demand is growing."

"And the testing stops when it gets to this point?"

"Of course. There's no reason to keep testing. We don't alter the product once it gets to this stage. As long as the test results fall within our parameters, then all that's left to do is to sort it into size and package it."

"And if it doesn't fall within the parameters?" Naila asked.

"We send it back and start again."

"I'm curious," Bradley said. "How likely is it that two different batches of fertilizer would share the same exact results in every test category?"

Ed chuckled. "Nearly impossible, I would think. There are so many variations. Our concern is only that the product meets our criteria and specific needs."

"What do you do with the samples after they're tested."

"We catalogue the batch and put the samples in storage."

"For how long?"

"What do you mean?"

"How long do you keep the catalogued samples once the batch is out the door?"

"Oh. The rules say two years, but Sarah insists we keep them for a minimum of four years."

"Why's that?" Naila asked.

"To cover her a . . . ah, I mean . . . to protect from unfounded accusations. She's smart that way."

"I see. Has the company had any problems with unfounded accusations before?" Bradley asked.

"Just business rivals' misinformation, as far as I know. It's becoming a very competitive industry."

"Can you tell us who those rivals are?" Naila asked.

"It's best if you ask Sarah for that information," Ed replied. "Shall we move on to the packaging area?"

"I thought Sarah would be rejoining us," Bradley said as he peered at the door Sarah had escaped through.

"I'm sure she'll find us," Ed said as he began to walk.

Ed had just finished talking about the bagging and storing practices when Sarah met up with them.

"I'm sorry to be gone so long. How was the rest of your tour? Did Ed answer all your questions?" Sarah asked.

"He was very helpful," Bradley replied. "I'd like to see the test reports for the previous twelve months."

"All of them?" Sarah raised her brows.

"Yes."

"Well, then, let's go to my office. This could take a while. Thank you, Ed," Sarah said over her shoulder as she began to walk.

"Cate is on line two," Madelyn said over the speaker.

Derek lifted the phone and said, "Really, Cate? You called Bradley?"

"He called me. I merely asked him to check on you. I know you can tell him things that you can't tell me. I thought it might help."

Derek sighed. He found it impossible to be angry with Cate when he knew how worried she was about him.

"Well, I'm fine. No more trips to the bathroom, if that's what you were wondering."

"Yes actually, it was. But that's not why I called."

"Is everything alright?"

"Yes . . . probably . . . most likely . . . I'm not sure," Cate stuttered.

"What is it?"

"I didn't want to call you. I know how much stress you're under already."

"Cate, what's going on?"

"I talked to Sheila, and she's really worried about Alex. She didn't get a postcard from him this week. She said she usually receives them like clockwork, so she's worried something's wrong."

"After one missed postcard? Honey, you know I love your sister, but she tends to jump to conclusions a little quickly, don't you think?"

"I know. But I could hear the worry in her voice. I just want to put her at ease if I can."

Derek rolled his eyes, then thought how fortunate he was Cate couldn't see him.

"What is it you want me to do?" He asked.

"I was wondering if you were keeping tabs on his travels. You know, like you did when Bradley went away."

"Why would I do that?"

"Because you are who you are. You do things like that."

"Cate, I don't monitor everyone's daily lives. I kept an eye on Bradley because he was an FBI agent. And because . . . well . . ."

"You are who you are," Cate said.

Exasperated, Derek said, "I don't know where Alex is but I'm sure he's fine. He's a very capable young man who's used to traveling. He probably lost track of time, that's all."

"He's somewhere in India. But I'm sure you're right. I just hoped I could give Sheila some concrete news as to his whereabouts."

"I'm sure she'll hear from him soon. I'm sorry but I've got to get back to work. I'll see you tonight," Derek said.

"Rusty and I will be waiting for you."

The initial annoyance Derek felt about Cate's call soon evolved to gratitude by way of appreciation. He understood Cate's desire to alleviate her sister's worries just as he felt a need to alleviate Cate's concerns. Such realizations amazed Derek—those moments when he knew that he and Cate were kindred spirits.

He made a silent promise that he would find time to see if he could determine where in India Alex Carson could be found.

DIVULGING DECEIT

After Sarah left Bradley and Naila alone in the storage area, Naila said, "Don't you think that if there were discrepancies in the tests and they knew that, we wouldn't find them here?"

"We aren't looking for discrepancies," Bradley replied.

"I don't understand," Naila said.

"We're looking for similarities. Exact duplicates. If Genetic Eco is trying to hide contamination, they would need to supply false test printouts from the equipment. The only way to do that is to test the same batch more than once under a new batch number."

"And Ed said it's nearly impossible to have identical readings." Naila smiled.

"This is the best way to find out if they're aware of the problems we found with their product."

From his briefcase, Bradley retrieved the report Dr. Howe had given him and read from it.

"M 0 5 2 2 9 8 0 2 1. Let's start with that batch. It's from the first reported case in Kansas. We'll work our way backwards from that report and see if we have any perfect matches."

The document was dated February 20.

"Four months ago," Bradley whispered. "He was here."

"Who was here?"

"Al-Haqani."

"How do you know that?"

"This morning Derek and Sam received word that al-Haqani crossed the Canadian border into North Dakota two days ago. After checking the activity of the passport he used, they discovered that he was also here four months ago."

"He's here? Now?"

"Maybe. It's possible he already left before they got their information. We don't know."

"What the hell are we doing here? We should be out looking for him!"

"I'm sure there're plenty of agents on the case, Naila. Our job is to investigate here so we can stop people from dying. And we need to be quick about it."

Naila sighed. "You're right."

After nearly an hour of comparing soil test results, Bradley said, "I haven't found any duplicates. How about you?"

"Nothing yet? We've gone back more than three months, Bradley. I don't think Genetic Eco knows anything about their product being compromised."

"I think you're right. We need to talk to Sarah."

Bradley and Naila were escorted to Meyers office where they found Sarah and her husband in deep conversation.

"Excuse us," Bradley said, "but we need a word with the two of you."

"Where are agents Mufti and Loukanis?" Naila asked.

"In the adjoining office going through our vendor list." Meyers pointed to a door on the side wall.

"Naila, could you ask them to join us, please?" Bradley asked.

With the six of them settled, Bradley began.

"I'm sure you must be wondering about the accusations against your company. First, let me apologize for the ruse. There is no corporate espionage complaint against you, as the director told you."

Sarah abruptly stood. Anger shot from her eyes. "What do you mean no complaint? What the hell is going on?"

"Please, sit down, and I'll explain. I'm afraid it's a lot worse than that," Bradley said.

Sarah's expression morphed to concern.

"You've undoubtedly heard about the so-called listeria outbreak in middle America right now?"

"So-called listeria? What are you saying?" Sarah asked.

"We have reason to believe that your fertilizer has been intentionally compromised and is the probable cause for the outbreak. We haven't determined how it was sabotaged or with what, but the CDC is working on it."

It was Meyers who then jumped to his feet. "That's impossible!"

"I'm afraid it isn't," Bradley said. "We've tested the fertilizer, Genetic Eco fertilizer, that we took from a farm in Kansas." Bradley handed Meyer's the CDC report. Meyers glanced at the paper, then handed it to Sarah, who inspected it thoroughly.

"This is from one of our bags of fertilizer?" She asked, her eyes wide.

"Yes, several actually. And it was tested multiple times. But the test report you have on file for that batch reads completely different."

"I would hope so," Sarah exclaimed. "These readings are completely wrong. How could this happen?"

"We were hoping you could tell us," Naila said. "If what you have told us is true, it would have had to have happened after the final testing. Somewhere between sorting and bagging."

"Of course I told you the truth. Why would I lie?" Sarah said.

Angrily, Meyers shouted. "That's enough. My wife doesn't lie. And nothing happens in this facility without us knowing. We have a security system. We would have been alerted if someone tampered with our product. What about after it was bagged and shipped? Maybe someone used a needle to inject something into the bags. That kind of thing happens."

"The outbreak is more far-reaching than the media has been told. We're not talking about a few bags here. That scenario is highly unlikely," Bradley said.

Standing behind Bradley, Agent Ayla Mufti spoke. "It's a new security system. Kind of expensive, too."

"How new?" Bradley asked, looking back at her.

Ayla Mufti looked at her notes. "Four months ago."

Bradley and Naila looked at one another.

"What made you upgrade the security system four months ago?" Bradley asked.

"Vandalism," Meyers barked. "Some kids got into the facility and spray-painted graffiti on the walls and tipped over some tables. General disruption stuff." When he saw the agents exchange knowing glances, he continued. "Nothing was stolen or tampered with. And there's no indication that anyone entered the sorting or shipping areas."

Bradley watched as Sarah's perfect posture melted.

Turning to her, Bradley asked, "Can you say for sure that no one went into those rooms?"

Realizing the implication, Sarah showed fear. "No," she sighed.

"This is ridiculous," Meyers yelled. "They were kids."

"Did they catch the culprits?" Bradley asked.

Meyers frowned.

"No," Sarah replied.

"We need to get the Centers for Disease control here immediately. You'll need to shut down this plant and place a recall on all the products produced after that date. We'll need a list of every store and farm you shipped to, all your employee files, and the names of anyone else who's been in these buildings in the last four months."

Bradley lifted his cell phone.

Meyers opened his mouth to object but promptly shut it when Sarah glared at him. The tension between them did not escape Bradley's attention.

Bradley moved out of earshot and dialed Sam's number.

"What have you got?" Sam asked.

"We need to get the CDC here. Genetic Eco Corporation had a break-in four months ago. It was made to look like a juvenile case of vandalism, but I believe that's when al-Haqani implemented his plan. We're pretty sure we can rule out collusion between the company and al-Haqani, but I wouldn't let them off the hook yet. There's something else going on."

"Like what?"

"I'm not sure yet."

"Well, figure it out quick. CDC isn't far away. Fill them in when they get there. Then I'm going to need you and Naila back here."

Bradley hung up and motioned for Naila to meet him by the door.

"I need to speak with Sarah alone, without Meyers. Can you keep him occupied?" Bradley asked.

"I'll get him working on collecting the employee files," she replied.

Bradley turned his wheelchair toward Sarah and said, "Sarah, I have a few more questions about the reclaiming process of the fertilizer. Could you take me back to the re-sorting room, please?"

"Of course."

In the hallway, Bradley asked if the un-sorted fertilizer was somehow sterilized before it went back through the manufacturing process."

"No. There's no need to. We clean the machines and containers on a regular basis, but the reclaimed fertilizer gets mixed back in with the raw materials. Oh, my God!" Sarah stopped walking. "You mean that if one batch of fertilizer was contaminated, then the reclaimed product would contaminate subsequent batches."

"It's possible, yes."

"But it would go through the testing process all over again."

"True. But you test the product to your specific parameters, not for actual ingredients. Is it possible that small amounts of contamination could go undetected?"

"I suppose it is."

"And, depending on the contamination, could it continue to germinate?"

"I . . . I don't know. Yes, I suppose." Sarah placed her hands on her face in an attempt to hold back tears. "This never should have been possible," came the muted statement.

"What do you mean?" Bradley asked.

"I've been after Meyers for two years to update the security system. He kept putting it off, saying we couldn't afford it."

Sarah removed her hands from her face, and Bradley saw only anger.

"Is that why there is so much tension between the two of you?" Bradley asked.

Sarah jerked her head and met Bradley's gaze.

"What do you mean? What tension?"

Bradley had always been good at reading people and situations. He was sure then that he knew the answer to his question, but he needed to make sure he hadn't missed something. Bradley turned his chair to face Sarah.

"Who was the woman you had words with in the sorting room a little while ago?"

Sarah exhaled hard. "She's one of the reasons we didn't have the money for the security system. You see, Meyers likes nice things! Nice, young things that he can hang off his arm in the casino."

A tear spilled from her eye.

"I'm sorry." Bradley gently replied.

"He thinks I don't know, but she's not the first employee I've had to fire. I've been replacing the money he's taken from the company with my own, and he doesn't have a clue. But now? All this? I can't do it anymore. The stockholders will eat us alive. My family's legacy is ruined."

Bradley paused, then said, "Maybe not!"

"How could it not be?"

"You may be able to salvage the family name if you become part of the solution. The CDC is going to need your help in determining how this happened. Your best move is to cooperate."

"Of course, I'll help. People are dying!" She paused, then said, "Ed, I need to talk to Ed. He's a remarkable scientist. No one knows more about fertilizer than Ed."

Bradley nearly countered her statement, thinking about Dr. Howe, but kept silent.

"The CDC are on their way. Don't let Meyers stonewall them."

"He won't be able to, because he won't be here!"

"Just one more thing. I need a sample of the raw fertilizer."

Bradley sent a text to Dr. Howe asking if she was still at the lab. She responded that she would be working for a few more hours that night. He responded that he was on his way.

HAM AND BEANS

The same CDC personnel that had flown with Bradley and his fellow FBI agents from Washington were led into Sarah's office. Bradley and Naila relayed everything they had discovered in the inspection, including Bradley's concern that there might be remnants of contamination in the raw fertilizer due to reincorporating reclaimed product. Agents Mufti and Loukanis would stay behind to finish gathering necessary information.

By then, Meyers was nowhere to be seen, the plant had stopped production, and Sarah and Ed were giving the CDC their full cooperation.

Back on the plane, Bradley called Sam.

"We're on our way back," Bradley told him.

"Good. We need your best assessment. What do you think his next move will be? Has he left the country? Or would he stay and watch? Is there more we should be looking for? This could be the most important profile you will ever dissect. Make it a good one!"

"What's happening with the CDC? Any progress in identifying the elements of the contamination?" Bradley asked.

"Nothing yet. They just issued a nationwide warning. It's just a matter of time before the public starts to panic. Hospitals in many states are already overfilled. The president is going to make a statement in the morning issuing a national emergency. I guess they didn't want the rioting to start tonight. Either way, the word is out."

"I've got something to drop off at Dr. Howe's lab. We'll come to the office right after."

Following the call, Bradley took a moment to imagine what might happen next. Panic would set in. People would rush to grocery stores only to find empty shelves. With police overburdened, looting would cause business owners to protect their property with force. Pure chaos would ensue! Just as al-Haqani planned.

"What did he say?" Naila asked.

"He wants to know what al-Haqani is going to do next. And you and I need to figure that out, fast!"

"There's no one on this planet that knows him better than you. Put yourself in his head. What would you do?" Naila asked.

The world around him began to spin, and Bradley's chest felt as if it were weighed down with searing, black tar. He had a notion to stand and run away but knew, even if his legs worked, the heaviness he sensed would be too much to carry. His breathing grew quick and shallow.

"Bradley! Are you alright?"

Naila's voice reached through the sludge and grounded him. He immediately took control of his breathing, then imagined the darkness seeping out of his body. The entire episode lasted only seconds.

"Yes, I'm fine," he replied in even, deep breaths.

It wasn't the first time Bradley had experienced hyperventilation due to anxiety. But he had gotten better at pulling himself out of it when it did occur. Normally, he chastised himself afterwards for being weak. However, under the current extreme circumstances, Bradley cut himself some slack.

Ignoring Naila's concerned expression, Bradley said, "Okay. What would al-Haqani do?" He then closed his eyes and pictured himself a young boy in Asadabad—the Afghanistan war all around him, family and friends dying, his school destroyed, and his country invaded by Americans. Minutes went by as his eyes darted, unseen behind his closed lids. His hands gripped the arms of his wheelchair until his knuckles turned white. His breathing grew labored, and sweat spilled down his cheek.

More worried than before, Naila prepared to bring him out of his thoughts, but then Bradley's eyelids shot open.

"He's still here!" he said. "Probably close to the border, but he's still here. He has several escape routes planned. But he won't leave through Canada again. And I'll bet he already ditched the car."

With her phone, Naila had recorded every word Bradley spoke. She could tell by his glazed-over eyes that he was still in al-Haqani's head, and she didn't want to interrupt his train of thought with questions.

He continued. "When he attended HEI, al-Haqani traveled around the country."

Bradley stopped speaking, reached into his briefcase, and retrieved a file folder. He ruffled through pages until his eyes focused on one. "DC, Texas, Florida, New York, California, Minnesota, Louisiana, and, of course, Massachusetts. He spent time in each of those states. Last year's attacks affected Massachusetts; Washington, DC; New York, California, and Minnesota. It always bothered me that we never connected Florida and Louisiana to any of his plans. He went to both for a reason. I think he's in one of those states. Probably Florida. If I were him, I would be in Miami. And I would have a boat waiting to take me to Cuba!"

Bradley paused, took a deep breath, then rapidly blinked his eyes. He glanced around as if he had just been awakened from a trance. In Naila's hand, he noticed the phone still recording.

He looked up at Naila and nodded. "Send it to Sam."

Ten minutes after Naila pushed send, Bradley's phone rang. It was Derek. "Sam's on another call. How sure are you about this, Bradley?"

"It's the only thing that makes sense. His plans have always been meticulous with no wasted steps. The only thing I haven't figured out is what, if anything, will happen in Louisiana."

"Hang on. Sam is finishing his call. I'll put you on speaker." Derek said.

Sam spoke. "Louisiana State Police found the SUV nearly submerged in Lake Pontchartrain. It was loaded with cement. Someone clearly never meant for it to be found. Lucky for us, it got held up on rocks."

"There's your answer, Bradley," Derek said.

"You might just be right about this," Sam said. "Get that plane back here. I'm going to Miami."

They ended the call with plans to meet Sam on the tarmac in Washington, DC.

The airplane's loading platform lowered Bradley and Naila to the pavement. Waiting for them nearby, Sam stood next to a small suitcase and his worn, black briefcase. Bradley got the impression the suitcase always resided in Sam's office for purposes like the one he found himself involved with at the moment.

While airline employees refueled Cessy, Sam updated Naila and Bradley on casualties. The death toll had more than tripled with warehouses used as hospitals. With still no news on what they were dealing with, he told them both to go home and get some rest.

Bradley and Naila watched Sam's plane take off before saying goodnight to each other. Each retrieved their vehicle from the airport's private parking area.

Bradley headed to the CDC lab. It was almost 9:30 when he opened the laboratory door to the near empty room. Audrey sat with her head bent, looking into what Bradley perceived as a very expensive microscope.

Remembering how he caught her by surprise that morning, Bradley cleared his throat to announce his arrival.

Audrey Howe jumped in her chair.

Bradley chuckled. "I'm sorry. I tried not to startle you."

Audrey wearily smiled and joked, "I actually think you woke me."

"It has been a very long day," Bradley agreed.

"How was Iowa?"

"Dark. But I brought you a souvenir."

Bradley reached for his briefcase and retrieved a vacuum-sealed plastic bag. "This is from Genetic Eco's raw fertilizer stock. They reclaim odd-sized processed fertilizers, mixing their sample back in with the raw materials. My theory is that the bacteria, chemical, or whatever it is we're looking for would leach from the processed stuff back into the raw. If that's the case, we have a lot more contaminated fertilizer than originally thought."

Audrey took the sample and walked over to a pair of machines that, Bradley thought, resembled a very large coffee maker and a very small dishwasher. He watched as she added the sample to the coffee maker then moved to an adjacent computer and typed on the keyboard. He could hear the machine at work.

"What is that?" he asked.

"I'm using liquid chromatography with tandem mass spectrometers. It's a two-step process for analyzing complex mixtures."

"How long will it take?"

"It could be an hour, maybe less."

"I'm sorry. I didn't mean to keep you here. I didn't expect you to give up the rest of your evening," Bradley said.

"It's alright. I wasn't leaving anytime soon. I've got other tests running. But if you need to leave, I can call you with the results if you'd like."

"I had planned to go back to the office, but now I don't have to. So, no, there's no place that I need to be."

"No?"

"No. My very good friend Cate is taking care of my dog. I had a feeling this might be a long night."

"Ah, that's very nice of your friend."

"Cate's one of the most generous people I've ever met," Bradley smiled.

Audrey returned the smile.

Bradley sighed. "I guess we have some time to kill. I don't know about you, but I haven't eaten all day. And I don't think take-out is going to be an option for a while. Does this place have a cafeteria or vending machines?"

"I'm famished. There's a small cafeteria on the first floor. We might be able to find something there that's safe to eat. They're closed for the day, but I have a key." Audrey reached into her lab coat pocket and retrieved a ring with multiple dangling keys.

"Let's go," Bradley said.

The reality of the day reinforced itself as they stared at nearly empty shelves in the cafeteria kitchen.

"Wow," Audrey sighed.

"Yeah."

"Isn't it strange how you can know a thing, but the enormity of it doesn't really register in your brain until you see evidence of it with your own eyes."

Bradley shuddered. "And tomorrow, everyone will see it. It's going to spark chaos."

Neither spoke for several moments. Then Bradley rolled his wheelchair over to a storage rack holding a stack of canned baked beans. He inspected one of the labels and noticed a printed canning date from the previous year. Next to the beans sat canned ham, also dated more than four months previous.

"All we need is some canned brown bread with raisins, and we'll have my childhood Saturday night meal," Bradley grinned.

"I prefer my brown bread without raisins, please," Audrey smiled.

"Well," Bradley said as he searched the rack, "I think we are both out of luck when it comes to brown bread. But ham and beans should do. Alright with you?"

"Sounds delicious. Here, let me," Audrey said as she reached for the items.

"You heat the beans. I'll take care of the ham." Bradley handed her a can.

Bradley cut two large slabs off the canned ham, wrapped the rest in plastic wrap, and placed it in the refrigerator. He also found canned pineapple rings that he pan-fried along with the ham and presented as garnish. The process felt very nostalgic, as his mother used to do the same thing when he was a child.

He plated the ham and pineapple and placed the two dinner dishes on the counter. "Voila!"

Audrey spooned steaming baked beans onto each plate. "I'll let the rest cool before I put them away. Let's eat."

Bradley slid a chair away from a nearby table and pulled his wheelchair into place. Audrey put the dinner plates on the table with plastic forks, knives, and napkins. Then Bradley reached and pulled out her chair.

"Merci."

They ate in silence for several minutes. Breaking the silence, Bradley asked, "So, what about you, Audrey? How does your family feel about you working this late at night?"

"They don't know I'm still working."

Bradley placed his fork on his dish and looked her in the eyes.

"What do you mean they don't know?"

Audrey chuckled. "It's not like it's a secret. This is my ex-husband's week to have our daughter. Although I'm sure Kevin knows I'm working late tonight, it was a contentious subject when we were married."

"Oh. I'm sorry. I didn't mean to pry."

"No, it's fine. We have a relatively workable relationship," she said as she scooped a forkful of baked beans into her mouth.

Bradley picked up his fork and did the same. A moment passed before he said, "You have a daughter?"

"Yes. Allison. She's eight going on twenty-three," Audrey laughed.

There is something soothing and maternal about her laugh, Bradley thought.

"Is she as smart as her mother?"

"Much smarter. She was reading at second grade level before she even started elementary school. And her math skills are astonishing." Audrey gushed. "Sorry. I get a little carried away when I talk about Allison."

"That's nothing to be sorry about. But her accomplishments are a reflection of excellent parenting. You should take at least some of the credit."

"Thank you, Bradley. That's very nice of you to say."

"I keep trying to take credit for my godchild's successes, but his mother keeps reminding me that we spent most of his childhood living three thousand miles apart."

"What's his name?"

"Alex. Alex Carson. He has a twin brother, Max. They're both very intelligent and successful but in completely different ways."

"How so?"

"Alex is the creative type. He's a writer. In fact, his debut novel is being made into a film."

"That's impressive. What about his brother?"

"Max is a geophysicist. He's very analytical. Both are doing quite well."

"Are they your nephews?"

"No, I'm an only child. They're my friends Sheila and David's sons. They live in California."

"It's got to be tough living so far apart."

"It is. I was just so honored that they would consider me to be one of the godfathers."

"Please feel free to tell me to mind my own business, but I'm curious. Why are you godfather to only one of the twins?"

Bradley chuckled. "My best friend Derek is Max's godfather. He's also Sheila's brother-in-law. It was a very democratic decision on their part."

"Well, Alex is a very lucky young man."

"Thank you," Bradley said as he lifted a speared piece of ham into the air to simulate a toast.

Audrey mimicked his move.

"It must be hard being separated from your daughter," Bradley said.

"It is. But Kevin and I both know it's important she have as much balance as possible. It makes it easier knowing she's only a few miles from me. I can pop in and see her anytime I want. The same is true for Kevin when she's staying with me."

"I admire the two of you."

"Don't admire us too much. It doesn't always go smoothly."

"What does?" Bradley asked.

"Good point."

After cleaning the cafeteria kitchen and locking up, they returned to the lab. The test on the fertilizer sample Bradley had brought was complete.

Audrey retrieved the report from the printer and examined it.

"Confirmed. The raw materials have been infected by the reclaimed fertilizer," she said. "You were right. The contamination goes well beyond that first infected batch. It's slight, but it's pushing the limits."

Dread seemed to fill the room.

ELEVEN FIFTY-NINE

While examining the map on his laptop, Max dined on an old, pre-packaged pastry tart. Heeding his mother's warning, he had cleared his shelves and refrigerator of suspect food items.

Using the mouse, he zoomed on Kolkata, West Bengal, India—the last place he knew Alex to be. Max and Alex used a cell phone tracking app to keep tabs on each other when traveling. Occasionally, one of them would turn off the app's access to allow some privacy, but those times were few and far between. It wasn't their habit to keep secrets from one another.

After more than a week without hearing from Alex, Max had checked the app. The tracking showed he had been in or around the Kolkata railway station three days prior. Since then, the app showed no additional movement. Either Alex had turned the app off, or he lost his cell phone in the vicinity of the train station, Max thought. But that would be unlikely. Alex is obsessed with his phone.

"He said he was going to Mother's House in Kolkata," Max said out loud to himself. "I'm sure he's fine. He probably hooked up with somebody and lost track of time," he chuckled, but not convincingly.

It had been two weeks. Two Saturdays without hearing from Alex. That had happened only twice before, and each time, Alex had warned him ahead of time that would be the case.

A chill ran through Max. He set the pastry on his desk and picked up his cell phone. The time on his home screen read 8:59

p.m. That meant it was almost midnight in DC. He would wait until morning to call his godfather, Derek.

Derek couldn't sleep. A glance at the clock showed the time as 11:59 p.m. He had lain his exhausted body in bed more than an hour before, but his thoughts would not cede to slumber.

Cate lay sleeping beside him. He rolled on his side to face her and silently watched her. A strand of her thick brunette hair had fallen across her cheek and splayed on the mattress. Derek gently swept the hair from her face and tucked it behind her shoulder.

He recalled the worry on her face when she found him in his office that morning. He hated that he had caused that look but was apprehensively thankful she had chosen that moment to stop in. Just to look up and see her there had washed away the bulk of his anxiety. At that moment he reminded himself there was nothing more important in his life than Cate. And no matter what the future held, he would always be grateful for that.

As he matched his breaths to hers, he felt a sense of tranquility, and the clutter in his head faded to whispers.

The last thing he heard before drifting off was the contented sigh of Rusty, who lay on the bed by Cate's feet.

Bradley rolled through his front door. The drive home had been worrisome. He had offered to follow Audrey to make sure she got home alright, but she insisted she would be fine on her own. He asked her to text him once she was home safely, but he wished he had been more forceful, as he had seen signs of unruly nocturnal activity already taking place in the city. In the suburbs where Bradley lived, the streets were quiet.

He checked his phone for a text and found nothing. He tried to convince himself that Audrey had made it home and forgot to text him. After all, he was sure she had more important matters on her mind. And going home to an empty house was discouraging to say the least. That's exactly how he felt at that moment without Rusty there to greet him. He rolled his chair toward the bedroom, exhausted from the day.

At 11:59 before he reached the bedroom door, his text tone sounded.

Audrey had caught a glimpse of what the near future promised when she saw a young man on Vermont Avenue throw an item through the glass of a storefront window. At that moment, she had wished she accepted Bradley's offer to escort her home.

As she rode the elevator to her seventh-floor condominium, she thought about Bradley. It had been a long time since a man had piqued her interest. She had been divorced for five years and had yet to go on a date. The invitations were there, but she just hadn't felt inclined to accept any of them.

Bradley seemed different. He was sweet, funny, and confident without being cocky or condescending. He had genuinely listened to her—and not only to those topics pertaining to the current crisis, but also to the small tidbits of personal details they shared. She felt him quite refreshing and easy to talk to.

Yawning, she set her purse on the hall table, then turned and deadbolted her door. The emptiness of her home caused momentary anxiety. But the more she thought it through, she was glad that Allison had been with her father that night. Audrey would not have been able to concentrate fully on her work if Allison had been home with her part-time nanny. She would have spent the day worrying about her.

And she certainly wouldn't have stayed at work so late. I would have missed the delightful dinner with Bradley, she thought, then smiled. But her smile quickly turned to a frown when she remembered how Bradley lit up when he talked about his friend Cate.

Cate is a lucky girl, she thought. She picked up her phone and texted Bradley.

Made it home fine. Thank you for keeping me company tonight.

She headed straight to her bedroom, kicked off her shoes, and collapsed on the bed. A moment went by before she heard the minute hand of her analog alarm clock tick to midnight. A new day had begun, and Audrey feared what it might bring.

BOUND BY BLOOD

Alex's hands and ankles were bound to a wooden chair. Loosely fastened around his neck, a burlap hood covered his face. Dried blood from the wound on his head tightened his cheek. The skin of his cracked lips curled like ancient parchment.

As best he could determine, it had been ten days since he'd been taken. It was difficult to track time without a semblance of sunlight or fresh air but the dirt floor beneath his feet grew cool. Approaching nighttime, he concluded for, he thought, the tenth time.

If they stuck to schedule, dinner would arrive soon. And so would the interrogation. He'd been told that what he received for food would depend on how he answered their questions.

Under the dark hood, Alex closed his eyes and prayed—something he'd done little of in his daily life, but at present seemed of great consequence. He asked for strength to cope with the terror that enveloped his mind, body, and spirit. He begged for insight about his captors. But mostly, he prayed that the last-ditch effort he implemented before his kidnapping would lead to his freedom.

"Your godson is on line two." Madelyn spoke over Derek's intercom.

Derek picked up the phone and tapped the button.

"Max, good morning. It's pretty early for you, isn't it?" Derek noted the clock in his office read 8:05, making it just after 5 a.m. in California.

"Yeah, a little."

Looking at the red dots on his computer's California map, a sudden moment of panic set in. "Is everyone okay?"

"Ah, yeah. Well, I think so. I don't know."

"Max, what is it?"

"I haven't heard from Alex. I'm a little worried."

Derek sighed in relief. "Yes, your aunt Cate told me your mother didn't get a postcard from him this week. I told . . . "

"It's more than that," Max interrupted. "I haven't spoken with Alex in more than two weeks—sixteen days, actually. But his phone hasn't moved in the last nine days. I haven't told mom or dad, but I'm really worried something's happened to him."

"Like what?"

"I don't know. Maybe he was mugged? Maybe he's in a hospital somewhere? Maybe he . . . " Max couldn't express out loud his next fear. "You know how he is, Uncle Derek. He trusts everyone. He's a walking target."

"Hold on, Max. Alex is a smart kid. He's been traveling alone for a few years. I wouldn't count him as an easy mark. I'm sure there's a good explanation, but why don't you send me everything you know about his whereabouts. I'll make some calls and see what I can find."

"Thanks, Uncle Derek. And please, don't tell Aunt Cate I called. She'll call my mom, and that will just upset her more."

"For now, this is between the two of us. Call me if you hear from him."

"I will. Thanks."

Derek hung up and sat back in his chair. It was one thing, he thought, that Cate's sister Sheila would jump to conclusions. But Max wasn't an alarmist. He was analytical and well-reasoned. It just wasn't like him to panic.

The afternoon before, having promised Cate, Derek had reached out to an old friend who worked for the Central Intelligence Agency. He asked him to track Alex down, knowing he was somewhere in India. He had yet to hear back from him, although he hadn't expected to so soon. After speaking with Alex and armed with new information, Derek decided to call his friend again.

"Madelyn, could you get me Eric Sampson, CIA, terrorism analysis unit, please."

"Right away."

A few moments passed before Madelyn's voice came over the intercom. "Mr. Sampson is on line one."

Derek picked up. "Eric, thank you for taking my call. I know things are a bit hectic right now."

"You always were the champion of understatement, Derek. If you're looking for information on Alex Carson, I don't have anything yet."

"Actually, I'm calling to give you some. It seems Alex's brother, Max, has been tracking Alex's phone. There hasn't been any contact, phone calls, or movement in nine days."

"Why would he track his brother's phone? Is there something you're not telling me, Derek?"

"No, nothing clandestine, I promise. He's a twin. They're very close. My godson is just worried about his brother who has fallen out of contact somewhere in India."

"Godson, huh?"

"Yes. Sorry to play the card but I'm more concerned today than I was yesterday."

"Send me everything you've got. Phone number, pictures . . . you know the drill."

"Thanks, Eric."

"I drink bourbon. The high-end stuff."

Derek chuckled, "I remember."

Derek checked his email. Max had already sent Alex's phone's tracking information, itinerary, lodging, and train schedules. Max had also taken photos of postcards and letters he received from Alex the previous month. Derek took time to examine the information, then forwarded everything to Eric Sampson.

His intercom buzzed.

"Yes, Madelyn."

"Agent Whitman is here to see you."

"Please send him in."

As Bradley rolled through the door, Derek closed the computer files pertaining to Alex. He made the quick decision to hold off telling Bradley that his godson could possibly be missing. He didn't wish to take the chance of worrying him unnecessarily.

Bradley entered and asked, "Any news from Sam?"

"They've retrieved the SUV from the lake. I guess it took some doing because it was full of cement bags. They're going through it now, but I think we all know they won't find anything in it that will help. Al-Haqani isn't that reckless."

"No, he's not. What about rentals? He had to have alternate transportation."

"Nothing yet. They're checking everything. What's happening with the CDC lab? Have they found anything yet?"

"Late last night, we confirmed that the contamination goes well beyond the initial tainted batch of fertilizer. Dr. Howe is hoping to get toxicology reports from the dead cattle and the detailed autopsy from the first victims today. She's confident the reports will shed light on what kind of substance we're dealing with." Bradley paused, then said, "The looting has already started. The city's about to explode—here and all around the country."

Derek grimaced. "Yeah. Well, the president is making his statement in about an hour. He's going to call for a nationwide state of emergency and won't rule out enacting martial law."

"I hope he's planning more than that. Someone needs to figure out how we're going to feed more than 330 million people."

"That's not for us to worry about. We need to concentrate on finding al-Haqani. Sam wants an updated profile."

"Derek," Bradley said tentatively, "I'm not sure I'm the best person to rely on for an accurate profile."

Derek narrowed his eyes and locked onto Bradley. "What the hell are you talking about?"

"He's been a step ahead of me this whole time. Ever since he hatched his plan. What if I'm wrong about Miami? What if Sam has put all our resources there and al-Haqani slips through the Canadian border?"

"First of all, we're still watching the Canadian border. Jonathan has a team there. And second, better than anyone, you know how profiling works. What do you keep saying? "The how and why gives you who?" How about "The who and why gives you how?" You know this guy better than anyone. But I get it. You can only do so much. That's why you're not the only person in this country working the case. Our success or failure will fall on all of us! A lot of us. And Ali al-Haqani is only one man."

Bradley looked Derek in the eyes and said, "I'll do my best."

"I know you will. And that's all you can do."

Bradley turned his chair and left Derek's office.

Derek sat back and took a deep breath. Then another. He could not afford to let his anxiety take hold. He made a decision.

"Madelyn. Could you get me Sahani Kumar in the Chelsea, Massachusetts headquarters, please."

"Of course," Madelyn replied.

Tightly wrapped in a blue cardigan sweater, Sahani Kumar sat in her sparsely decorated, taupe-colored Chelsea office.

What should have been early spring weather had returned to late winter chills, and whoever controlled the heat in the FBI headquarters had not gotten the metaphorical memo.

The steaming cup of break-room coffee was all she had to keep warm. When the telephone rang, she was reluctant to pull her hands away from her ceramic coffee mug.

"Hello?" she answered.

"I hope I'm not catching you too early. Have you got coffee in hand yet?"

"Derek?"

"Who else would risk calling you before your second cup?"

"How are you? I'm asking as your psychologist, not your friend?"

"Considering my wife found me hunched over the toilet in my office yesterday, I'd say I've been better."

"What can I do to help?"

"Can you come? I'm not the only one who is feeling the pressure."

"Are you talking about Bradley?"

"I'm talking about everyone, Sahani. The resident psychologists are good, but they aren't you. I could really use your help."

"Work it out with Nick, and I'll be on the next plane out."

"Done. Thank you."

"Hang in, Derek. Remember, you may think the weight of the world resides on your shoulders, but you have an obligation to evict it. None of us are alone."

Derek chuckled. "That's what I just told Bradley."

"You've always been the first to hand out good advice but the last to take it. Why is that?"

"I don't see it that way."

"I know you don't. I'll see you this afternoon."

Sahani hung up and started searching for flights to DC.

When news broke of the rapid spread of deaths the day before, Sahani had thought about reaching out to Derek. Knowing he would be extremely busy, she chose not to. But she had hoped he would reach out to her. After speaking with him, she got the idea that the latest threat was even more dire than the broadcasts had reported.

She dialed her home number. When her wife answered, she asked her to pack her a bag and told her to pay careful attention to the news.

Pre-empting typical morning programming, news networks took over the airways. Television screens flashed headlines such as, "Death virus steamrolling across America," "Food shortage imminent," and 'Is this the End of Days?" None of the reports were accompanied by facts, only fear. Although they reported that the CDC categorized the outbreak as listeria infection, speculation ran rampant.

Once the public learned that more than thirty-thousand people had already died and more than two hundred thousand were hospitalized, panic spread like fire in a wheat field.

It was six-thirty when Cate heard the first police siren. Derek had warned her to keep the doors locked and not go outside, so instead of taking their routine morning walk, she and Rusty curled up on the couch in front of the television. Her stomach churned as she watched events unfold.

The day before, when Cate left Derek's office, she had gone to the local fish market and purchased as much seafood as she could fit in her freezer. Then, at the bulk-item store, she filled a large cart with imported canned and dry goods as well as toilet paper and water, just in case the tap proved unsafe for drinking. It was the dog food that she stressed over most. Checking the dates, she purchased the oldest bags of dry food in stock.

Cate desperately wanted to talk to her sister Sheila but knew Sheila was probably blissfully unaware, being three hours behind, of what had begun to transpire.

By seven o'clock, the sirens were deafening. Cate and Rusty hadn't moved. Video of mobs clambering to get into grocery and department stores broadcast desperation and terror. Car fires, indiscriminate thefts, and senseless vandalism filled the downtown streets.

Cate didn't wait any longer. She called Sheila.

"Cate? It's awful early." Sheila answered.

"Get up now! You and David have to go get Mom and Dad and bring them back to your house. Bring all of their safe food with you. Keep your doors locked."

"What's going on?"

"All hell is breaking loose! Go now before people wake up and see the news. I'll call Mom and Dad and have them start packing. Hurry!"

"Okay!"

Cate had called her parents. It took some convincing, but they agreed to go to Sheila and David's. "Call me when you get there," Cate said before she hung up. All she could do then was wait.

MIAMI

With more than one million registered vessels, Florida was considered the boating capital of the world. Miami-Dade County alone boasted nearly seventy-five thousand registered craft.

"How the hell are we supposed to watch every port and boatyard in South Florida," a voice from the back of the packed Miramar FBI office asked.

"We'll need to spread ourselves thin," Sam Houghton said. "It's not ideal, but it's all we've got. He's here. And it's imperative that we apprehend him, preferably alive. We can't let him slip through our fingers.

"We've already got people positioned at the busiest ports," he continued. "You've got updated photos of the subject. He most certainly will have adapted his appearance, so stay aware. No one leaves their post until replacements arrive. We've got more agents flying in to help.

"Your assignments will include check-in times, and you'll each be given a code word. Memorize your code word. Do not, I repeat, do not forget to use the code word when you call in. If you spot al-Haqani, don't try to apprehend him alone. Call in using your code word and help will arrive. Any questions?"

"What if he doesn't use a boatyard?" another voice asked.

"We're working on that. But with the chaos happening in cities and towns right now, his escaping by boat makes the most sense," Sam answered.

"Anything else?" Sam waited, but all he heard were murmurs from the large group of FBI personnel. "Alright, pick up your assignments and get going."

Glad that al-Haqani had not been particularly careful in his youth, Bradley combed through credit card and cell phone records and everything else he could find pertaining to Ali al-Haqani's trip through Florida nearly ten years before. He had amassed restaurant, gas station, and motel receipts from throughout the state. Most were one-time purchases that told Bradley al-Haqani had merely passed through those areas.

Hours passed, and he was no closer to discovering al-Haqani's exit strategy. He decided to take a break and see if there was any edible food in the breakroom. As he coasted by the elevator, the doors opened, and an agent walked out. But it was the person still standing inside the elevator that caught Bradley's attention.

"Sahani?" Bradley said, sounding more like a question than a statement.

Sahani reached out to hold the elevator door open.

"Hello, Bradley."

"What are you doing here?" Bradley asked.

With her suitcase, Sahani stepped off the lift and allowed the doors to close behind her. "I'm on my way to see Derek."

"He called you."

Sahani didn't respond.

Bradley smiled. "I'm glad you're here. Derek has been a bit . . . anxious, shall I say?"

"And how about you?"

"I'd be kidding myself if I said I wasn't."

"Hopefully we can chat while I'm here?" Sahani asked.

"I would like that, thank you. Oh, and congratulations. I heard you got married."

"How did you know that? We kept it very low key." Sahani smiled.

"I'm FBI," Bradley grinned as he rolled away.

Derek opened his office door for Sahani. "Thank you for coming," he said.

"Of course. You know you can call me anytime," Sahani replied as Derek took her luggage and set it aside.

"How was your flight?"

"The flight was fine. It was the cab ride from the airport that got a little scary. Luckily, my driver knew his way around the mob scenes."

"Christ, Sahani, I'm sorry. I should have thought to send a car to pick you up. Son-of-a-bitch."

"No, Derek. I'm perfectly capable of getting myself from Point A to Point B. Stop berating yourself."

"I'm not berating myself. I just should have thought of it."

"You're berating. That's the most swear words I've ever heard you use. And I'm not even sure I can call them swears. Relax. Sit down. You look awful."

Derek unconsciously adjusted the collar of his blue dress shirt. He had already discarded his tie. He reached for the intercom. "Madelyn, could we have two coffees, please. One black."

"Absolutely," Madelyn's voice sounded.

"You remember how I take my coffee?" Sahani asked.

"I'd be a pretty poor FBI agent if I couldn't remember that," Derek smiled.

Sahani laughed. "I've missed you. How are you? And I don't want the abbreviated version."

Derek thought for a moment, then said, "I feel like I'm on the world's largest roller coaster without any restraints, and it's just by chance that I haven't been thrown out yet. And I know there's another wild turn up ahead. And, oh, by the way, roller coasters make me sick."

Madelyn knocked before entering with the coffee.

"Thank you," Derek said.

Once Madelyn left the room, Sahani asked, "Have you been getting sick? I mean, more than the one time you mentioned?"

"No. Just that one time."

"Well, okay, good."

"Good?"

"Yes! You can't expect to be unaffected by the events around you. You wouldn't be human if you were. Now, I'd be more worried if you were getting physically ill every day or multiple times a day. Remember the last time that happened to you? After the bombing? It's just a warning sign. Let's roll up our sleeves and figure this out, shall we?"

Derek sat back in his chair, threw his head back, and sighed.

"Okay. Where do we start?"

In the near empty office bullpen, frustration was getting the better of Bradley as, unsure of where to look next, he hastily shuffled files. A manila folder fell from the pack and spewed paper onto the floor.

"Goddamn it," Bradley yelled. Someone looked up from across the room, then shifted focus back to their computer.

Bradley bent in his chair and picked up the documents one by one. Each was a photocopy of credit card statements. When Bradley reached for the fifth sheet of paper, something on it caught his eye.

Out loud he read, "Cocoplum Café. Cocoplum Café. Cocoplum Café."

Three times that December week, Ali al-Haqani had patronized the Cocoplum Café in Coral Gables, Florida—part of Miami-Dade County. Bradley quickly picked up the rest of the documents and searched through them.

His eyes widened as he read. He found a receipt for a four-day stay at Fairwinds Motel not far from the café. He searched his browser for boatyards within the vicinity and found several private marinas and three public boatyards within twenty miles—ten miles north and ten miles south.

His heart pounded, and his hands began to shake. Am I grasping at straws? he asked himself. No, I don't think so. Derek. I need to talk this through with Derek.

He darted out of the bullpen and rode the elevator to the sixth floor. He raced his chair to Derek's office, but before he could push through the door, Madelyn headed him off.

"You can't go in there. He's with someone."

"I have to talk to him now. Please. Get him on the intercom and tell him it's an emergency."

Madelyn did as he asked, and a moment later, Derek opened his office door. Bradley could see Sahani sitting behind him.

"Is Cate alright?" Derek asked.

"Yes, yes. This isn't about Cate. I know where he is, Derek. I think I know where he is. But I need to run this by someone. I need to know I'm not crazy."

Derek turned to Sahani and told her he would be right back. "The coffee room. Let's go in there. Madelyn?"

Madelyn replied, "Got it. No one in or out."

They entered the coffee room and shut the door. Bradley told Derek what he had found. "Is it too simple? Am I crazy?"

"Simple doesn't mean wrong," Derek said. "Al-Haqani was a kid, barely twenty years old. He was planning his revenge, but he had no way of knowing anyone would scrutinize his college expenditures, right?"

"Right!"

"Every other trip he took while in the states has played a part in his plan. It makes sense that this would be the final piece. I think you may have found Ali al-Haqani's exit point!"

Derek hurried out of the coffee room with Bradley on his heels. On his way by Madelyn, he said, "Get Sam on the phone."

They rushed into Derek's office. Sahani stood, clearly recognizing something had happened.

When Madelyn buzzed, Derek picked up the phone.

"Sam!" he shouted.

Sahani looked at Bradley and asked, "Should I leave the room?"

Bradley shook his head.

"We know where he's going. I'm going to put you on speaker. Bradley's here."

Derek pressed a button on his phone, then turned and looked at Sahani. "I'm sorry, Sahani. Would you mind waiting outside?"

"Not at all." She looked at Bradley with raised brows. He shrugged his shoulders as she left the room.

"Go ahead, Bradley," Derek said.

"We think he's in the Coral Gables area. Ten years ago, he stayed for four days at a place called Fairwinds Motel. He had to have been casing the area. My guess is his exit point will be within a ten-mile radius either north or south of that point, give or take. There are three public boatyards and more than a few private marinas. But that's the area where we think you should place your focus."

"I'll redisperse now. Send me everything you've got," Sam said, then hung up.

Derek and Bradley sat in silence for a moment. Then Derek went to the door to bring Sahani back into the room.

"You two look like death warmed over," she said.

Both breathed deeply. Sahani knew each was experiencing a great surge of adrenaline and a spike in blood pressure. "Look at me, both of you. Watch me breathe." She slowly breathed in, then out. It took only a few cycles before each had matched her rhythm. "Better?"

Derek nodded, and Bradley grinned.

"Bradley, get that stuff to Sam right away," Derek said.

"I'm going," Bradley replied, then turned his chair and left the room.

That morning, Dr. Audrey Howe woke to the sound of sirens causing the morning fog in her brain to dissipate quickly. Remembering the vandalism she had seen the night before, her first conscious thought was to make sure her daughter was safe.

She sat on the edge of the bed, picked up her phone, and dialed her ex-husband's number.

"This is awful early even for you," Kevin answered.

"I need to know she's okay."

"She's fine. She's sleeping, like I was."

"I'm sorry. The panic has already started. You need to keep her home today. It won't be safe outside for anyone."

"I know. I've been watching. Is this thing as bad as they're making it sound?"

"Yes. You threw out the foods I told you about, right?"

"Yes, Audrey. Don't worry. We'll be fine. I have plenty of ready-to-eat rations and water. How about you? How are you holding up?"

"I'd be better if I could see Allison, but I'm okay. It's going to be a long day. Could you have her call me when she wakes?"

"Yes, I will."

"And Kevin?"

"Yeah?"

"I'm sorry I always gave you a hard time about doomsday prepping. I'm grateful you did."

"Well, I was bound to do at least one thing right in my life," he chuckled. "You be safe out there."

"I will," Audrey answered as she hung up.

Later that morning after analyzing necropsy reports of the dead livestock sent from the Atlanta CDC lab, Audrey began to form a theory. While waiting for the detailed autopsy reports of the Kansas couple, she set up several targeted tests on the Genetic Eco fertilizer. It'd be several hours before she received initial results.

Meanwhile, Audrey researched the possibility of whether her theory was plausible. To do that, she thought it'd be helpful to read every research paper that Ali al-Haqani had written.

At 11:30am, she reached out to Bradley via text message.

Can you send me Haqani's research materials?

I'll email them asap. Found something?

Just theory. Waiting for more info.

Text me your email.

With what she had learned thus far, and of all the scenarios she had played out in her head, she kept returning to one. And the idea of it not only made her shudder but also fascinated her. If she was right, Ali al-Haqani was not only schooled in biology but history as well.

Rather than drive more than five hours to Sacramento to pick up Sheila and Cate's parents, David had used his contacts to charter an airplane. Janet and Bill Wayland met them at the airport, and the four were safely back in Hollywood Hills by 9:45 a.m.

"Was all this really necessary," Bill asked? He had opposed leaving their home, but his wife, Janet, had insisted they follow Cate and Sheila's advice.

"Yes. According to Cate, this is very necessary," Sheila answered.

"Shush, Bill," Janet said, then turned to Sheila and David and informed them, "He's always irritable when he doesn't get his sleep."

"Godammit, Janet. Don't talk about me like I'm not in the room."

Janet swatted her hand dismissively at Bill, then said, "I thought Max would be here."

"I called him from the plane. I'm sure he's on his way," Sheila answered.

"That was a nice little jet you commandeered, David," Bill said. "How much does something like that set you back?"

"Bill!" Janet screeched. "That's rude and none of your business."

David smiled. "Just one of the perks of my business, Bill. When people want something from you badly enough, they'll give you just about anything."

"And what will you have to give in return?" Bill asked, triggering a nasty glare from his wife.

"Probably a small acting part in one of my movies for a wife, daughter, niece, or more likely, girlfriend," David chuckled.

"Hollywood!" Bill said, shaking his head.

Sheila heard a car in the driveway. "That must be Max," she guessed as she raced to the door.

With a suitcase and laptop, Max entered and gave Sheila a hug.

Janet, Bill, and David went to greet him.

"How was the drive?" David asked.

"It's getting a little crazy out there. I swung down Rodeo Drive to check on your shop, Mom. So far, it hasn't been touched. Crowds seem to be building up at supermarkets, pharmacies, and gas stations."

"Medications! I hadn't thought of that," Sheila said as she turned to her parents. "Do you have enough of your medications?"

"How the hell many meds do you think we're taking? We're not on our deathbed, you know!" Bill barked.

"Oh, for crying out loud. Take the luggage to our room and start unpacking. I'll be up in a minute," Janet told Bill.

Bill grudgingly did as he was told.

"This whole thing has got him nervous," Janet said. "He won't admit it, but I think he's worried."

"It's okay, Mom. We all are. Why don't I make some coffee, and then we can call Cate." Sheila suggested.

"You're going to make coffee?" David asked.

"Yes! I can make coffee. I've watched Daisy do it thousands of times," Sheila responded.

"Who's Daisy?" Janet asked.

"Our housekeeper and cook. She's wonderful. She makes the best mocha macchiatos."

"Where is Daisy?" David asked.

"I sent her home. She should be with her family."

Janet nodded in agreement, then said, "Well, then. Why don't you show me what we've got to work with for food. Max, could you bring the cooler that's sitting by the front door into the kitchen, please? We brought what little food we had from home."

"Sure, Grams."

"Then you can fill me in on what you and your brother have been up to," Janet said as she made her way to the kitchen. She didn't see the panicked look on Max's face. But it didn't escape Sheila!

OLD NEWS

The clink of chains alerted Alex to the arrival of his captors. He heard a lock click, then the scrape of rusted metal accompanied by a squeak as he imagined the room's door slowly opening.

Several pair of feet shuffled on the dirt floor. Three of them again, Alex thought. But only one ever spoke.

Alex easily understood his captor's halted English, but the man's vocabulary was limited. Alex had previously surmised that the man's education hadn't taken him outside of Afghanistan.

When his kidnapper spoke, he used the Persian language Dari, also known as Farsi. A moment later, someone lifted the hood off Alex's head.

Alex squinted to adjust to the small amount of light that seeped through the open door. The scene was set much the same as every evening since the interrogations started. The inquisitor stood directly in front of him while the other two lurked in the shadows.

"You will talk now?" the heavily bearded man asked. He wore an ornately embroidered tan tunic, loose fitting tan pants, and brown sandals. A simple tan cap sat on top of his head.

"I'll tell you my life story if you'll just let me out of here," Alex replied.

"Yes, but not so trustful."

"I've told you the truth."

"No. You don't say right. Who do you bring to us?"

"I don't bring anyone. I don't know what you mean. I'm just a writer. I write books."

"You spy to us."

"No. No spy. I'm writing a travel book. About traveling in your country. And Pakistan, and India."

"Who do you bring?"

"I don't understand the question."

The man raised his voice. "Who do you bring?"

"No one. I bring no one. You have my journals. Read them. I just wanted to see your country."

"You say no thing. You not be trustful. You stay." The man started to leave.

"No. Wait. Please," Alex pleaded. "It's a mistake. I'm not a spy. I'm just a writer."

The man's cold, dark eyes fixed on Alex. "You spy. You stay." Then he said something in Farsi and walked away.

The hood slipped over Alex's head, then he heard the shuffling feet, the rattle of chains, and a click. He knew he would soon be given naan and water for his evening meal.

As frustrating as the interrogations were, Alex favored the interaction. As best he could determine, he was held for six days before his jailers began to ask questions. During those six days, the only people he had seen was the woman covered with a hijab who brought him food and the man who accompanied her. The woman never looked at him or spoke. The man only mumbled as he untied Alex's hands to allow him to eat. Not long after, the man would return to retrieve the empty dish and re-bind Alex's hands.

Rather than think about his family and to keep a clear head, Alex repeatedly recalled the circumstances that led him to captivity. He remembered taking the train from the Howrah Railway Station in India to the region of Jammu and Kashmir as he imagined the clacking of the rails and rocking of the railcar.

The territory had always intrigued him because of long-standing border disputes between India and Pakistan as well as India and China. In his head, he tried to list the decades of legal challenges and legislative actions he had read about, ticking them off one by one on his chilled fingers. He brought to mind the violent uprisings and armed insurgencies that eventually prompted the Jammu and Kashmir Reorganization Act of 2019 that dissolved the state. The union territory was then restructured and governed federally by the Union Government of India.

Alex had always told people he could write a mountain of books about the region and still not tell its complete story. Chapter headings began to form in his head, averting him from sinking into despair over his situation.

Jammu and Kashmir had not been Alex's intended destination. He had continued to the Durand Line, a 1,660-mile border between Pakistan and Afghanistan. Although internationally recognized as the border between the two countries, Afghanistan refused to recognize it. From a political and strategic standpoint, the Durand Line was considered one of the most dangerous borders in the world. And, for Alex, that certainly proved true.

It took the driver forty minutes to get Sam and his five-person staff from Miramar FBI headquarters to Coral Gables Hyatt Regency. Sam had booked the only available room to suit their needs—the two-level Presidential Suite. The front door opened to a tan-splashed white-tiled hall with a kitchen to the left, bathroom to the right, and an open-spaced living and dining area straight ahead. The modern décor consisted of a brown, tan, and black color scheme. The ten-foot rectangular walnut dining table quickly filled with laptops, printers, briefcases, and radios.

The master bedroom and bathroom resided on the upper floor and overlooked the living room. No one took time to explore. The hands on the analog kitchen wall clock pointed to 1:42.

"Get these laptops online right away," Sam barked to no one in particular.

"Yes, sir!" a young man replied.

"Are you the technician?"

"Yes, sir."

"What's your name?" Sam asked the man.

"Walt Harper, sir."

"Walt. How long before we're up and running?"

"Ten minutes, sir."

"Stop calling me sir. Get it done."

"Yes, sir . . . I mean, okay."

"Listen up everyone," Sam said as he unfolded a paper map and laid it on the table. "I want constant communication between us and agents posted in our prime zone at these positions." One at a time, he pointed to nine red-circled locations on the map, including the former Fairwinds Motel, three public boatyards, and five private marinas. "We'll monitor them by text or radio. You each have a list of agents' assignments and code words. If an agent checks in without using their code word, proceed as if everything is fine and report it to me immediately after. This guy is smart, resourceful, and without conscience, but as far as we know, he has no reason to think we know he's here. Let's keep it that way. Any questions?"

The four agents kept silent.

"Okay. How we doing, Walt?"

"Almost there, si . . . almost done."

"It's Sam. My name is Sam."

"Yes, sir, Sam." Walt said, then shook his head.

Sam smiled in return.

Three minutes later, Walt informed Sam that communications were up and running. Only Sam had direct communication access to all field agents including those stationed outside the prime zone.

"I want you to stay by my side, Walt." Sam pointed to the empty chair next to him. "I may need help navigating this system."

Walt's eyes widened with excitement. "Anything you need . . . Sam."

For the next thirty minutes, Sam peppered Walt with questions. He familiarized himself with the cutting-edge technology that Walt had implemented. By using cell phone signals, Sam could see real-time locations of each agent. Walt had also activated a feature where Sam could click on any agent and his or her name and code word would pop up on the computer screen.

Sam zoomed onto the computer image to display the prime zone. The satellite image of the area made him feel as if he were there.

"This is good, Walt. Very good."

"Thank you. Now, if you hit this little icon here, it will tell you the last time that agent checked in."

"Really? What if an agent misses their check-in time?"

"You'll get an alert. Right here." Walt pointed to the bottom right of the screen.

Just as he did, a red alert appeared.

Sam stiffened. According to the alert, Agent Rojas should have called two minutes before. Sam was about to click on Rojas's position when the alert box turned from red to green and displayed a message confirming a completed communication with the agent.

"Okay," Sam said. He took a deep breath and sat back in his chair, then he dialed a call on his cell phone.

The phone rang four times before Derek picked up.

"Derek, we're up and running in Coral Gables. Any new information on where he might be?"

"Nothing, Sam. I've got people still looking, but I had to pull Bradley. He's headed back to the CDC."

"What's happening there?"

"Dr. Howe has something. She thought Bradley's research may be able to help. I'm hoping that's a positive sign."

"We could use it. We've got this area locked down as best we can. Call me with any news."

"Same here."

Sam hung up.

On the other side of the table, an agent wearing headphones stood and held his right hand out in front of him as if demanding an oncoming car to stop.

Sam looked at his computer screen. Walt had already zoomed on the location of the agent on the other end of the phone call. Agent Gloria Diaz was one of two agents stationed at Cyprus Yacht Club on Prado Boulevard in Coral Gables. She positioned herself on the north side of the property while Agent Wilson Wallace monitored the south side.

When Sam looked back at the agent on the telephone, Walt said, "That's Agent Simms on the phone with her."

"We have confirmation, Agent Diaz." Sam heard Agent Simms reply before Simms hung up on the call.

"She didn't use her code. She called in on time but didn't use her code," Simms said excitedly.

Sam turned to Walt and said, "Get me the other agent, Wallace, now!"

Walt clicked a few keys on the laptop. The ringing of a phone came through the speakers.

"Agent Wallace," a voice answered.

"Wallace, this is Director Houghton. We require visual confirmation that Agent Diaz is still at her post."

"Yes, Director. One minute please," the voice answered.

Moments passed before the voice returned and said, "I do not have a visual on Agent Diaz. I repeat, I do not have a visual with my binoculars. Shall I abandon my post to check on her?"

Sam only took a moment before replying, "Yes. Proceed with extreme caution. Backup is nearby." Sam hung up, then alerted mobile units to head to the area. Once units were deployed, he phoned the Coast Guard.

Sam cringed when the radio exploded with chatter. This is it, he thought. If we don't catch him now, we've tipped our hand. Ali al-Haqani will be in the wind again.

Sam dialed one more phone number, then said, "Bring the car around."

"So, what's this theory?" Bradley asked without preamble as he entered Audrey Howe's laboratory.

"Bradley! I didn't expect you."

"I thought I could help you with the reports. I'm very familiar with the contents."

"Right. Well, I hope I'm not wasting your time. I have no real evidence yet of what this is except that it is some type of fungus. We're still analyzing the samples."

"But you said you had a theory."

"Yes, but it's a bit . . . old."

"Old? What do you mean?"

"What do you know about Claviceps purpurea?"

Bradley's face went blank. "You got me."

"The genus Claviceps includes roughly fifty species of fungi. I have isolated one specific species known as C. purpurea. This particular fungus is parasitic to grasses and grains. When a spore of C. purpurea infects the crop, it forms a kernel known as sclerotium. Sclerotium remains dormant until conditions are right, such as the onset of spring. Then it begins its fruiting stage. After that, the plant infection process is akin to a man impregnating a woman."

Bradley's eyebrows raised.

Audrey continued. "If the fungal spore has access to the stigma, the pollen grain may develop in the ovary during fertilization. Once infected, it leaches in the soil and spreads quickly and easily. It's also spread by wind and insects."

"And if directly eaten by livestock?" Bradley asked.

"The ergot alkaloids invade the animal's system and wreak havoc with circulation and neurotransmission. Symptoms may vary by species, but the results are the same."

"And humans?"

Audrey indicated an unpromising expression.

Bradley took a moment to digest the information. Then said, "I've heard that word before, ergot. What is it?"

"Why am I not surprised you've heard of it? Ergotism dates back a hundred million years and was the first recognized form of toxic mold poisoning. The ergot sclerotium contains high concentrations of alkaloid ergotamine. This led some physicians in the 1830s to experiment with medicinal uses, including childbirth-related issues and migraines."

"But it's toxic?"

"It's a fungus like penicillin is a fungus. But eventually they found the risks outweighed the benefits and stopped using it. But ergotism poisoning dates back much further than that. How familiar are you with Peter the Great?"

"The Russian tsar?"

"The same. In 1722, as his forces waged war on the Ottoman Empire, his army ate bread made from poisoned grain. It was documented that his troops suffered severe burning sensations, nerve contractions, and loss of limbs—their hands and feet just fell off. Epidemics of the disease have gone by many names, but mostly it is known as St. Anthony's Fire because of the burning. Over the centuries, tens of thousands of people have died from ergotism."

"Wait. St. Anthony's Fire! I've heard of that." Bradley slapped his hand to his head. "Of course! How stupid!"

"What is it?"

"Al-Haqani's last communication. He included St. Anthony's prayer. He told us what to expect, I just didn't see it! Dammit!"

"How could you possibly have known that? When was his last communication?"

"Three days ago. I know him—how his mind works. I should have caught that. I could have stopped this!"

"No, you couldn't. There's no way anyone could have stopped this once the fertilizer hit the fields. And that happened months ago. Besides, there's more to it than that."

"How much more?"

"I'm not sure, but this isn't a typical spore of ergot sclerotium. It's been modified."

"How?"

"I don't know yet. But he had to do something to disguise the diseased crops. Ergot is very easy to spot. Farmers would have seen it and destroyed the affected crops to keep it from spreading."

"So, he made some sort of hybrid fungus?"

"It would seem so. I need to see all his research, whatever you can get your hands on."

"He experimented back in college. That might be the best place to start." Bradley reached for his briefcase, retrieved several folders, and laid them on Audrey's desk.

"I haven't seen news today. What's happening out in the world?" Audrey asked.

Bradley returned the same unpromising expression Audrey used earlier. "Bedlam."

By then, the president had made his public address, and the American people realized that the situation was more dire than initially reported. Across the country stores were broken into, looted, and burned. Fear gripped the nation. And with fear came disorder and lawlessness.

The reports Derek and Sahani watched sparked physical pain in Derek's body. The thousands of deaths seemed unfathomable to him. But it was the cruelty of a terrified nation baring its teeth that made him sick. Television reports showed mothers fighting each other for baby food and talked of home invasions of the elderly. Synagogues and churches burned for no reason, and the streets exploded with gunfire. One report focused on a young man—no more than sixteen years old, Derek thought—who had been shot in the back. A bystander told the reporter that he died for a gallon of milk.

Derek shot up from his chair and ran into his office bathroom. Sahani retrieved the television's remote control and turned it off.

When Derek returned, he apologized to Sahani.

"My God, Derek! How could you not feel sick after watching that?" Sahani asked.

"I didn't see you kneeling beside me in the bathroom."

Sahani scooted to the edge of the couch, leaned forward, rested her elbows on her thighs, then cupped her hands. "That's because I don't feel responsible for what's happening. Because I'm not. And neither are you."

"I know that."

"No, Derek. You don't. You might be able to say the words, but deep down, you don't believe them. Deep down, you think you should be able to save the world." Sahani paused. "You know, I completely understand why you and Bradley are so close. When it comes to a savior complex, you two could be twins. You've just been able to hide it better. Even from yourself."

Derek was about to reply when his phone rang. He glanced at the caller's ID. It was Bradley.

"Yeah, Bradley. What have you got?" He noticed Sahani's lips curl.

"I missed it, Derek. I'm sorry. I should have seen it, but I missed it."

"Missed what?"

"Saint Anthony. Al-Haqani told us what was about to happen. Saint Anthony's Fire! He's modified a centuries-old fungal epidemic and somehow managed to cloak the symptoms so growers had no idea their crops were contaminated."

Not understanding exactly what Bradley meant by Saint Anthony's Fire, Derek did grasp the concept he relayed. "Have they isolated it? Do they know how to counter it?"

"No. They're still working on it. But we've wasted valuable time. I've wasted valuable time."

"Look, I don't know how you think you should have picked up on the Saint Anthony connection, but we had the best minds in the country analyzing that communication, including you, and they all missed it. You can't put this on yourself, Bradley."

"No one knows him like I do. I blew it. I'm going to stay here at the lab and see if I can help Dr. Howe figure this out. Any news from Sam?"

"Last I heard, he moved his team to Coral Gables."

"It's going to take a miracle to catch this guy."

"We'll get him." Derek hung up. When he turned to look at Sahani, her expression conveyed an "I told you so" reaction. "Alright! I get it."

"The question is," Sahani asked, "can you continue to live with it?"

Derek pondered her question. He knew something felt different, he just didn't know what. Surprising himself, he responded, "I don't really know."

"How's Cate?"

"Cate? She's fine. She's worried about her family, but she's holding up okay. She's home, alone. Well, she has Rusty to keep her company."

"And physically? Has she recovered fully from the . . . ?"

"Yes," Derek cut her off. "Just a slight limp and occasional headaches. But she's doing great."

"Why didn't you want me to finish my question, Derek?"

Derek looked confused. "What do you mean?"

"You knew I was asking about the bombing, but you stopped me before I could say the word. Why is that?"

"No. I just anticipated your question. I'm sorry I interrupted."

"No. You cut me off so I wouldn't say the words out loud. Tell me something. When is the last time you thought about the limousine bombing?"

Derek ran his hands over his face and sighed. "I dreamt about it last night."

"And what did you imagine just now when you saw the image of that young boy lying on the sidewalk?"

A tear threatened to fall from the corner of Derek's eye. He quickly wiped it away. "I saw Cate. It was Cate lying on the sidewalk." He cleared his throat to help squelch his emotions.

"Okay. Now we're getting somewhere."

"How did you know?"

"I know you, Derek. It wasn't too difficult to figure out. Now let's work on how you're going to deal with this, shall we?"

PULLING THE PIN

"Agent Diaz is unconscious," Sam heard Agent Wallace say over his cell phone.

"Units are almost there. Tell me what's going on," Sam said.

"A crowd has gathered. I can't see anything. Should I stay with Agent Diaz?" Wallace asked.

Sam struggled with the decision. The right thing to do was to tend to Agent Diaz. But, in doing so, Ali al-Haqani could escape. "Stay with her until help arrives."

Sam turned to Walt. "Get an ambulance there now! The rest of you, come with me."

The car waited for them at the entrance. Once inside, Sam called the Coast Guard and alerted them to the immediate situation.

The usual fifteen-minute drive to Cyprus Yacht Club from the hotel took them only eleven minutes when they met up with the ambulance and followed it to the marina. Sam noticed several government vehicles scattered in the lot and wondered how many agents were on scene. Sam jumped out of the vehicle as soon as it stopped. Agent Diaz was conscious and sitting up. Blood dripped from the side of her head. Agent Wallace knelt by her side.

"I've got this, Wallace. Go find him," Sam said.

Wallace and the four other agents disappeared through the crowd. Two Coral Gables police officers stood by the ambulance.

Sam waved them over. He showed his credentials to the officers and said, "Get this crowd out of here."

"Diaz, did you see which way he went?" Sam asked.

Diaz raised her hand to her bleeding head and shook it slowly. "No, sir. I'm sorry."

"Don't you worry, Diaz. You did great. You alerted us. We'll take care of the rest. Now let these people take care of you."

EMTs had arrived with their equipment. Sam moved away to give them space. Radio chatter became hectic, and Sam recognized the need for order.

"All units," he said into his radio, "report positions."

As the crowd dispersed, Sam could see landmarks and identify the areas the agents targeted. Based on the information, he repositioned a few to unmanned locations.

He glanced back at Agent Diaz, who seemed to be regaining her strength. She lay on the stretcher and swatted at one of the EMTs when they tried to insert an IV into her arm.

"Diaz, let them do their job," Sam said.

"Yes, sir," Diaz replied.

With the IV inserted, the EMTs rolled the stretcher to the ambulance and slid Agent Diaz into the back.

"You're going to be fine, Diaz," Sam said before they closed the ambulance doors and drove away.

Sam surveyed the area. Several buildings lined the marina. He had no idea how many boats were docked, but it was more than he had hoped. He knew it would take some time to check the structures and each vessel, so he picked up the phone and called Bradley.

"What's happening, Sam?" Bradley asked as he answered his phone.

"He's here. He disabled one of our agents at the Cyprus Yacht Club. Does that place have any meaning to you?"

Bradley quickly scanned his brain for any recognition of the name.

"No. There weren't any receipts or transactions from there. But if he knows you're there, he's going to try to throw you off."

"Yeah, I'm sure he will. We've got good coverage, though. And the Coast Guard has been alerted. Even if he gets by us, he still has to get by them."

"Good luck, Sam."

"Yeah. Call me if you get anything new."

"Will do."

Sam placed his phone in his pocket and turned to the group of local police officers that had amassed.

"Who's senior here?"

"I am." A tall, broad-shouldered man stepped forward. "I'm Sergeant Boxer."

"Sam Houghton, FBI." The two shook hands.

"Sergeant, we need all entry and exit points manned. Do your officers know the situation?"

"Yes. We were briefed."

"Have they got photos?"

"They do."

"Excellent. Position your people at every egress point. This guy is slippery, Sergeant. And extremely dangerous."

"Understood."

Sergeant Boxer gathered his officers.

Sam could only hope al-Haqani hadn't had the opportunity to slip away before backup had arrived. He comforted himself knowing al-Haqani couldn't possibly have anticipated their preparedness. Unless, Sam thought, someone had warned him.

He considered how al-Haqani had crossed the Canadian border undetected, then felt a pit in his stomach.

"They're on his tail." Bradley spoke on the phone. "He's at the Cyprus Yacht Club in Coral Gables."

"Right where you said he would be," Derek replied.

"Let's just hope we weren't too late. Sam said he injured one agent already."

"Any idea who and how bad?"

"No, Sam didn't say."

"I'll look into it. Anything new at the lab?"

"Audrey thinks she knows how he did it. She's running more tests now."

"Audrey?"

"Dr. Howe. She's isolated elements that are not normally associated with ergot poisoning. She thinks al-Haqani engineered this new strain to go undetected and to spread more quickly."

"Any idea how to counter it yet?"

"I don't have a grasp of the chemistry behind it, but it sounds like it's possible. She won't know until she has conclusive results. It seems the Atlanta CDC office is about to issue a statement detailing the process for cleaning the diseased fields."

"How can they do that without being certain what they're dealing with?" Derek asked.

"Audrey told me if the sclerotia, the fungus, is buried at least four inches, it can't germinate. So if farmers destroy infected crops and then perform a deep plow in their fields, the fungus will die."

"How long before they can replant?"

"I don't think they know that yet. I suppose it depends on the current tests. But it's good to know that it can potentially be destroyed."

"What about the victims? Have they got a treatment?"

"Yes. I'm told the CDC and World Health Organization have a plan in place. They may not be able to save the most vulnerable, but now that they know what type of infection they're dealing with and because it's not a completely unknown epidemic, they're confident they can fight it."

"That's good news, Bradley."

"It damn sure is. Now, we just need Ali al-Haqani in custody."

"Sam will get it done. Are you coming back to the office?"

"I'd like to stick around for Audrey's test results unless you need me back there," Bradley replied.

"No, you stay and get as much information as you can."

"Call me if you hear from Sam."

"Will do." Derek hung up. "Hmm. Audrey."

"Excuse me?" Sahani asked.

"Oh, sorry. Nothing. Listen, I've got some things to take care of. Can we talk again later?"

"Of course. I'll go check in to the hotel. Call me when you're ready." Sahani stood.

"I'd ask you to stay with us at the house, but I think I know what your answer would be."

"And you would be correct," Sahani smiled. "It wouldn't be ethical."

"Would dinner be ethical? Cate asked if you would join us. Besides, you won't find any open restaurants."

"I hadn't considered that. Thank you, yes. I would love to join you."

"I'll call you when I'm leaving here and pick you up at the hotel."

Bradley sat at the desk in the CDC lab and flipped through files in hopes of finding information about Ali al-Haqani's exit plan. He felt increasingly frustrated and useless after an hour went by and he hadn't found anything of substance. And there was still no news from Sam or Derek.

Audrey bounced from scientist to scientist as she checked test reports and discussed options.

Suddenly, Bradley noticed the room went completely quiet. All heads, including his, turned and faced Audrey standing in the center of the laboratory reading from a sheet of paper.

"This is it!" Audrey said, excitedly. "We've got it! Send this to Atlanta right away. Send it all!"

Several sets of scientists' hands quickly tapped keyboards. Those not sending reports hooted and hollered in celebration. Bradley rolled his chair over to Audrey. Expecting a smile, he received a stone-cold expression.

"What is it?" Bradley asked.

"Who is this man?"

"Someone who has spent his whole existence thinking only of destroying us."

"And he may have. This is extraordinary." She lifted the paper in her hand. "The pathogen he created is not only fungal but bacterial and viral as well. He somehow merged three of the deadliest elements of infection and found a way for them to coexist—not only coexist, but thrive. His research and conclusions are flawless. Under normal circumstances, it may have taken us years to figure out what he'd done. And by then, well, who knows?"

"What do you mean under normal circumstances," Bradley asked.

Audrey looked at Bradley with confusion and considered her words. "You really don't know?"

"Know what?"

"It could have taken us months just to discover the source of the soil contamination, but you handed us the information. And if it weren't for the reclaimed fertilizer that you brought back from Iowa, well, we wouldn't have a clue how the infection mutated, never mind discover all the elements of the infection. Bradley, you led the horse to water. All we did was drink."

Bradley laughed. "You might be right about the horse, but I think you have me on the wrong end of it. I just collected manure. You did all the work."

"You really don't see it, do you? I don't think you understand. None of the current treatments would kill this infection. Not alone, anyway. It will take a three-way attack to slow its progression and, hopefully, destroy it. But now, because of the information you provided, we know that."

"I just did my job," Bradley said, matter-of-factly.

It seemed to Bradley that Audrey wished to say more, but she slowly curled her lips into a smile, then laughed.

Bradley did the same.

The ringing of Bradley's telephone soon interrupted their pleasant moment. Thinking it might be Sam, he quickly reached for it.

"Bradley, it's Cate," he heard.

"Oh, hi Cate," Bradley said as he glanced at Audrey, then moved his chair back to the desk to allow her to finish her work.

"I know things are crazy, but Rusty really misses you. You have to eat dinner anyway, so I want you to come here. Sahani will be joining us, and Derek promised me he would be home at a reasonable hour. I'm guessing that's around 8pm."

"Okay, Cate. That sounds great. I miss Rusty too."

Cate huffed. "And what about me?"

"Yes," Bradley laughed. "I miss you too." Then he hung up the phone.

Audrey had walked to a file cabinet next to the desk and overheard the exchange.

"It looks like I have dinner plans," Bradley said.

"That's terrific. You should celebrate tonight. Cate, is it?"

"Yes. And a friend is in from out of town. I hadn't really thought about food. I don't think I have much at home to work with."

"It's lucky you have Cate looking out for you. I guess we're done here. I'm going to head to my office to make some phone calls and write reports. It's been a pleasure working with you, Agent Whitman." Audrey stuck out her hand.

Bradley took her hand and, instead of shaking it, just held it. "Yes, a pleasure," he smiled.

Audrey pulled her hand from his and walked out the door.

Instead of feeling a sense of accomplishment and a job well done, Bradley felt sad. He had enjoyed working with Audrey, perhaps more than he'd realized. He gathered his reports, stuffed them into his briefcase, then headed back to the J. Edgar Hoover Building.

He found Derek pacing in his office.

"It's been an hour and a half. No word from Sam. What the hell are they doing down there?" Derek asked.

"What happened to the optimism you had on the phone earlier?" Bradley replied. "Relax. If he's there, Sam will find him."

"That's the big question, isn't it? If he's still there."

Bradley sighed. "I came to tell you that Audrey and her team have isolated the composition of the fungal infection. She seemed confident doctors now have the information they need to establish a targeted treatment. Medically, it seems we'll have this epidemic under control soon."

Derek stopped pacing. "That's great news! It's incredible that they got it done so fast."

"She was very impressive."

"Dr. Howe?"

"Yes." Bradley smiled. "She is . . . well, brilliant!"

Derek smiled.

"What are you grinning at?" Bradley asked.

"Nothing."

Starting from the outer edges of the marina to the middle of the property, agents and officers searched every building and boat. During the search, they thoroughly inspected every vessel that tried to leave. Ali al-Haqani was not sighted.

Sam had acquired a map of the marina from the harbormaster. With the map lying on a picnic table at the edge of the parking area, Sam checked off grids as they were searched. He surmised that if al-Haqani were there, he must have been in one of the larger yachts moored along the center boat slips. And his agents were closing in.

Carefully, Sam climbed on top of the picnic table and surveyed the property. He scanned the water's edge and watched an agent and officer move from one vessel to another. His peripheral vision then caught movement at the far end of the parking lot. Someone emerged from the back of a windowless white van and headed toward the south end of the marina, an area that had been searched more than an hour before. He wasn't sure why, but something didn't seem right about it.

It took a moment, but then he understood. He picked up his radio and contacted Sergeant Boxer.

"Sergeant! Have any white vans entered the marina parking lot in the last hour?"

"One moment," the Sergeant replied. Seconds later, he responded, "No. The only vehicle allowed in was an SUV driven by an FBI agent."

"Thank you, Sergeant."

Sam climbed down from the tabletop and motioned for two police officers to join him. "Come with me," he said.

Rather than communicate by radio, which Sam assumed al-Haqani would be monitoring, he decided himself to investigate the person from the white van.

To the officers, he said, "Do you see that white van at the end of the parking lot? Someone just got out of it and is walking toward the marina. We need to find that person."

"Yes, sir," the young officers said enthusiastically.

As they got closer, Sam caught a glimpse of someone moving between vehicles, then behind a storage shed, and then again on the dock. Still too far away, Sam couldn't determine if it was Ali al-Haqani. However, with certainty he identified the person as male. When he and the officers rounded the storage shed, the man was nowhere to be found. Sam had a decision to make.

He picked up his radio. "I want agents on the south side of the marina to backtrack to the south end of the dock. Keep your eyes open for a single male dressed in dark clothing."

Sam turned and looked behind him. Several agents appeared and began to walk toward him.

In an instant, normally serene Biscayne Bay exploded with machine-gun fire. Sam took cover behind a palm tree as wood splinters from the dock and trees became deadly projectiles. He heard a scream. One of the officers lay on the dock. A pool of blood began to form by his side. Sam searched for the second officer. He found him crouching behind a garbage can just fifteen feet away. He looked back to where the approaching agents had been and saw nothing.

Suddenly, it was quiet.

The injured police officer moaned. Sam knew they had to get him to cover. He got the attention of the second officer and pointed his index finger first at him and then back at himself. Then, with two fingers, he pointed to the injured officer and then toward the shed behind them.

The second officer nodded.

Sam held up three fingers. He dropped the first finger, then the second. When the third finger dropped, both men rushed toward the injured officer and lifted him by his shoulders.

Gunfire erupted from two directions. Sam and the assisting officer were in the crossfire. He could feel the breeze of bullets as they whizzed by his head.

As quickly as they could, Sam and the assisting officer dragged the injured man behind the shed to safety.

Sam examined the officer who had a bullet hole through his right side. "It's a clean wound," he said. The bullet went in and out."

To the wounded man, he said, "You're going to be fine." He took off his white button-down shirt and ripped it into strips. He tied a few of the strips together and wrapped them around the wounded officer's waist as a bandage. "Put some pressure on the wound," he said to the second officer.

Shots continued from both sides. But from his fresh vantage point, Sam could identify where the unidentified man was shooting from. "He's in a black and white speedboat in Slip Number 43."

Sam surveyed the immediate area. He determined that, if he backtracked through the parking lot, he might be able to approach the speedboat from the opposite side.

"Call an ambulance and stay with him," he said to the officer who helped.

Sam crouched as he retraced his path back to the line of vehicles. Stopping only twice to glance at the shooter's position, he quickly made his way further south through the parking lot. During the second glance they made direct eye contact. Sam positively identified the gunman as Ali al-Haqani. An ice-cold chill swept Sam's body. Before he could reach a safe position with a clear line of fire, he heard the engine of the speedboat rev.

Sam frantically searched for agents who'd been closing in on the boat slip. He couldn't see any close enough to stop Ali al-Haqani from leaving.

Without hesitation, Sam pulled his forty-five-caliber firearm from its holster, sprinted onto the open dock, and emptied the fifteen-round clip into the boat. Simultaneously, al-Haqani reached into his jacket pocket, pulled the pin from a grenade, and tossed it in Sam's direction.

The explosion knocked Sam off his feet and sent shrapnel into his body. He felt as if his leg was on fire. But there was no fire, only smoke. And when it cleared, Sam could only watch as Ali al-Haqani sped away from the marina.

"Sam, are you alright?" Agent Simms asked as he reached him.

"Dammit, where's my radio?" Sam asked.

Another agent found Sam's radio nearby on the dock. "It looks undamaged."

Still lying on the dock, Sam grabbed the radio from the agent.

"This is Sam Houghton. Coast Guard be advised that the suspect has just left Cyprus Marina in a black and white speedboat. He's heavily armed."

"Coast Guard will intercept," the reply came.

"I hope so," Sam said under his breath. Then, to Simms he said, "Help me up."

"Sam, I don't think that's a good idea."

"Why not?"

"Uh, your leg is pretty messed up."

Sam lifted his head and looked at his blood-soaked leg. "Shit! Did I get shot?"

"I don't think so. I think it might be shrapnel from the grenade and pieces of the boat dock. Just stay still. It doesn't seem to have hit a vein. Help is on the way."

"Son of a bitch!" Sam yelled. "This guy is always one step ahead of us. How did he know we were here? How did he know to hole up in that van instead of leaving after he took out Diaz?"

Sam slapped his hand on the pavement, then winced as a pain shot through his body.

"Easy, Sam. Don't move," Agent Simms said.

Sam sucked air through his teeth, then released his breath. "The officer who was shot, how's he doing?"

"I don't know. I came straight to you." Simms turned to the agent who had retrieved the radio and said, "Why don't you go check on the officer and report back?"

The agent nodded and left.

"What's his name? That agent."

"I don't know him."

"He's not with the Miami division?"

"No. I've never seen him before."

"Maybe he came in from Tampa Bay or Jacksonville," Sam said, feeling a bit groggy.

"Not unless he's new."

"Are you saying that he's not Florida FBI?"

"Not that I know of. Like I said, he could be new."

"Maybe," Sam said softly. The hair on Sam's arms raised.

Several minutes passed before the agent returned. Sam's eyes were closed. "Is he alright?" the agent asked Simms.

Before Simms could respond, Sam's eyes popped open and focused on the unknown agent.

"Officer Haskel is being tended to now. He seems to be doing fine," the agent said.

His words halted, Sam said, "That's great news. Thank you, Agent . . . ?"

"Raskins, sir. Tom Raskins."

"Raskins. Are you with the Miramar division? I don't remember seeing you this morning." Pain was visible in Sam's cloudy eyes.

"I'm hoping to be. I'm checking out the area for a possible transfer. I'd heard what was happening here and thought I may be able to help."

"Ah!" Sam said. "We appreciate the help. Where's home base?"

"Grand Forks, North Dakota."

Sam slowly nodded. The sound of ambulance sirens grew close. "Here they come. Dammit!"

"What is it, Sam?" Simms asked.

"I left my notebook and map on the picnic table near the harbormaster's office." Sam said.

"I'll get them," Raskins quickly offered, then turned and walked toward the parking lot.

"Simms," Sam whispered, "I want you to quietly take Agent Raskins into custody."

"What?"

"Al-Haqani has someone inside. Raskins might be our guy."

"How do you . . . son-of-a . . .." Simms voiced trailed off.

"And be careful," Sam said.

MOB SCENE

"Director Richards, you have Deputy Director Mendez here to see you," Madelyn said through the intercom.

"Thank you," Derek replied with the push of a button. "Send him in."

Derek stood, and Bradley turned his chair to face Mendez as he came through the door.

"Mike?" Derek spoke, knowing something important must have happened.

"I'll leave you two to talk," Bradley said.

"No need. This concerns you, too," Mike replied. "Sam is on his way to the hospital. He just called me from an ambulance. He's going to be fine, but . . . " he paused, " . . . Ali al-Haqani slipped through."

"What happened to Sam," Derek asked.

"Grenade shrapnel," Mike responded.

"Grenade?" Bradley asked.

"What the hell was he doing so close?" Derek asked.

"I asked him the same question," Mike said. "He wasn't in any condition to get into it. Sam needs you to check on an agent named Tom Raskins. He's supposedly with the Grand Forks, North Dakota field office."

"North Dakota. Does Sam think he's our leak?" Derek asked.

"It would make sense." Bradley said.

"The guy just showed up at the marina. If he is who he says he is, it's a good bet Sam's right. But, it could be someone posing as Agent Raskins. Florida is looking into it, but Sam wants you to check it out."

"Okay."

"What's the word on al-Haqani?" Bradley asked.

"It's in the Coast Guard's hands now. We haven't heard anything yet." Mike replied. Just then, Mike's phone rang. "It's Director Rhoades."

"Bradley and I can step out," Derek said.

Mendez bobbed his head as he answered the phone. "Yeah, Stu?"

Derek shut the door behind them. They waited in Madelyn's outer office. Several minutes later, Derek's office door opened, and Mendez waved them in.

"We just got confirmation. The Coast Guard has Ali al-Haqani in custody! It was a battle. The Coast Guard lost a boat, and two mariners are in critical condition. It seems al-Haqani had more grenades in his arsenal."

"Are they sure it's him?" Bradley asked.

"Positive identification. We got him! I've got to go make arrangements for his transfer to FBI custody. Congratulations, gentlemen!" Mike exclaimed as he shook their hands.

"And the same to you, Mike." Derek smiled.

When Mendez left the office, Derek and Bradley were speechless. The two just stared at each other and smiled. Finally, Derek said, "Let's get to work on this Tom Raskins. I'll check out his current status. You dig into his past."

"I'm on it," Bradley said as he steered his chair to Derek's door. "If we can wrap this up in time, I'll see you for dinner."

"You will?"

Bradley laughed. "Yes. Cate called and invited me. And, since I don't have any edible food at home, I accepted."

Derek laughed. "Just don't tell her that's the only reason you accepted. You'd break her heart."

Bradley stopped laughing. "I would never want to do that." He left the room feeling better than he had in a long time.

Sheila, David, Janet, Bill, and Max spent most of the day sitting in front of the television watching the news. With each hour, the stories became more horrendous. Sheila had become so worried she had forced David to lock every window in the house, including those on the third floor. She also had him set the house alarm so they would know if anyone tried to break in while they were there.

Come late afternoon, Janet and Bill announced they were going to lie down for a nap. That gave Sheila the opportunity to corner Max and ask him about his earlier reaction.

"Why did you look panicked when my mother asked you about Alex?" Sheila asked Max.

"What are you talking about?" David asked.

"Shush, David. I'm talking to Max."

"You're acting like your mother," David replied, then received a glaring look from Sheila—one that resembled her mother's.

"Max?" Sheila asked.

"I don't know what you're talking about. I wasn't panicked."

"Well, what were you, then? Something is going on, and I want to know what it is."

"I don't know what it is," Max replied.

"Do you mean you don't know what your mother is talking about? Or you don't know anything about Alex?" David asked.

Max paused, then decided he shouldn't keep quiet any longer. "I don't know where Alex is. I haven't heard from him in two weeks. He doesn't answer his phone and hasn't returned calls. And . . ."

Sheila stiffened. "And what?"

"We have this phone tracking app on our phones. We use it to keep track of each other when we're traveling. But . . ."

"Max, what is it?" David asked, getting worried.

"Alex's phone hasn't moved in nine days!"

"Oh, my God!" Sheila's hand went to her lips. "I knew something was wrong. Why didn't you tell us this sooner? Oh, my God!"

Max said, "He may have just lost his phone, Mom. It could be in a lost-and-found somewhere."

"Or it could be lying in a ditch," Sheila screamed.

"Is everything alright down there?" Janet yelled from upstairs.

"Yes, Janet," David said. "Sheila just got excited about something. Sorry!"

"Okay," Janet replied.

"Let's take this conversation into the study," David said.

With the study door closed, David asked Max, "When was the last time you talked to Alex?"

"Sixteen days ago."

"Oh, my God. Oh, my God." Sheila began to shake.

David took hold of her and sat her down in the desk-side leather chair. "Where was he?"

"He said he was in West Bengal, India. In Kolkata."

"Did he say where he was going?"

"No. We just talked about the city. And he asked me about work. Nothing unusual."

"We need to call the police," Sheila said. "We need to report him missing."

"I already called Derek," Max said.

"You called Derek? You thought it important enough to call Derek, but you didn't tell your own parents?" Sheila yelled.

"I didn't want to worry you. I figured Derek would find him and that would be that."

"When did you talk to Derek?" David asked.

"Early this morning."

"Have you heard from him since?"

"No. Nothing yet."

Sheila picked up her phone. David reached for it and took it out of her hand.

"What are you doing?" Sheila asked.

"I think this will go better if I talk to Derek," David said. As he handed Sheila back her phone, he pulled up Derek's number on his own phone.

Derek picked up on the second ring. "Hey, David. Is everything alright?"

"That's what I'm calling to find out. Max told us he called you this morning. I need to know if you found Alex."

There was a pause on Derek's end. "I don't have any information yet, David."

"Can you tell me what you're doing to find him? I mean, should I fly to India and start looking somewhere?"

"No, that wouldn't be productive. Give me a little more time. I've got people looking into it. Good people. We'll find him."

"I don't know if I can just sit here."

"It's the best place to be. Especially with everything that's going on. Just give me a little time."

"Alright. But just a little. Call us with anything you find out. Any time of day or night."

"I promise. I will." Derek paused. "I'm sure he's fine. Give Sheila a hug for me, will you?"

"Thank you, Derek." David hung up.

"Well?" Sheila asked.

"He's got people looking into it, but there's no news yet. He said he needs a little more time."

"I think you were right!" Sheila said. "I think we should go to India and find him. Then, if Derek comes up with any information, we'll already be there."

"I think we should do as Derek asked," David replied. "But to be ready, I'm going to put a jet on standby."

"What about Gram and Gramps?" Max asked.

"They need to know, Max. We can't keep this from them," Sheila said.

"I'm sorry, Mom. I should have told you sooner. I . . . I thought maybe he met someone, or . . . I guess I just didn't want it to be anything to worry about."

Sheila jumped from her chair, walked to Max, and hugged him. "I know what you mean."

Audrey stuffed reports into her briefcase, switched off the office light, and took the elevator to the first floor. Her thinking had been, if she left while it was still light outside, she would not be subjected to the vandalism and lawlessness that had consumed the city. She'd been wrong.

The glass-front vestibule resembled a movie screen showing a war film. The National Guard lined the entrance as a mob of angry people threw any item within reach at the soldiers. The guardsmen held see-through shields to protect themselves. The noise was deafening. A woman with a bullhorn incited the crowd, hollering something about the inept government and its inability to protect the people.

Audrey froze inside the lobby. It would be impossible for her to get to her car without passing through the throng, which she had no intention of doing. She had just decided she would spend the night in her office when her cell phone rang.

"Hello, Audrey. It's Bradley. I'm sorry to bother you, but I'm investigating a possible suspect in the al-Haqani case and had a question I'd hoped you could help me with. I'd do the research, but this is time sensitive."

"Of course, Bradley. What is it?"

"Can you tell me what a phytopathologist does? I know it has something to do with plant pathology."

"Three of the scientists in my lab are phytopathologists. They study disease in plants caused by infectious organisms and environmental conditions."

"Do they specialize in certain areas? I mean, do they concentrate on bacterial or fungal diseases?"

"No. They study all plant diseases that aren't insect- or parasitic-related. Bradley. If you're asking if a phytopathologist could have created or helped to create this disease, the answer is a definite yes."

"That's exactly what I'm asking. Thank you."

"You're welcome."

"I'm sorry I bothered you at home."

"Oh, I haven't made it home. There's an angry mob between me and my car. I may be staying in my office and eating ham and beans tonight."

"Have you called the police?"

"The National Guard are here protecting the building."

Bradley paused, then said, "I'm leaving here in about thirty minutes. I'll come by and get you."

"That's not necessary. I'm fine here."

"What about your daughter? I'm sure she wouldn't want you to sleep in your office. Besides, I have a couple more questions to ask, if you wouldn't mind."

Audrey considered her options. "Alright, thank you. I appreciate it."

"I'll call you when I'm leaving here. Sit tight."

"What more can I do?" Audrey smiled as she put her phone in her purse. What are you doing, she thought. He's in a relationship. All the good ones are.

She entered the elevator and returned to her office to wait for Bradley's call.

The age-old question of whether a little white lie may be justified in some cases had Bradley feeling a twinge of guilt. He didn't know what made him do it. He had been researching Tom Raskin's background when he uncovered that Raskins had graduated from HEI the same year as Ali al-Haqani with a degree in biology. His specialty was plant pathology. That led Bradley to think of Audrey.

With little hesitation, Bradley had picked up his phone and called Audrey with the question he already knew the answer to. And, to his delight, it turned out better than he could have imagined. He would get to see her again. And, for the first time since Laney passed away, Bradley again felt the nervous excitement of meeting someone special.

Few agents remained in the bullpen at 7:30. Sitting behind his desk, Bradley smiled. The finished report on Tom Raskins shot out of the laser printer across the room. He had emailed the information to Derek but knew Derek preferred to read such things on paper.

Bradley brought the report to Derek's office. "Madelyn, what are you still doing here?"

"If he's here, I'm here," she replied.

"No worries. I'm about to get him out of here," Bradley grinned.

Madelyn announced Bradley. Over the intercom, Bradley heard Derek reply, "Send him in." Then, "Go home, Madelyn."

Derek looked up as Bradley entered.

"It's him. Raskins must have met al-Haqani in college—another HEI grad. He holds a degree in biology. I've confirmed that, with his background, he could have helped al-Haqani create the pathogen."

"He's only been in the FBI for six years. His application states a desire to make a difference in the world," Derek said.

"I guess he accomplished that," Bradley replied.

"I'll call Mendez."

"Then we've got some celebrating to do. I'll see you at the house." Bradley started to turn his chair.

"Bradley, wait! There's something I have to tell you."

Bradley turned back to Derek. "What's up?"

Derek paused. "A situation has come up. I'm not sure if it's anything to worry about yet, but . . ."

"What situation?"

"Nobody has had any contact with Alex in more than two weeks. The family is worried."

"My Alex?"

Derek looked at Bradley with confirming eyes.

"Two weeks? Why the hell am I just hearing about this?" Bradley barked.

"Cate mentioned something yesterday, but I just got the details this morning. Apparently, Alex is good about sending postcards home every week, but Sheila didn't get one this past week. I assumed Sheila overreacted. But Max called this morning and said he checked the tracking app he and Alex use on their cell phones. Alex's phone hasn't moved in nine days."

"Jesus!" Bradley spat.

"There could be multiple reasons for that. Maybe Alex lost his phone."

"But you don't believe that, do you?"

Derek took a deep breath, then looked at the floor. "I don't know what to believe."

Bradley asked, "Where's the cell phone located?"

"The Howrah railway station in Kolkata."

"I know that place. I've been there. It's one of the largest and busiest train stations in the world. A lot of bad things happen there."

"Where do the trains go from there?" Derek asked.

"Everywhere! You should have told me what was going on sooner. I can get on the next plane and go find him."

"And look where? We don't have any idea what's happening."

"Well, we can't just sit here!"

"I've got a CIA contact looking into it. He's one of the best intelligence guys in the business. Let's wait and see what he comes up with before we make any rash moves."

"I need to talk to Max," Bradley said.

"Let's go to the house. We'll call him from there."

"Alright, let's go!"

Then Bradley remembered his commitment to Audrey. "Dammit! I've got to make a stop first, but I won't be long."

"I've got to fill Mendez in on Raskins. I'll see you at the house."

Madelyn was still sitting at her desk when Bradley left. The light-heartedness he had felt upon entering Derek's office had disappeared and the happy anticipation of seeing Audrey again had become a speed bump in Bradley beginning the search for his godson.

On my way. Meet you at the front door. White Silverado truck, Bradley texted Audrey when he got in his truck.

Ok, Audrey replied.

The city streets swarmed with National Guard personnel. Some clashed with angry citizens, while others assisted residents safely to their homes. All were armed with semi-automatic rifles.

If he weren't in such a hurry, Bradley may have stopped to identify the person who threw a piece of wood at his truck on Fourth Street Southwest. Instead, he continued driving then took a left onto East Street Southwest. He came to an abrupt halt when a National Guardsmen stepped in front of his truck and held his hand up signaling Bradley to stop.

Bradley opened his window and showed the young man his badge. Speaking loud enough to be heard over the bullhorn, he explained his purpose and intention and was soon waved through. Several of the troops cleared a path through the crowd for Bradley to inch his vehicle to the front.

He watched as one of the soldiers met Audrey at the door and walked her to his truck.

"Thank you," Audrey said to the young man.

The guardsman nodded, then waited until she was safely in the vehicle before closing the door behind her. He cleared a path for Bradley to move away from the mob.

"Well, that was interesting," Audrey said. "Thank you for this."

"You're welcome. Where are we heading?" Bradley asked.

"If you could just get me to my car. It's in the lot to the left."

"I don't think it's a good idea for you to drive home alone tonight. I just had someone throw stuff at my truck. I'll feel much more comfortable if I drive you home, or to a friends."

"But my car. I need to get to work tomorrow."

"I'll pick you up in the morning. I really don't think it's safe tonight. The guardsmen may have a better handle on things tomorrow."

"No. That would be too much trouble. Bring me to Kevin's. Head to Vermont Ave."

"Your ex-husband's?"

"Yes, I'll stay in Allison's room, and Kevin can drive me to work in the morning. That way, I get to see my daughter, and I won't be a bother to you any longer." Audrey began to type into her phone.

"You're not a bother. In fact, I was . . ." Bradley stopped himself. How could he ask her for a date when he could be heading to India soon.

"Was what?"

Bradley paused. "I wanted to ask you about the process for developing the treatment for al-Haqani's mutated infection."

"Oh. We've already started. We know what works on everything individually, so we'll try combinations of all of them to see what works best. We've got people working 24/7. Atlanta is testing a recent vaccine for bacterial infections that seems promising. Preliminary tests show we can at least slow down the progression. That will give us more time."

Bradley wanted to tell Audrey that they had captured Ali al-Haqani, but the news was still considered classified. He also thought to mention his missing godson. Anxiety had been building inside him, and he felt the need to talk to someone. It surprised him that that someone was Audrey Howe. But he kept it to himself, and the anxiety grew.

For several miles, they drove in silence.

"Is everything alright?" Audrey asked.

"Yes, why?"

"You seem pre-occupied." Then Audrey remembered. "I've kept you from your dinner date with Cate and your friend."

"No. I'll still be on time for that. I was just thinking about everything that's happened today."

"Things do change quickly, don't they," Audrey said.

Bradley sighed. "Yes, they absolutely do."

"Take this left up ahead."

Bradley turned left and, following Audrey's instructions, stopped the truck in front of a three-story, single-family, brick home.

"This is it."

Bradley shifted the truck into park. The front door of the home opened, and a tall, fit man with a thick crop of black hair stood in the doorway.

"Well, thank you for your chivalry. It's a rare quality these days." Audrey said.

"It was my pleasure. Enjoy your evening with your daughter."

"Enjoy your dinner date."

Bradley was about to mention that the friend he, Derek, and Cate were having dinner with was not a date. But it seemed too complicated at that moment. "Goodnight."

"Goodnight."

Bradley watched as Audrey climbed three stairs to the front door. The man Bradley assumed to be Kevin rested his hand on the small of her back and guided her inside. From what Bradley saw, they did not appear to be a typical divorced couple.

During the drive to Derek and Cate's, Bradley contemplated how the evening had gone wrong so quickly. Just two hours earlier, he was ready for a celebration. Ali al-Haqani was in custody, and Bradley had allowed himself to think about having a romantic relationship. Things had been looking up.

But Alex. His godson. The closest thing he would ever have to a son of his own, Bradley thought, was missing. Bradley wouldn't let himself think the worst. He couldn't bear it. The closer he got to the house, the more his concern grew. As he drove, he convinced himself that if he had known sooner that something was wrong, he could have fixed it.

If it hadn't been for Rusty enthusiastically greeting him at the door when he arrived, Bradley may have launched into a rant when he saw Cate. With Rusty resting his seventy-pound body on Bradley's lap and licking Bradley's face, Bradley had time to recognize his old way of thinking. It's what Sahani Kumar called his savior complex. And he was grateful Rusty had prevented him from attacking Cate—the closest friend he had other than Derek.

"God, I've missed you," Cate said to Bradley. "What can you tell me? About the epidemic? About Alex?"

"Derek just told me about Alex. I didn't know. I wish you had called me right away, Cate."

"I didn't know what to think. I still don't. Tell me what you know."

Bradley moved his chair into the living room. Rusty stayed by his side. "I don't know anything. Derek will have to fill us both in when he gets here."

"They're just pulling in now," Cate said, looking out the window.

Bradley reached for Rusty and stroked his head. "I've missed you, buddy."

"He's been my only comfort," Cate said.

"Yeah, he's good that way."

The front door opened, and Sahani entered followed by Derek, who carried a briefcase.

Bradley turned his chair and intercepted Derek before he reached the living room. It seemed Bradley's anxiety had found a landing spot. "I can't believe you knew about Alex all day and didn't tell me. What the hell were you waiting for?"

"Hold on! I don't know anything. What should I have told you? Alex didn't send a postcard to his mother so he must be in trouble? And, by the way, he may have lost his cell phone?"

"That would have been better than keeping me in the dark!"

"I don't know if he's missing or if he's somewhere in the mountains and just can't communicate. You've been there! You know what it can be like!"

"It's been two weeks!" Bradley said, heatedly. "That's a long fucking time not to hear from him."

Derek put his briefcase on the floor, bent at the waist, and placed a hand on each of Bradley's wheelchair arms. His eyes narrowed and locked with Bradley's. "Really! Because we didn't hear from you for more than a year. Tell me, Bradley, what should I have done then?"

"Derek!" Cate shouted.

Rusty moved to Bradley's side. Under his silky black coat, his muscles tensed, and his lip began to quiver.

Derek had never seen Rusty in protection mode, especially directed toward him. He slowly removed his hands from the chair and backed away.

"Easy, boy," Bradley said, stroking Rusty's head. "Sit."

Rusty did as he was told.

"What the hell was that?" Derek asked.

"He doesn't like people getting in my face," Bradley replied.

"And I don't like being second-guessed."

Bradley had his mouth open to speak, but Sahani interrupted him. "Gentlemen! Are you done?"

The two looked toward Sahani.

She continued. "It's been a very long couple of days for both of you, and there is a lot of stress in this room right now. You might want to take a deep breath and rethink where this conversation is going."

Derek and Bradley glared at each other for a moment, then Derek picked up his briefcase and stormed down the hall to his den. He closed the door behind him.

"He's doing the best he can," Cate said to Bradley. "And it's eating away at him." Cate turned and headed to Derek's den.

"Shit!" Bradley spat.

After a moment, Sahani smiled. "So, how has your day been?"

Bradley took a deep breath and bowed his head.

"There's a classic folktale that reminds me of you and Derek. It's about two brothers. Together, they worked the family farm. The older brother is married and has a family. The younger brother is single.

"Every day, they would split evenly—their bounty—until one day, the younger brother decides it's not fair that he takes half because he only has himself to feed. So, each night he takes a bag of grain and dumps it into his brother's bin.

"At the same time, the older brother thinks his younger brother should get more than half of their harvest because he had no wife or children to take care of him. So, every night he empties a bag of his grain into his brother's stash. That continued for years until one night, the brothers met, each carrying a bag of grain to the other's bin. They smiled, dropped the bags, and hugged."

"That's a nice story," Bradley said.

"You two have always filled each other's buckets, Bradley. And when one of you needs a little extra, the other provides, no questions asked. I think right now, you both need a little extra. So, it might help if you concentrate on filling the buckets instead of emptying them."

Bradley nodded. "I don't know why I did that. It's just . . . Alex is . . . he's like . . . ."

"Go ahead."

"I'll never have a son, Sahani. Or a daughter. That dream died when I lost Laney. Alex is the closest I'll ever come to having a family."

"You're still a young man. Who's to say you won't fall in love again and have a family. As far as I can tell, you haven't opened up to the possibility. Could it be your unfounded guilt is the only thing holding you back?"

"All I know right now is that I have to find out what's happened to Alex."

"Don't you mean we? He's Derek and Cate's nephew, too."

"Yes, we." Bradley slowly shook his head. "I need to apologize to Derek."

"I think that's a good idea."

The den door opened, and Derek and Cate walked into the living room. Bradley turned his chair to face them.

"I'm sorry," Derek and Bradley said in unison.

"I should have told you sooner," Derek said.

"It's been a crazy day. I get it. I shouldn't have jumped on you like that," Bradley replied.

"I didn't mean to bring up old wounds, you know, you being gone. It wasn't right."

"It's fair game. I deserved it. But maybe we need to talk that whole thing out once and for all. Put it behind us for good."

"I agree. But we have a more pressing situation right now."

"Yes, we do. What are we going to do about it?" Bradley asked.

"We'll start with what we know," Derek replied.

"Can we please get some food into you?" Cate asked Derek. "You both look like death warmed over. And the langostino casserole is ready. Talk while we eat."

After dinner, Derek called Max. He asked Max to repeat everything he knew about Alex's movements and itinerary. Bradley, Cate, and Sahani listened on speaker with Sheila, David, Janet, and Bill on conference call.

"And there's nothing else to add?" Derek asked.

"Not that I can think of."

"Derek, what about these people you said you have looking into this? Have you heard from them yet?" David asked.

"No. Not yet, but it's still too early to expect anything. I'll make some calls in the morning and see if they've got any leads."

"I'm not going to sit here forever, Derek," David said.

"I know you're frustrated. So am I. But if we start poking around on our own, it will just present a whole new set of problems. You've got to trust me, David."

"Derek, it's Bill. You know I trust you implicitly. But I don't see how us going to India to look for Alex would be a problem."

Derek hesitated before answering. He didn't want to worry his father-in-law any more than necessary, but it seemed he could not afford to skirt the issue any longer. "Bill, here's the honest truth. If something has happened to Alex like a kidnapping or, God forbid, something worse, whoever is responsible won't hesitate to do the same to you when you start asking questions. That won't do anyone any good, least of all, Alex."

"Oh, my God! Is that what you think has happened?" Sheila screeched.

"No, Sheila. We have no evidence of anything like that. Look, just give me some time."

"Bradley?" David asked.

"I agree with Derek. We've got very little information right now. But I promise you, we will find him."

Derek looked uncertainly at Bradley. Then said, "Yes, we will!"

MAESTRO?

He was groggy when he woke. Sam slowly adjusted his eyes to the bright lights. When he tried to lift his head, he felt a surge of pain run through his left leg.

"Dammit," he muttered.

"I wouldn't do that, Sam."

The voice came from the far corner of the hospital room. Ignoring the suggestion, Sam lifted his head and winced as he watched Deputy Director Mike Mendez rise from a chair.

"Tell me we got him, Mike."

"I thought Agent Simms told you before you went into surgery," Mendez replied.

Sam took a moment to reflect. "Yeah, I remember now. The Coast Guard."

"He's secured."

Sam rested his head back on the pillow. "Then what are you doing here?"

"Checking on you. And making arrangements to transfer al-Haqani to our custody."

"Have you talked to him yet?"

"We'll get to that. Let's talk about you first. The surgeon said they took twelve pieces of shrapnel and wood out of your leg. He said you were lucky none of them struck the femoral artery or you could have bled out. The question is, Sam, what were you doing on that dock?"

"All available agents were busy searching boats in the marina. I saw someone in the parking lot, I didn't know it was him at the time and followed him."

"And got into a gun and grenade fight."

"That wasn't the plan, Mike."

"Well, whatever the plan was, it was damned stupid. You could have been killed."

"And you would've done it different, how?" Sam asked.

Mendez paused, then grinned.

"How are Agent Diaz and the officer who got shot?" Sam asked.

"They're both going to be fine. Now, tell me about Tom Raskins."

Sam grimaced as he shifted on the bed. "When Simms told me that he didn't know Raskins, I got suspicious. Then Raskins told me his home office was in North Dakota. That's where al-Haqani crossed the Canadian border several times. It seemed too much of a coincidence. Was I right?"

"You were. He's in custody. Seems he and al-Haqani were schoolmates."

"Alright. We've talked about me and Raskins. What about al-Haqani? Have you talked to him?" Sam asked.

"Not exactly."

"What do you mean?"

"He's not readily accessible."

"Where is he?"

"The Coast Guard is holding him offshore on a cutter. It's too risky to bring him in until some order is restored in the streets."

"That could take days, weeks!"

"As it turns out, we've got time. He's refused to speak to anyone. Instead, he indicated a need for pen and paper and wrote a note saying he'll only talk to an FBI agent by the name of Maestro."

"Who the hell is Maestro?" Sam asked.

"I hoped you would know. We don't have any agents by that name and al-Haqani won't tell us where to find him, or her."

"Have you run the name through the alias files?"

"Yes. Nothing. We sent a memo to all department heads. In the meantime, once he arrives in port, I've arranged for al-Haqani to be transported to Coleman Federal Correctional Complex in central Florida."

"What's the plan to restore order?" Sam asked.

"Beginning tomorrow at 6 a.m., the president is enacting martial law."

"The entire country?"

"Yes. It's chaos out there! Law enforcement can't keep up. The president doesn't really have a choice. He's setting a civilian curfew from 6 p.m. to 6 a.m., excluding law enforcement and emergency personnel. Military troops are already moving into place, and checkpoints are being established. Until the military has control of the streets, the best place for Ali al-Haqani is on that Coast Guard cutter."

"This Maestro. How do you figure they fit into this?" Sam asked.

"I don't know. It's possible it's another corrupt agent. Either way, we need to find them. Preferably before we're ready to move al-Haqani."

Derek had been searching the FBI database for anyone who might have a connection to the name Maestro when he received a call from CIA terrorist analyst Eric Sampson.

Eric said, "We found Alex's cell phone. It was deliberately wedged into a concrete crevice behind one of the train platforms. The information his brother had gotten from the tracking app took us right to it. One of our operatives retrieved it and is charging the battery to go through it as we speak."

"So he didn't just lose the phone."

"No. It looks like he hid it there. Probably in somewhat of a hurry, too. There were less exposed places he could have found in the area if he had had enough time."

Derek swallowed hard. He found it difficult to keep emotion from his voice. "What . . . ", he cleared his throat, " . . . what platform was it near."

"The Himgiri Express. It makes thirty-one stops, ending at the Jammu Tawi station in Jammu and Kashmir."

"Pakistan?" The name caught in Derek's throat.

"The Union Territory." Eric replied. "Derek. I'm going to ask you again. Is there something that you're not telling me?"

"He's not an agent, Eric. He's a writer. An author. He's been traveling South Asia—India, Bhutan, Nepal. He's a kid."

"Okay. I had to ask. He may not have been going all the way to Jammu Tawi. We're trying to determine his intended destination, but record keeping has never been a priority in the region. The good news is that, since the COVID pandemic hit, the railway instituted a policy to record passenger destinations for contact tracing."

"What are the odds that he even got on the train?" Derek asked.

"I don't know. If someone grabbed him off the platform, they could have taken him anywhere from there. I'm sorry. I wish I had better news."

"I appreciate your help. You'll keep me posted, right? Everything you learn!"

"I will."

Derek hung up and sat back in his office chair. The thought of telling Sheila and David that their son may have been abducted on a train platform in India had his stomach wrenching. And Cate! She loved her nephews as if they were her own. Derek feared the news would bring up terrible memories of Cate's two miscarriages and their subsequent inability to have children of their own. How much more could she take? Derek asked himself.

After several moments of contemplation, Derek picked up the telephone and dialed Sheila and David's number. It was early in California, a little after 6:30 a.m., and even though they weren't typically early risers, Derek knew Sheila and David would be awake.

The conversation was difficult. Devastated by the news, Sheila wailed uncontrollably. In the background, Derek could hear Janet trying to console her. At first, David was quiet, leaving Bill to ask most of the questions. Finally, David spoke. "What is the plan, Derek?"

"I'm going to see the FBI director today. We'll see what legal and political options we have. Then, we'll develop a plan."

"I've got a jet on standby," David replied.

"Okay. Hang in there."

Derek sighed as he disconnected the call. He punched a button on his intercom and said, "Madelyn, could you ask Agent Whitman to come see me?"

"Right away," she replied.

Waiting for Bradley, Derek called Cate. She didn't immediately weep at the news, but Derek could hear the fear in her voice. When she couldn't hold back tears any longer, she found it difficult to speak.

"I'll come home, Cate."

"N . . . n . . . no! You d- . . . do everything . . . you can to bring him back! Do you hear me?" Cate's words got stronger as she spoke. "Everything you can!"

"I promise," Derek replied.

There was a knock at Derek's door.

"Cate, Bradley's here. I'll call you in a little while, alright?"

"Bring him home, Derek!"

Cate hung up.

"Come in," Derek said.

Bradley rolled through the door. "What happened?"

Derek filled him in on the conversations with Eric, Sheila and David, and Cate.

"I'm glad I left Rusty with Cate. He might be some comfort to her," Bradley said, then asked, "What about Max? What did he say?"

"He wasn't there. He must have been on his way to work. I'm sure David would have talked to him by now."

"We need to talk to him. Maybe he'll have an idea where Alex was headed."

"I'm more concerned with where he was and why someone would want to harm him. There's been no ransom communication. If this was a kidnapping, the family would have been contacted by now."

"Maybe he saw something he shouldn't have seen? He's an inquisitive kid," Bradley said.

"That's very possible. But I hope you're wrong."

"What about the phone? He must have hidden it there for a reason."

"Yes, to give us his location?"

"Maybe. But think about this. If you were at an unfamiliar train station and found yourself in immediate danger, what is the likelihood you would have time to find a crevice in the concrete behind the train platform to stash your phone?"

Derek's eyes widened. "He knew he was in danger!"

"And, if the person or people coming after you saw you ditch the phone, wouldn't they take it with them?"

"He got rid of the phone ahead of time."

"And why hide the phone from his assailant unless there was something on it that he didn't want them to see."

"Like someone's identity or an explanation of some sort."

"There's something on his phone that's going to help us figure this out. Maybe even help us find him."

"The CIA is on it. Eric told me he would keep me posted."

"Do you think Max had any way of monitoring Alex's communications—like he did with tracking?"

"Let's find out," Derek replied.

The call to Max didn't provide any new insight. Derek had been correct that David had filled Max in on the latest developments, and Max was clearly distraught.

"I should have known something was wrong," Max told Derek.

"He's half a world away, Max. There was no way for you to know."

"Still. I should have," Max said before they hung up, agreeing to stay in constant contact.

Derek was unable to console Max like he had hoped, and that inability to make things better for his godson hurt him deeply.

After several minutes of complicated silence, Derek said to Bradley, "There's nothing more we can do but wait. In the meantime, I have to get back to my database search."

"Before I leave, have you heard any news about Sam?" Bradley asked.

"He had successful surgery last night and is recuperating in the hospital. Deputy Director Mendez is with him."

"Wow. The big guns!"

"He's down there trying to get al-Haqani safely transferred to a federal facility."

"Has anyone talked to al-Haqani yet?"

"No. Al-Haqani is demanding to speak to an Agent Maestro, but nobody in the bureau seems to know of anyone by that name."

Bradley's face turned paper white.

"Bradley? Are you alright?" Derek asked.

When Bradley didn't respond, Derek came out from behind his desk and approached him. He had seen it happen before. Occasionally, Bradley would begin to hyperventilate, his blood pressure would spike, and he'd go from pale white to beet red in moments. But this time, Bradley didn't breathe heavily, and his face remained white.

"Bradley, what's happening?"

Bradley blinked, then looked at Derek. "Maestro?"

Derek, feeling less concerned, replied, "Yes. Agent Maestro. Do you know him—or her?"

Bradley could only nod his head.

"Where do I find them? Who is it?"

Bradley looked Derek in the eyes, and replied, "It's me!"

"What do you mean, it's you?"

Bradley explained his college nickname and told Derek how he found the phrase maestro move on the back of one of Ali al-Haqani's research papers. He also explained how, after seeing the name on al-Haqani's paper, he thought maybe his college professor had used the nickname for other students.

"But now I'm not so sure," Bradley said.

"Do you think your professor mentioned you in classes after you graduated?"

"I know he did. He told me he used my papers to inspire his students. I spoke with him last year about al-Haqani. He told me that al-Haqani and I would match wits perfectly. He said al-Haqani was the static to my concerto."

"What the hell does that mean?"

"It means that it's no coincidence I'm working this case. It's what al-Haqani wanted. He wanted to match wits and show me—and the world—that he is the ultimate maestro."

"You've got to get to Florida," Derek said.

"I can't go to Florida, not with Alex missing!"

"Ali al-Haqani is willing to talk. But only to you! You have to realize how vital that is."

"It's not as important as my godson!"

"What about Sam? What about the thousands of people who have died at al-Haqani's hand? What about the thousands that you might be able to save by talking to him? You know I'm right."

"I know you're right. But there's more to it than that. I don't know if I'm up to it. He's been steps ahead of me this whole time. I don't think my head is clear enough to go head-to-head with him."

"Dammit! Enough!"

Stern-faced, Derek leaned and placed his hands on the arms of Bradley's wheelchair and looked him straight in the eyes. "I've let you wallow long enough, Bradley! No more! These doubts you've fabricated are all in your head! Don't you understand?

We wouldn't have al-Haqani in custody if it weren't for the work you've done? We wouldn't know the cause or the treatment of all the people who could have died if you hadn't used that completely fucked up and beautiful brain of yours!

"News flash! You're not perfect! Get the fuck over it and get on a plane to Florida! And tell that bastard that there's only one goddamn maestro in this world!"

Out of breath and red-faced, Derek stood, then took a step backwards.

Silence.

Then, stone-faced, Bradley said, "That may have been the best pep talk you've ever given me."

"I'm calling Mendez, then I'm going to see the director. Get your go-bag!"

Alex thought about the message he left behind. Surely, they would have gotten it by now. And though he didn't know exactly where he was, he hoped he had been correct in his assumption. "They're good at what they do. They'll figure it out," he mumbled.

But he wasn't sure how much longer he could hold on. Given limited food and water and sweating out most of the liquid, Alex knew he was dehydrated and guessed he had lost nearly twenty pounds since he was taken. He used those details to keep his mind sharp. He counted pounds, days, footsteps, and voices. He listened to insects, rodents, chains, and locks. He thought about every place he had traveled and every story he had written. He strategized how best to stay alive. But the one thing he would not allow himself to think about was his family. He couldn't bear it.

It was time. Chains rattled, the lock clicked, and three pair of feet shuffled in. Then the hood lifted. Once his eyes adjusted to the minimal light, he saw the bearded man standing before him.

"Who do you bring to us?" the man asked.

Alex dropped his chin to his chest and rocked his head back and forth. "You're going to have to start asking me different questions, because I can't answer this one any other way. I bring no one."

"You think you . . . over smart me?" The man spat in Alex's face.

Alex attempted to shake the spit from his cheek. "Outsmart? Do you mean outsmart? I don't think I outsmarted anyone. I just want to go home."

"You lie. I outsmart you. Man from CAI. I take you, spy!"

"I'm not a spy. I don't work for the CIA, CAI, or FIB. How many times do I have to tell you? I write books. You can keep asking me, and I will keep telling you. Because I am not a spy!" he yelled.

The bearded man turned and said something in Farsi to the two men in the shadows. The hood was placed back on Alex's head.

Alex listened as the three left the room, then chained and locked the door.

Alex knew he would not be getting any food or water that night.

ON REFLECTION

Derek arranged for Bradley to meet Deputy Director Mendez in Sam's hospital room at 1 p.m. He coordinated with the driver of a wheelchair accessible van to pick Bradley up at Miami airport and transport Bradley to the medical building.

When he arrived, Bradley knocked quietly on the closed, private-room door. Deputy Director Mendez greeted Bradley at the door.

"Hello, Director."

"Call me Mike." They shook hands.

"Bradley. Good to see you," Sam said with a tired smile.

"And it's great to be seeing you, Sam, in one piece, give-or-take."

Sam grinned. "Right. Mike told me about Maestro. What do you think this is all about?"

"I wish I knew. I didn't know I was on his radar. But, if I had to guess, I'd say it's about his ego."

"How so?" Mike asked.

"He wants to prove he is the only person worthy of the name. I don't think he likes playing second fiddle. For anything. Professor Forsythe was right about one thing."

"What's that?" Sam asked.

"He said al-Haqani was a master at turning cohesion into chaos."

"Ain't that the truth," Sam replied.

"Let's go, Bradley. Sam needs his rest, and we need to talk strategy," Mike said.

Sam objected. "Wait a minute. I want to hear this. Talk strategy here."

Mike replied, "Maybe you should have thought of that before you stepped in front of a grenade, Sam. Get some rest. I'll try to come see you before I head back to DC. Let's go, Bradley."

Bradley heard Sam grumbling as they left the room.

The transport van waited near the entrance, and the driver pulled up to the door when she saw Mike and Bradley come out.

Once settled in the van, Mike said, "Take us to the Miramar office, Jenny."

They weren't in the van more than a minute when Mike said, "I heard about Alex Carson. He's your godson, isn't he?"

Surprised, Bradley replied, "Yes."

"The director is making the case a priority as much as legally possible. He's in direct contact with the CIA."

"I appreciate that, Mike. I confess, it's got me a little distracted."

Mike grinned. "Derek said you'd say something like that."

"That's because it's true."

"Derek also said that half of your attention is better than most people's full attention."

"Well, Derek's never been very good at math."

Mike chuckled. "I think I'll trust his judgement anyway."

They didn't discuss Ali al-Haqani until they sat privately in one of the Miramar offices.

"What's our priority with al-Haqani?" Bradley asked.

"First, how to definitively combat his virus."

"And second?"

"Make certain there's nothing else on the horizon."

"What makes you think he'll tell me anything?"

Mike pulled a copy of the note Ali al-Haqani presented to the Coast Guard captain who tried to interrogate him.

Bradley read.

> I will tell you everything you want to know. But I will only speak to one FBI agent. Maestro.

"What I don't understand is why he didn't use your name? Why the riddle?" Mike asked.

"I'm no psychologist, but it seems he's flexing his informational intelligence muscles."

"How so?"

"He wants us to believe he knows everything about us."

"And does he?"

Bradley paused. "Individually, I doubt he does. But collectively? As in, FBI tactics and personnel? He's been studying us most of his life and has been multiple steps ahead of us since his college days. Maybe longer."

"Yet, he knows personal things about you."

"His profile suggests a severe competitive nature. I think Professor Forsythe unwittingly ignited a grudge match between the two of us. Unfortunately, I didn't know the match existed until now.

"That could work to our advantage," Mike said.

"How?"

"Maybe he'll want to show you up—point out every mistake you've made or detail you missed."

"Wow! Thanks for the pep talk."

"I know you're not that thin-skinned, Bradley. You know what I'm saying. You said it yourself. We've been trailing this guy from the beginning, and he's enjoyed every minute of it. Maybe he'll want to flaunt his prowess. And the only way to do that is to explain how he accomplished everything—how he created the virus, how he got across the border undetected, and how he infiltrated the fertilizer plant."

Bradley thought for a moment, then replied, "But I can't be submissive. He won't respect that. I'll have to take an adversarial position. I think we'll get more information that way."

"Okay. You know him better than anyone."

"There's one thing I do know for sure," Bradley said.

Mike raised his brows.

"Ali al-Haqani plans to dominate the conversation. I've got to find something that will throw him off his game."

"Well, you better figure it out soon. We're taking a chopper to the Coast Guard cutter in three hours."

The two discussed strategy for the next forty minutes until Bradley suggested that he should spend time reviewing al-Haqani's files.

"Agreed. I'll leave you to it," Mike said. "Let me know if you need anything."

Sitting alone in the office, Bradley's initial thought was *How can I get ahead of this guy?* It wasn't long before he realized he couldn't. It was too late for that. But it did give Bradley an idea. *I don't have to get ahead of him now. I just have to keep up with him. And to keep up with him, I need to understand why he's gone to all this trouble.*

Bradley felt a surge of excitement. The burden of thwarting al-Haqani's next move had been shed. If al-Haqani had another surprise for them, it would have already been implemented. Bradley hoped that was not the case. But it meant he could shift focus from the how to why.

Bradley's briefcase overflowed with information on Ali al-Haqani and he had read each report several times.

Al-Haqani's recorded rhetoric concerning the US/Afghan war made it clear that was the underlying reason for al-Haqani's actions. But there had to be more, Bradley thought. *What would it take for me to commit my entire life to vengeance?*

One by one, Bradley pulled sheets of paper from his briefcase. He dismissed the first dozen or so reports, then stopped when he came to al-Haqani's communication received two days before. Bradley took a moment to reflect on how much had happened since then.

He reread the letter.

> Who laid the foundations of the earth, that it should not be removed forever. Thou coveredst it with the deep as with a garment: the waters stood above the mountains. At thy rebuke they fled; at the voice of thy thunder they hasted away. They go up by the mountains; they go down by the valleys unto the place which thou hast founded for them. Thou hast set a bound that they may not pass over; that they turn not again to cover the earth.

> Something is lost, and it cannot be found. Let me rather lose all things than lose God, my supreme good. Let me never suffer the loss of my greatest treasure, eternal life with God.

Nothing in the first paragraph suggested to Bradley anything other than the topic of the virus itself and that Ali al-Haqani took responsibility for the attack. The section quoting St. Anthony's prayer, the patron saint of lost things, originally thought only to be a hint about the virus itself, now read differently to Bradley.

"He lost someone. Someone very important to him," Bradley said out loud. The idea did not surprise Bradley. It would have been nearly impossible for the Afghanistan war not to have personally affected al-Haqani. His childhood home of Asadabad had been devastated. But, Bradley thought, the fact that there was no information in his background to suggest who he had lost is of interest.

Two hours later, Mike entered the office. "It's time to go."

Audrey looked into the telescope and frowned. In the mix, she thought she had found an element hiding and disrupting the cells' ability to ward off the epidemic. But the bacteria rallied and overpowered her attempt.

The Atlanta office was not having any better outcomes.

As she documented her findings, her cell phone rang. She smiled when she saw it was Bradley.

"Audrey? Can you hear me?" Bradley asked over a loud disturbance. Audrey's first thought was that he had been overtaken by a mob.

"Bradley? Are you alright?"

"I'm fine. I'm in a helicopter. I have a hypothetical question for you."

"Um, okay."

"If you had a chance to ask the creator of this virus a question, what would it be?"

"Can you? I mean . . . "

"Purely hypothetical," Bradley reiterated over the sound of the rotors.

"Of course. Let me think how to phrase this. We know he found a way for the three basic infections to coexist—viral, fungal, and bacterial. But there's a hidden element that prevents the cells from recovering when treated properly. There's something else. I would ask what that missing element is."

"Okay."

"Where are you?"

"Somewhere . . . er . . . Atlantic Ocean."

"Well, tha . . . nar . . . it . . . wn."

"What?" Bradley asked.

"I said, that doesn't narrow it down."

"No, I gu . . . s'nt. Audrey, I've been thin . . . When . . . is . . . ver . . . we could go out to dinner?"

"No. I . . . ldn't. What about . . . ?" Audrey asked.

"What?"

" . . . about . . . ate?"

"I'll . . . all . . . you."

The phone went dead.

Audrey stood with her mouth agape. Had Bradley just asked her on a date? And ignored her when she asked about Cate? Anger then sadness ran through her. She had thought Bradley was different. She thought he was one of the decent men she had been told still existed in the world. But she was beginning to think that was a fairy tale.

Did she say no? Bradley asked himself as he tucked his cell phone away. Maybe I heard her wrong. Or maybe I didn't. He pulled his phone back out and checked for a signal. There was none.

Mike elbowed Bradley and pointed. "There's the Coast Guard cutter up ahead. Are you ready for this?"

"I guess we'll find out," Bradley replied.

Setting a helicopter down on a cutter in the Atlantic Ocean seemed to Bradley like trying to land a paper airplane on a table twenty feet away during a windstorm. But the pilot executed it perfectly. With the engine idling, a Coast Guardsman opened the side door of the chopper and slid a ramp out the door and onto the boat's helipad. Bradley navigated his chair slowly down the ramp onto the boat's deck.

At the base of the ramp, a woman with a brunette ponytail sticking out the back of a navy-blue ball cap stood tall and erect. She wore a starched navy-blue collared shirt with cuffed short sleeves and perfectly creased slacks to match. The name of the cutter, USCGC Eagle (WMSL-878), was stitched in gold block letters on the front of her hat and captain's patches attached to her collars. "Hello, gentlemen. I am Captain Sanchez. Welcome aboard. Please follow me."

Once they were clear of the helipad, the helicopter rotors picked up speed, and soon the chopper lifted from deck and headed back to land.

In single file, Bradley, then Mike, followed Captain Sanchez through a narrow doorway, leaving only inches to spare on either side of Bradley's chair. They passed a set of stairs, one set going down to a lower level and one set going up. At the end of the hall, a metal gate blocked their way. The captain pushed a button, and the gate opened to reveal a cargo lift. Once the three were inside, the captain closed the gate and pushed a button. The cargo lift lowered them below decks.

When the gate opened, Bradley saw two uniformed men standing guard outside one of the closed doors of the hallway.

"Has he given you any trouble?" Mike asked the captain.

"None. Other than not talking, he's been very cooperative," the captain replied.

Mike looked at Bradley, "Are you ready?"

Bradley sighed deeply. "Let's do it."

Small and cramped, the room filled with Ali al-Haqani's presence. He sat on the opposite side of a metal table. His body was wrapped in chains, and he wore handcuffs bound by a short section of chain to the table.

One of the guards followed Bradley into the room and stood by the door. Seeing the chains, Bradley felt confident in asking the guard to leave them alone. Silently, he complied. He left the room and closed the door behind him.

Two bottles of water sat on the table, one close enough for al-Haqani to reach and one on Bradley's side of the table. Bourbon would have been better, Bradley thought as he settled his nerves and pushed his chair to the table.

Each inspected the other. Al-Haqani wore black from head to toe. With his dark skin, thick black hair, beard, and moustache, his outfit augmented his ominous aura. Bradley figured al-Haqani, muscular and fit, must have outweighed him by nearly eighty pounds. In return, Bradley was well aware of the person Ali al-Haqani was seeing, and he recognized he would need to dispel that first impression quickly.

"Finally, I am face-to-face with the Maestro himself," al-Haqani smiled.

Stone-faced, Bradley replied, "It's more of a pleasure for you than for me, I assure you."

"Ha! You may be right. You appear much weaker than I had envisioned."

"Yet, I'm not the one in chains."

"Allah's plan."

"FBI plan, actually. Let's get on with this. I'm a busy man."

"You are half a man, my friend. And you need me. This I know."

"Your plan fell short, Ali. We don't need you for anything."

In a flash, Ali al-Haqani became angry. Forgetting about the chains, he lurched from the chair and tried to stand. But the handcuffs and chains prevented him from doing so, and the cuffs bit into his skin. "You disrespect me and my father?"

Bradley not only expected the response, he welcomed it. It was considered bad form to call a male of the Islamic religion by his first name upon a first greeting. And by ignoring his last name, the name of Ali's father, Bradley knew Ali would consider it disrespectful. As intended, Bradley had hit a nerve.

"You're going to lose your hands if you keep doing that."

"And you will lose more important things than your hands."

"Can we get this over with?" Bradley said. "What did you want to tell me?"

Ali al-Haqani regained control and smiled. "Ah! I finally see the Maestro in action. Professor Forsythe spoke of you as if you were the next coming of your savior, Jesus Christ. But I believe you may have fooled him. You are no savior. You are a sponge who soaks up all the water, leaving none for those close to you. Yet, you expect them to feed your ego to keep your sponge afloat. We are not so different, you see. But I have embraced my hollow existence. And you still cling to hope. But hope only reminds you of who you could have been."

Al-Haqani's words were eerily similar to something Amanda Lessing, the Pathside Predator, had said to Bradley just before he killed her two years before. Bradley did his best to hold his composure in spite of the burning he felt in his gut.

"I am curious about one thing," Bradley said. "This little virus you've concocted. Our scientists have already dissected it, but I've been a little busy and haven't had a chance to read the findings. Other than finding a way for the three types of infections to coexist, what makes it so special? I mean, a high school student could have done that."

A flicker of anger brushed across al-Haqani's face. Then he grinned. "This is you trying to get information from me? You must work on your approach. However, I did make a promise, under Allah, to the captain of this vessel. So, I shall tell you. The key is in a single strand."

"A single strand of what?"

"Ah, much time has gone by since you sat in a classroom. Forsythe would be further disappointed in his dear Maestro."

"It bothers you to know that I'm the one and only Maestro, doesn't it?"

Al-Haqani's left cheek twitched. "You are no Maestro. You are a mistake of nature. The product of an inefficient virus. And to think I once regarded you as a worthy adversary."

"I must point out once more that I'm not the one in chains here. I'm free to leave this room, this ship, anytime I want."

"But you won't."

"And why is that?"

"Because you have more questions."

"A single strand of what?"

"That would be too easy. I assure you, by telling you this I have kept my promise in the presence of Allah."

"Why make that promise? What have you got to gain by it?"

Al-Haqani smiled once more. "You are here."

Bradley thought it time to rattle the man.

"You said hope is a reminder of who one might have become. Is that because of your brother, Omid?"

Al-Haqani's jaws clenched at the mention of his brother, and his eyes bore into Bradley's.

Bradley continued. "Omid. The name actually means hope, doesn't it? He died in the hospital bombing when he was seventeen, so he never got to be the man he could have become. You were fifteen years old at the time. That must have been very difficult."

Anger infused al-Haqani's complexion with blood-colored overtones. "You dare to speak of my brother!" Al-Haqani spoke through gritted teeth.

"It wasn't easy to uncover the records, Ali. But I did. Your brother was visiting your mother after a difficult childbirth. Isam and Imani, your infant twin sister and brother, perished that day as well. You lost your whole family because of that bombing. Your father committed suicide a week later and left you all alone. I can't imagine what that must have been like for you."

"I don't need your pity, just your blood." Anger seemed to seep out of every pore of al-Haqani's body. His knuckles turned white as his tight fists produced sculpted forearms and biceps. Bradley sensed a rise in al-Haqani's body heat and knew his heart pounded in his chest. But, for a moment, he saw the Afghani's eyes weaken.

Al-Haqani took two deep breaths then picked up, the full bottle of water and drank until the bottle was empty.

Bradley thought he had succeeded in upending Haqani's agenda. But he wasn't prepared for al-Haqani's response.

"And you, sponge. You have lost someone dear to you, also. But that was by the hand of your God. This time, it will be my hand reaching into your forsaken soul."

"I think you're being optimistic about your current position."

"And you are being naïve. You may have learned about my family, but so have I learned of yours. I know more about your family than you will ever learn. About the boy you think of as your own." Al-Haqani formed a grimacing smile.

A lump formed in Bradley's throat, and his hands began to shake. Then the room seemed to go dark and cold.

"Alex," Bradley said.

"You've abandoned him too, in his time of need." Spittle appeared at the corners of Haqani's lips. "You've absorbed all the water for yourself and left none for those you supposedly care for." Mucus dribbled from al-Haqani's mouth and landed on his chest.

"Where is he?" Bradley growled. He didn't recognize his own voice as it hurled from his lips. The overwhelming urge to jump from his chair and wrap his hands around al-Haqani's throat made him fumble with the wheelchair joystick. "Where's Alex?" he howled again.

The door swung open, and a guard rushed in just as Bradley rounded the table and reached al-Haqani. Bradley was about to reach his hands out and grasp al-Haqani's throat when al-Haqani's head began to jerk forward, then back, and his chest heaved heavily. Thick white foam bubbled from his mouth like shaken champagne gushing from the neck of a bottle, and Bradley knew then what had happened.

"Get a doctor," Bradley hollered to the guard. "You son-of-a-bitch! Don't die on me now!"

Al-Haqani looked Bradley in the eyes and formed a grin with his foam-filled mouth. His heaving chest went still, and his head gently dropped to the side. His dark eyes still focused on Bradley.

Mike ran into the room. "What the hell happened?"

"The water. The fucking water bottle. He must have put something in it before I came into the room. He waited until he . . . he waited . . ." Bradley's face turned pale, and he began to breathe heavily. Aware of what was happening to him, he tried to control his intake of air. Once his chest began to heave, his face turned red.

"Jesus! Did you drink the water?" Mike asked.

Bradley shook his head side-to-side and raised his right hand with his index finger pointing up, indicating for Mike to wait for a response.

The doctor entered the tiny room and saw Bradley in distress. As he approached, Bradley managed to say, "Hyper . . . vent . . . tilating."

The doctor immediately closed Bradley's mouth and blocked one nostril.

"What are you doing?" Mike asked.

"Slowing down his breathing. This should only take a moment."

Bradley nodded his head and swatted the doctor's hand away.

"Save . . . him," Bradley said, pointing to al-Haqani. Then he closed his mouth and breathed through his nose. He felt himself gaining control and before long was able to speak. "He's got Alex, Mike. He's going to kill Alex."

"What? Did he say where? Or how?"

"No. He waited until the poison kicked in to tell me. That's what this meeting was all about. He had this planned. His revenge for getting caught. Mike, you have to tell Derek. I don't think I can . . ."

Mike Mendez put his hand on Bradley's shoulder. "I'll take care of it."

It took three telephone transfers before Derek was able to speak with the Kolkata consul general, Miranda Parks.

"Yes, Mr. Richards. I have been in contact with the CIA about this matter. Unfortunately, I don't have any additional information at this time."

"Additional information? That means you had information to share?"

"I'm sorry. But you will have to contact the CIA directly, sir. I can't help you."

The conversation had been alarmingly short.

Derek called Eric Sampson.

"Hey," Sampson said when he picked up the call.

"Eric, what's going on? Kolkata consul general indicated she passed information to the CIA. What did she have?"

Eric cleared his throat, then spoke quietly.

"Listen. I can't do this here. Meet me at the old place at five o'clock."

Eric hung up.

Derek slammed the desk phone back onto the receiver. He looked at his watch. It was nearly 3:30.

He paced in his office. He had a bad feeling about the last two telephone calls. He asked himself why the CIA would withhold information about Alex's disappearance. Of course, he could think of many reasons, none of which had anything to do with Alex.

Although CIA and FBI occasionally cooperated on investigations, each had its own area of focus. CIA investigated only foreign countries and citizens while prohibited from collecting data on US citizens and entities. They have only an intelligence gathering function without any law enforcement ability.

FBI has law enforcement capabilities within the United States with restriction from investigating foreign entities.

That is why, Derek understood, gathering information on a case involving a US citizen on foreign soil often proved difficult. But he wasn't about to give up. He had some time before he would meet Eric at their old stomping grounds.

Derek's thoughts quickly turned to Bradley's interrogation of Ali al-Haqani. He knew it was too soon to expect to hear from either Bradley or Mike, but that only served to increase his anxiety. At the moment, it seemed to Derek that, if he wanted to obtain any information about his nephew, he would have to find it himself.

He tapped his computer's keyboard and searched the phrase, Himgiri Express passenger list. After following several dead-end links, Derek found the one he wanted. His expectations for using the list to find the information he wanted weren't high, but he was desperate to try.

The website page allowed for entering the passenger name, travel date, passenger train name, and destination. Only the travel date and train name were marked as required fields for data entry. Derek entered Alex's name, travel date of April 21, and Himgiri Express. In seconds, the information appeared.

Alex Carson

12331 HIMGIRI EXPRESS Howrah Jn to Jammu Tawi Fare

1 Adult 2A 2,895

21 April 2023 11:03 IST

Derek sat back in his chair. His square jaw clenched as his internal temperature rose and his face turned crimson. *That's all it took? Why hasn't Eric told me about this? And what else isn't he telling me?*

After allowing himself a few moments to fume, the information took center stage in his brain. Alex had purchased a ticket to the Union Territory, one of the most dangerous borders in the world.

"What were you thinking, Alex?" Derek said to no one. "And what are you hiding, Eric?"

Derek printed the ticket information and stuck it in his shirt pocket. Then he went back to his computer and started to dig deeper.

At 4:40, still harboring anger, Derek left his office and headed to Ralph's Bar & Grill.

While at Northeastern University, Derek and Eric had become fast friends and made several jaunts via train to DC during school breaks. After graduation, each had gone their separate ways but reconnected when Derek accepted his current position and moved to DC. Both had been surprised to discover that their former favorite haunt, Ralph's, was still in business.

Derek spotted Eric sitting in the back corner. When he reached the table, he took the paper from his pocket, unfolded it, and slammed it down in front of Eric. Eric glanced at the document then displayed a sullen expression.

"Why are you keeping me out of the loop?" Derek asked angrily.

Eric replied, "Sit down . . . , please."

Derek paused, then took a seat across from Eric. A glass of bourbon was waiting for him.

"You're not the only one who has orders to follow, Derek. I shouldn't even be here."

"Why?"

"Because this is a highly classified situation."

"Who took my nephew?"

"I don't know."

"But you have something. What is it?"

"I'm sorry, Derek. I can't."

Derek hit the table with his fist. "Goddammit, this is my nephew! My family!"

"I know. That's the only reason I'm here right now."

Eric paused. Derek could sense his internal struggle.

"Shit!" Eric glanced around the bar. "You and I never had this conversation."

"I understand."

"We traced Alex to Jammu and Kashmir. And because Alex left his phone at Howrah Station, we think Alex may have suspected someone was after him."

"Why would anyone be after Alex?"

"I don't know. Maybe he saw something he shouldn't have. Maybe he trusted the wrong people?"

"What else?"

"It's possible whoever took him followed him onto the train."

A lump formed in Derek's throat. "There's more, isn't there?"

Eric frowned and sat silent for a moment. Then he leaned in and whispered. "From there, we're pretty sure Alex traveled into Afghanistan by way of Khyber Pass."

Derek's jaw dropped. "What?"

"Then he disappeared. We think that's when he was taken."

"Afghanistan? Why would he willingly go into Afghanistan? This doesn't make any sense."

"I don't know."

"What's your next move?"

"You know I can't tell you that."

"I swear, Eric. I'm on a jet to Jalalabad if the CIA doesn't keep me in the loop."

"You'll get yourself killed."

"I'll take that chance."

"Don't be stupid, Derek. You don't know the area. You don't know the people."

"Then I'll find someone who does." Derek stood. "I mean it, Eric."

Eric sighed. "Let me see what I can do."

Derek got into his car, leaned his head on the headrest, and took multiple deep breaths to try to calm himself. Amid his fourth cleansing breath, his cell phone rang. It was Mike Mendez.

"Mike! How did it go?"

"Where are you?" Mike asked.

"In my car."

"Pull over."

"I'm parked. What's going on?"

"Ali al-Haqani is dead. He took some kind of poison. He must have had it with him the whole time."

"Goddammit. So, we didn't get anything from him?"

"Bradley was with him when he died. Derek, al-Haqani is responsible for Alex's abduction. He told Bradley just before he died."

Derek couldn't speak. Horrible pictures flashed through his mind. Each of them was worse than the previous. He heard a voice that seemed far away.

"Derek!" Then again. "Derek!"

Derek managed to utter, "Yeah."

"Are you alright?" Mike asked.

"I . . . yeah. I'm okay. Is he dead?"

"Yeah, al-Haqani is dead."

"No, I mean Alex."

"I don't know," Mike replied.

"He's in Afghanistan," Derek said, as if in a trance.

"Who's in Afghanistan?"

"Alex. I just found out."

"How?"

"It doesn't matter. But I . . . I've got to call you back," Derek said as he saw Eric coming out of the bar.

"Wait!" Mike said.

Derek disconnected the call and jumped out of his car.

"Eric!" he yelled across the parking lot.

Eric looked up, saw Derek waving his arms, and started walking toward him. Derek jogged to meet him.

"Ali al-Haqani took Alex," Derek said when in earshot.

"Al-Haqani? I thought he was in the states?"

"He is. But I just got confirmation that he was behind the abduction."

"Confirmation by who?"

The information was classified, but if Alex were still alive, Derek knew it was the only way to help him. Derek decided right then that he would disclose only the information that suited his purpose. "Ali al-Haqani himself."

"You've got him?"

"We do."

"I'll get right on it," Eric said as he turned and hurried to his vehicle.

Derek returned to his car and dialed Mike's cell phone.

"Sorry, Mike. I had to take care of something quickly. What happened?"

Mendez relayed the events to Derek, adding that since his death, they had discovered a torn lining in al-Haqani's shirt where he must have carried the poison.

"It was easy to miss," Mike explained.

"How's Bradley?"

"He's shaken, but he'll be alright. He's on the phone with someone from the CDC. He was able to get information about the virus before al-Haqani drank the water."

"Would you have him call me as soon as he gets off the phone? I'd like to hear his impressions of the conversation."

"I will." Mike paused. "We're going to do everything we can to find him."

"Yes," Derek agreed, "we are."

TOO CLOSE TO HOME

To take advantage of satellite communications, Bradley sat on deck near the helipad on the Coast Guard cutter and dialed Audrey's cell phone.

"Hello," she answered.

"Hi. I've got some information for you," Bradley muttered. "I don't know how much help it will be, but it's all I could get."

"Are you okay?"

"Yes, why?"

"You sound, I don't know. You just don't sound like yourself."

"It's been a tough day."

"I'm sorry."

"If I told you that the key to the virus is in a single strand, would that mean anything to you?"

"Ribonucleic acid. It could mean the key is hidden in RNA, not DNA." Audrey paused. "That makes sense! That might be it! You're a genius!"

"No, I'm a messenger."

"Either way, this may be exactly what we needed. I've got to get right on this."

"Okay."

"Bradley, are you sure you're okay?"

"I've been better. I've got to go. Good luck." Bradley hung up the phone. Every part of his body felt heavy, even those parts he could not feel, as if all the blood in his body had been replaced by lead.

He gazed at the Atlantic and concentrated on the sounds of the ocean lapping at the sides of the boat as they made their way to port. I pushed him too far, Bradley thought. And I may have gotten Alex killed.

"Bradley," he heard from behind.

Bradley turned to see Mike standing on deck.

"I just got off the phone with Derek. He wants you to call him."

Bradley shook his head. "I don't know what to say to him."

"What do you mean?"

"I may have just gotten his nephew killed."

Mike's eyes grew wide as if surprised by Bradley feeling guilt over al-Haqani's death. "Now, hold on there, son! This madman had his plan, and he was going to implement it no matter who was in that room with him."

"I pushed him."

"You did your job. You got the information out of him that I asked of you. If anyone is responsible, it's me. And I'm sure Derek knows that. Besides, he has some information you might be interested in hearing."

"What information?"

"Call him," Mike said, then turned away.

Bradley took one more look at the ocean before dialing Derek's number.

"Bradley," Derek answered.

"I'm sorry, Derek. "I pushed him too hard."

"That's bullshit! The bastard intentionally put you in that position. Keep your head afloat!"

Like a sponge, Bradley thought.

"Are you still there?" Derek asked.

"Yeah, I'm here. Mike said you had information."

"I think Alex is somewhere in the Nangarhar province of Afghanistan."

"Where did you get that?"

"It doesn't matter. It's reliable. We need to talk to someone who knows that region."

"We should talk to Zayt. If he doesn't know the area himself, I'm sure he knows someone that does," Bradley said.

"I hadn't thought of Zayt," Derek replied. "Will you call him? If he can't come to us, we can go to him."

"I'll call him right now. Have you told Cate and Sheila?"

"No, not yet."

"What are you going to tell them?"

"I can't tell them about al-Haqani. But, I won't lie to them about where we think Alex is."

"When you talk to them, tell them . . . tell them . . ."

"Yeah, I know. No words. When are you coming back to DC?"

"As soon as possible."

"Call me when you get here," Derek said, then hung up.

Bradley found Zayt's contact in his phone and pressed the call icon.

Zayt's real name was Warrick Gaines, but nobody ever used it. He and Bradley had met seven years before during a murder investigation in Chelsea, Massachusetts. Not only did Bradley consider Zayt one of his closest friends, they had become business associates in Zayt's successful efforts to create a tiny home community for the homeless. Bradley felt sure that Zayt, a three-tour Afghanistan military veteran, could provide valuable insight.

"Maestro!" Zayt happily answered.

Bradley cringed at the use of the nickname. "Hey, Zayt. How are you?"

"Got sixty left in the tank!"

"What the hell does that mean?"

"Look it up, analyst! How've you been, dude?"

"Too much to tell over the phone. We need your help."

"We who?"

"Me and Derek. We need to find someone in Afghanistan. In the Nangarhar Province. Do you know it?"

"Yeah, I know it well. I spent a full tour in that region. It's not a great place to lose someone."

"Alex is missing, Zayt. We think that's where he is."

"Your Alex? The kid?"

"Yeah. Can you get to DC?"

Zayt paused. "Yeah, I'll just need to make some arrangements here."

"Thanks, Zayt. Text Derek your flight info. He'll send someone to pick you up at the airport. I'll see you when I get there."

"Get there? Where are you?"

"Headed into a Miami port. I'll explain later. See you soon."

Bradley felt a small glimmer of hope as he hung up the phone. He texted Derek to let him know Zayt would be getting in touch and that he would need to pick him up at the airport.

Alone on deck, Bradley recalled his conversation with al-Haqani. He had said, "This time, it will be my hand reaching into your forsaken soul." Not "... it was ..."—"... it will be ..." That told Bradley that Alex was still alive. But he knew they had to find him fast. Once word got out that Ali al-Haqani was dead, Alex would most likely suffer the same fate.

Bradley found Mike talking with the captain.

"We'll be in port in an hour," Mike told Bradley.

"We can't let it be known that al-Haqani is dead. As soon as his captors find out, they'll kill Alex," Bradley said.

The two moved onto the deck to speak privately.

Mike said, "He must have had a way to contact whoever has Alex. By text, email, something to let them know his intentions."

"Did the Coast Guard find anything on the boat? A computer, cell phone?"

"Yes, both. And I'm sure they're password protected. I've got a tech guy standing by in Miami."

Bradley slammed his hand on the wheelchair arm. "Dammit! Can't they move this tug any faster? Why can't we take a helicopter back?"

"By the time they got a crew together and got out here, we'd be back in port. Take a break, Bradley. Use this time to regroup."

Bradley turned his focus to the ocean. But he wasn't thinking about water, he was thinking about sand—the desert. Ali al-Haqani had never done anything without reason. He would have held Alex someplace of significance. But al-Haqani was a well-traveled man, and Afghanistan was ripe with underground bunkers and mountain caves. They would be looking for a specific grain of sand in a desert.

Sheila, David, Max, Janet, and Bill sat in a circle around David's cell phone.

Derek's voice came through the speakerphone. "We think Alex may be in the Nangarhar province of Afghanistan. Can any of you think why he may have been heading into Pakistan or Afghanistan?"

Sheila gasped, then turned to face her son. "Max?"

"No! He told me he was going to explore India. He never said anything about going to either of those places. He knew I would have told him he was crazy."

"Maybe that's why he didn't tell you?" Derek asked.

"I don't know," Max replied. "None of this makes sense. Why would he go there? His book is about India."

"Sheila? David? Did Alex ever express interest in that area?"

"Yes. He was fascinated by the region. Especially Jammu and Kashmir. He always said he could spend his entire career just writing about the area's history. But he wouldn't go there alone. He knows how dangerous it is. He's not a reckless kid."

"No," Derek agreed. "He's never been reckless."

"What do we do now?" David asked.

"Do you still have that jet standing by?"

"I do."

"Send it to me!" Derek said.

Derek's mood matched the dark clouds that rolled into DC as the sun set. Raindrops the size of buckshot hammered his windshield. The methodical whoosh of wiper blades barely overpowered the sound of drops hitting the glass, and thunder rumbled in the distance where flashes of lightning lit the night sky. It's coming, Derek thought.

He parked his car along the curb at the airport's ground level Terminal 1. He knew Zayt would not have checked a bag, so he wouldn't need to wait long. He texted Zayt to tell him that the SUV was black, told him exactly where he was parked, and gave him the license plate number of the vehicle. Through the heavy rain, he found it difficult to tell if Zayt was one of the people who already stood under the covered terminal exit.

The passenger door opened, and Zayt quickly squeezed into the front seat with his overnight bag and closed the door.

Derek had forgotten how big he was. Not tall, but solid and muscular. Raindrops clinging to his dark skin seemed to shimmer.

"It's good to see you, Zayt. Have you gotten bigger?" Derek asked.

"Only around the middle." Zayt smiled and held out his hand.

The two shook hands, and Derek said, "I don't believe it for a minute. You look like you could still be special forces."

"You're looking pretty fit yourself. That beautiful wife of yours must be taking very good care of you."

"That she is. She can't wait to see you."

"Oh? I assumed we'd be going to your office. Bradley said you were going to have someone else pick me up."

"Yeah, well, there've been some developments that are better discussed outside my office. I'm taking you home. I hope you're hungry. I'm sure Cate will go above and beyond."

"Food? Real food? We've been scrounging for everything we can find to keep the residents fed. Things are looking mighty tough back home."

"I know. Supposedly, the first shipments of food from overseas are due tomorrow. Food is already coming in from South America, but it's the people on the west coast that have the advantage. Some of it will make it east, but most of it won't. Cate managed to fill the freezer with seafood and locally sourced foods before the supermarkets closed."

"She happened to go shopping just before this happened?" Zayt eyed Derek.

"I . . ."

"Relax. I know you're an honorable guy. And, working with Cate all those years, I know she keeps her pulse on the food market. It's in her blood. So, tell me what's going on."

Careful not to divulge confidential or classified information, Derek explained the situation using words and phrases such as the perpetrator, my old friend, and theoretically.

Back when Bradley worked for Derek in the Chelsea headquarters, Zayt had unofficially assisted Bradley in some instances. Derek rarely learned of Zayt's involvement until it was too late. To say the two had gotten off to a rocky start would be an understatement. Eventually, Derek and Zayt came to an understanding and a friendship evolved. But Derek had never before asked for Zayt's help, and Zayt didn't want to disappoint.

"Okay. Let me see if I've got this. The perpetrator is behind the kidnapping but did not perform it and is now dead. Your old friend gave you reliable information on Alex's general whereabouts, but won't divulge how he or she knows, and you think your friend knows more and is holding out on you. And, theoretically, Alex knew all along he was being followed? I'm sorry, that one just doesn't make sense to me."

"Me, neither. If Alex thought he was in trouble, why wouldn't he go to the embassy or local law enforcement?" Derek asked as he pulled off the highway. The rain had slowed as the storm moved south of the city. "But at this point, it doesn't matter. What matters is finding and freeing Alex. And we need to be quick about it. If the kidnapper finds out the perpetrator is dead . . ."

"Yeah!" Zayt said.

"Here we are," Derek said as he pulled up to the house.

The brick house sported a black door and black window shutters. A wheelchair ramp had been installed to the left of the front steps, and a row of small shrubs lined the front and inclined in size with the ramp. A flower bed decorated the right side of the stairs. Zayt could see Cate's sense of style in the house's curbside appeal.

When they were halfway to the front door, it opened, and Rusty bounded out and ran to Zayt. Rusty's nubbed-tail butt wagged so hard he almost lost balance before he reached Zayt.

"Rusty, old pal. I didn't expect to see you here!" Zayt smiled.

Rusty jumped with excitement and then ran circles around Zayt.

"Looks like he missed you!" The voice came from the door.

Zayt looked up and saw Cate as stunning as ever. A smile creased his cheeks, and he took only one step to mount the three stairs in front of the door. Lifting her off her feet, he wrapped Cate in a bear hug.

Cate giggled as he twirled her in a circle.

"My goodness, Zayt. Have you gotten bigger?" Cate asked.

Zayt laughed, placed her back on the floor, and said, "You are as beautiful as ever, Cate."

"God, I've missed you. How is the REACH community doing? And how are Tasha and Shea?"

"Honey," Derek said, "you could at least let him actually walk into the house before you bombard him with questions." Derek took Zayt's overnight bag and set it by the table in the foyer.

"Really, Derek. I'm sure you've already heard about the gang back home. It's my turn. Come into the living room, Zayt," Cate said.

Cate grabbed Zayt's hand and led him to the couch. Rusty stayed by Zayt's side. Her euphoria of seeing Zayt lasted only seconds. Although Derek hadn't told her, she understood that Zayt was there to help with Alex. "Thank you for coming."

Cate's hand was still in his. Zayt placed his other hand over hers and said, "I will always come when you need me."

"Cate? Do you mind if we eat now? We have a lot of work to do." Derek said.

"I thought Bradley was coming?"

"He is. But it's going to take him a little longer to get here," Derek told her.

"Can you get in?" Mike asked as he stood over Walt Harper's shoulder.

With Ali al-Haqani's laptop sitting on the desk in front of him, the young technician replied, "Oh, I'll get in. It's just going to take a little time."

"We don't have the luxury of time," Bradley said.

"Well, what can you tell me about him?" Walt asked.

"What do you mean?" Mike asked.

"Even though everyone knows your password shouldn't contain personal information like birthdays, anniversaries, or your dog's name, that's what most people do. So, what can you tell me about him?" Walt raised his brows.

"Bradley, this is your territory," Mike said.

"Al-Haqani was not like most people," Bradley said.

"You'd be surprised at some of the weak passwords used by even the most cautious people. Besides, it's the best option we have if you need this done fast," Walt replied.

All the information Bradley had learned about al-Haqani spewed from his mouth. Walt took notes, nodding his head and underlining the facts he considered most probable. When

Bradley stopped talking, Walt started typing into the laptop's password field.

The laptop accepted the seventh password attempt.

"How the hell did you do that?" Mike asked.

"The keyboard. Look at the keys. You can see that the I and M keys are more worn than the others. From the information you gave me, I chose what I thought would be most important to the person who set the password. You said his siblings all died at the same time. Isam, Iman, and Omid. The combination of all three names uses four I's and three M's. That was the most probable option."

"Huh! The keyboard." Mike smiled as he inspected the keys more closely. "Let's see what he's got on there."

"I've got to go," Bradley said. "My flight leaves in two hours."

"I'll let you know if we find anything," Mike said.

It was nearly ten when Bradley arrived at Derek and Cate's. He hadn't been able to sleep on the plane. His mind whirled with questions as to how and why Alex was in Afghanistan. He had a vision of Alex being kidnapped in India, bound and gagged in the back of a beat-up truck, and driven through the mountains along bumpy dirt roads into Afghanistan. He also pictured a frightened Alex held at gunpoint in a dingy, cold room, wondering if he would ever see his family again. Several times, Bradley shook the images from his head and tried to sleep, but it never came.

Derek and Cate expected him, so there was no need to knock. Rusty stood at the door when he entered, then jumped onto Bradley's lap and licked his face.

"I missed you too, buddy. Where is everybody?" Bradley checked the kitchen and living room but saw no one. "Hello?"

Cate came out of the bedroom at the end of the hall—the room they called Bradley's.

"Bradley, you look exhausted," Cate said while hugging him.

"I passed exhausted two hours ago."

"And I bet you haven't eaten, either. I have a plate ready for you. I'll heat it up. Come into the kitchen."

"Where's Derek?"

"He and Zayt are in the den."

"I should go in . . ."

"Not until you've eaten something," Cate demanded. "I've got your room ready. You're staying here tonight."

"Am I?"

"Yes. That is not up for discussion. Besides, I know the three of you won't be sleeping any time soon, no matter how much you need to."

A chime from Bradley's cell phone alerted him to a new text.

Nothing from the laptop so far. Techs are working on cell phone.

Feeling frustrated, Bradley replied to Mike Mendez,

OK.

"Sorry about the interruption," Bradley said.

"Are you kidding? I don't think I've had an uninterrupted conversation with Derek in years."

Just as she did then, Cate generally had the ability to lift Bradley's spirits. He grinned and followed her to the kitchen. "Have you talked to Sheila?"

"She's completely distraught. I thought about flying to California to be with her, but I know I'm needed here."

Startling them both, the doorbell rang.

"Are you expecting anyone else," Bradley asked.

Derek and Zayt came out of the den and looked down the hall toward the front door.

Through the opening from the kitchen to the hall, Cate asked Derek, "Are we expecting anyone?"

Derek shrugged and headed to the door. Bradley, Cate, and Zayt followed.

"We brought the jet," David said when Derek opened the door. Sheila and Max stood beside him.

"Oh, Sheila!" Cate ran to her sister. They hugged and cried.

"What are you doing here, David?" Derek asked.

"I told you. We brought the jet."

"You shouldn't have come. What if someone tries to contact you at home?" Derek asked.

"Bill and Janet are there. We couldn't just sit there."

Hesitantly, Derek moved from in front of the door to allow them to enter. He lowered his gaze and rubbed his forehead. "You know I didn't mean for you to bring the plane personally. What do you think you'll be able to do here? What were you thinking?"

David took a defensive stance. "I was thinking that my son has been kidnapped halfway around the world, and I wasn't going to sit on my ass and do nothing about it!"

All eyes focused on Derek and David.

Derek opened his mouth to respond, but before he could, Bradley interjected, "It's good to see you, David. And you, too, beautiful!" Bradley smiled at Sheila. "Max. You're looking good." He hugged Sheila and shook David and Max's hands.

Cate moved to Derek's side and linked her arm with his. She pleaded with her eyes for him to accept the situation. Derek sighed and said, "Alright, then."

To Zayt, David said, "I didn't know you were in DC."

"I just got in tonight," Zayt replied.

David's brows cinched, and he glanced at Derek.

Wanting to diffuse the tension in the room, Cate said, "I've got fresh coffee in the kitchen and plenty of seafood casserole. Why don't we go in there?"

"We have work to do. Bradley?" Derek asked.

Bradley rolled his chair toward Derek but stopped abruptly when Cate said, "Bradley is going to eat something first. No arguments."

Looking first at Derek, then Cate, Bradley said to Derek, "I'll be in in a few minutes."

Derek, then Zayt, turned to walk down the hall. David and Max followed. When Derek noticed, he turned and asked, "What are you doing?"

"I told you, Derek. I'm not going to sit on my ass! And I won't be left in the cold. This isn't just another FBI investigation. This is my boy we're talking about."

"And my brother," Max added.

"It's not a good idea," Derek said.

"It's not up for debate," David replied.

Derek exhaled deeply, then turned. The four entered the den and closed the door behind them.

"Well, that went well," Cate said, then pursed her lips.

"I'm sorry, Cate. We didn't mean to upset Derek. But we just couldn't sit at home waiting for the phone to ring," Sheila said.

"He's not upset," Bradley replied. "He's worried. And he doesn't want you to be any more worried than you already are."

"I don't know if that's possible." Tears ran down Sheila's cheeks.

Cate wrapped her arms around her sister and held tight.

Tension filled the room when Bradley entered the den. Derek and David stood face-to-face only inches apart.

"Whoa!" Bradley said. "What's going on?"

Each took a step back from the other, eyes still locked.

Zayt spoke. "There's a disagreement about the jet's passenger list."

"I didn't know it had been decided that we would go to Afghanistan," Bradley said.

"It hasn't," Derek said, adamantly.

"Then what's the trouble?" Bradley asked.

"Ask him," Derek pointed to David.

"David?" Bradley asked.

"We can't do anything from here," he replied.

"But you could get him killed by going there!" Bradley responded. "Don't be a fool. This isn't about your need to protect your son. This is about finding Alex and getting him safely out of captivity. This can't be about you, David. This has to be about doing what's best for Alex. Believe me, I understand your frustration and anger. I've been there."

David's face reddened. "You think I'm being selfish?"

"I think you're being a father. And that's not what Alex needs right now. He needs trained soldiers. Once he's safely home, he'll need you more than ever!"

David backed away and dropped himself onto the den's leather couch. He sat still, his eyes gazing straight ahead. Max took a seat next to him.

The room filled with silence. Then Bradley asked, "What did I miss?" He eyed the open map on Derek's desk.

The paper map was well worn. Some of the folds were torn from extensive use. Red and black circles and arrows marked the map, and handwritten notes lined the edges.

"Is this yours?" Bradley asked Zayt.

"Yeah. I didn't hold on to much from back then, but I couldn't part with my maps." Zayt quickly recapped what Bradley had missed. "This is the Nangarhar Province," he said while circling a section of the map with his forefinger.

Then he stabbed his finger on the paper and said, "This is Jalalabad, its capitol. The airport is over here," he pointed to its location, "and the Kabul-Jalalabad road runs here." Zayt traced the route of the road that connects Kabul to Jalalabad and on to Khyber Pass and Peshawar. "It's one of the busiest major roadways in Afghanistan. It's a strong agricultural area. The road serves as a trade route to export olives, dates, lemons, and other crops. We confiscated many shipments of breadseed poppy during our deployment."

"Breadseed poppy?" Derek asked.

"Opium," Bradley answered.

Derek nodded.

"This, right here by Khyber Pass," Zayt continued, "is the Spīn Ghar mountain range where we went after Osama bin Laden in the Battle of Tora Bora."

Zayt's eyes darkened. "We didn't succeed. There's a series of caves in those mountains. Easy for someone to slip away if being pursued. But you could say that for almost any area in the region. Like I told Derek, this is not a good place to lose track of someone." Remembering David and Max were listening, Zayt sheepishly lowered his head.

"So how do we narrow this down?" Bradley asked.

"To start, I'm going to put added pressure on my source. If that doesn't work, we'll take things into our own hands," Derek said.

Bradley had never known Derek to disregard the limits of his position. But it sounded to Bradley as if Derek were prepared to put his career on the line to save his nephew. And, Bradley thought, if that was the case, Bradley would be right by his side.

They strategized for two more hours before retiring.

Cate had assigned sleeping arrangements. Zayt would sleep on the den couch, Max on the living room couch, Sheila and David in the upstairs guest room, and Bradley with Rusty in his room.

Before turning in for the night, Derek knocked on the guest bedroom door. When David opened it, Derek said, "I'm sorry! I didn't mean to attack you like I did. You coming here took me by surprise. I can't imagine what you're going through."

"Thank you," David said, "but there's no need to apologize. You were right. I was thinking about my need to do something, not what's best for Alex. I don't want to add to the problem. But, if it's alright with you, we'd like to stay here. Sheila needs her sister, and I need to know what's being done to find my boy."

"Of course," Derek replied. "Get some rest. Tomorrow's going to be a long day."

FRIEND OR FOE?

Bradley was making coffee when Derek came into the kitchen and turned on the small television that sat at the end of the breakfast bar.

"Mornin'," Derek said.

"Mornin'," Bradley replied.

As he ate dry dog food from his bowl, Rusty ignored Derek.

"At least he's eating now," Bradley said. "He really doesn't like dry dog food. Especially old dog food."

"That's because you've spoiled him."

"No. Your wife has spoiled him," Bradley said as he pointed to the box of Twinkies sitting next to the food bag in the pantry.

Derek chuckled and turned up the television volume.

Zayt walked into the room. "Coffee?"

"Working on it," Bradley said.

On the television, a pretty, blonde woman stood in front of the Atlanta CDC building and said,

> The Atlanta headquarters of the Centers for Disease control has issued a statement concerning a vaccine for the listeria epidemic. In part, it reads, "We are pleased to announce that we have a viable vaccine that is proven to combat the current epidemic. Pharmaceutical labs are in the process of producing high quantities of the vaccine, and doctors will begin to administer it as it becomes available.

"Nice job, Bradley," Derek said.

"It wasn't me. It was Audrey—Dr. Howe," Bradley replied.

Derek grinned and shook his head.

"What did you do?" Zayt asked Bradley.

"Yeah, what did you do, Uncle Bradley?" Max asked as he lifted his head from the living room couch.

"Nothing. Who's having coffee?" Bradley asked as the last drips drained from the coffee grounds.

All responded affirmatively.

After pouring coffee, Bradley picked up his cell phone and texted Audrey.

Congratulations!

Moments later he received a return text.

Couldn't have done it without you!

Bradley grinned. He didn't notice the three sets of eyes focused on him.

Just then, Cate walked into the kitchen and, as always, turned down the volume of the television. "What's with the goofy looks, fellas?"

Bradley looked up from his phone and scanned the faces around the table. Cate was right. They each shared a stupid grin.

"What did I miss?" Bradley asked.

"Nothing at all," Derek replied.

The moment of levity felt good but didn't last long.

"All we have is locally sourced eggs for breakfast. How about a scramble casserole?" Cate asked.

"Sounds great," Max said unenthusiastically.

"Okay," Zayt muttered.

"Yeah, good," Derek mindlessly agreed.

"What can I do to help?" Bradley asked. Cooking always helped Bradley think. And he needed the distraction more than ever.

Cate smiled at Bradley and steered him toward the stocked vegetable bin in the pantry. "You can chop some veggies. I'll work on the eggs. Oh, and there's a block of cheddar in the fridge."

David and Sheila joined them for breakfast. Conversation centered on the day's strategy. They decided that Zayt would spend the day with Derek. David, Max, and Sheila would stay at the house with Cate and document on a computer everything they knew about Alex and his trip. And Bradley would meet with Mike Mendez when he and Sam got back from Florida. Bradley hoped Walt, the technician working with Mike, had found something of use on al-Haqani's laptop or cell phone.

It was 7 a.m. when Bradley got off the elevator and headed to the bullpen. He nearly collided with another wheelchair as he rounded the corner.

"What are you doing here?" Bradley asked.

Sam sat with his left leg sticking out in front of him and supported by the wheelchair's raised leg rest.

"I work here," Sam replied.

"Shouldn't you be home recuperating?"

"I already tried that," Mike said as he came out of Sam's office.

"I can sit in this damned chair here as well as at home. What's the difference!" Sam barked.

"I can make a list if you'd like," Bradley said, "starting with proper circulation. You should be in bed."

Sam ignored Bradley's remark. "Can we get started?"

"Right," Mike said. "Let's go back to your office, Sam. I'll call Derek and see if he's here yet."

"He is," Bradley said.

Back in Sam's office, they waited for Derek to arrive. When Derek walked into Sam's office alone, Bradley wondered where Zayt would be waiting.

"We think al-Haqani was tracking Alex's cell phone," Mike said.

"For how long?" Derek asked.

"Almost two months," Mike replied.

"I don't understand," Sam said. "Why would he track someone like Alex?"

"Because of me," Bradley said. "He told me. Al-Haqani said he knows more about my family than I will ever know. He knew how important Alex is to me. I don't know how, but he knew."

Derek reached for Bradley and put his hand on his shoulder.

"So, did he take Alex as insurance?" Sam asked.

"Spite," Derek answered. "He watched him. But he didn't take him until Alex presented him with the opportunity."

"What was Alex doing in Afghanistan?" Mike asked.

"We don't know. He's writing a travel book on India. As far as anyone knows, he wasn't supposed to be near Afghanistan. His parents and brother are going through all their communications to see if there's anything to suggest otherwise. Are we sure he wasn't taken by force into the country?"

Mike nodded. "Our intelligence says he was alone when he crossed the border."

"And after he crossed?" Bradley asked.

"We don't know. If they took him into the mountains, he could be anywhere by now," Mike said.

Derek stood. "I've got to make a phone call."

Zayt sat on the couch and watched Derek's television. When Derek stormed into the office, Zayt turned if off. "What's the news?"

"Alex was being tracked."

Madelyn was not due to arrive for another half hour, so Derek looked up Eric Sampson's cell phone number and dialed it himself.

Without pleasantries, Derek lit into him as soon as Eric answered. "You have Alex's phone. Why didn't you tell me al-Haqani was tracking him. You must have known that."

"Take it easy, Derek."

"Don't fucking tell me to take it easy! We go way back, Eric. I don't want to fuck things up for you, but I will if you don't start telling me everything you know!"

There was silence on the other end of the phone.

"Eric!" Derek yelled.

"Alright! But not over the phone. I'll come to you. Give me an hour."

"One hour!" Derek said, then slammed the phone onto its base.

"Well?" Zayt asked.

"I don't know. We'll see."

"Could you really fuck things up for him?" Zayt grinned.

"I could, but I won't. But he doesn't need to know that!"

Twenty minutes later, Madelyn buzzed Derek. "Good morning, Derek. Agent Whitman is here to see you."

"Send him in. And good morning," Derek said.

"Mike got a call from Walt, the technician working on al-Haqani's phone. Walt thinks al-Haqani was trying to hack into Alex's email and text accounts. There's no evidence he succeeded."

"Why would he need Alex's emails and texts if he already had Alex?" Derek asked.

"He was thorough. Like a dog with a bone," Bradley said.

Derek knew what Bradley was thinking. He was thinking that he and al-Haqani were very much alike. But Derek knew that wasn't true. There was a major difference between the two, and he would keep reminding Bradley of that difference. "Your information saves lives, his took them."

Bradley dismissed Derek's remark and asked, "Did you call your friend?"

"He'll be here in about forty minutes," Derek said.

"With his tail between his legs," Zayt added with a smile.

When Eric arrived, Derek sat behind his desk, Zayt on the couch. Bradley had placed himself to the right of Derek's desk, facing the door.

"What the hell is this?" Eric asked Derek. "Who are they?"

"Relax, Eric. Agent Whitman, this is Eric Sampson, an old college friend." Derek placed an unusual inflection on the word "college." "And this is Zayt."

"I thought we'd be alone," Eric said.

"If we had cut through the bullshit earlier, we could have done this on the sly. But I'm running out of time."

Eric reached inside his suitcoat and retrieved a thick file.

Derek's eyes widened when he saw the amount of information it held. "How long have you had this?"

"Not long," Eric replied. "Some of it you already know."

Derek opened the file. The room went dead quiet as he read. Some pages he flipped through quickly, others he lingered over. The deeper he got into the file, the redder his face got.

"You had this information two days ago! You knew al-Haqani was tracking Alex's phone. You knew it all! I gave you everything I had, and you gave me nothing." Derek fumed.

"I'll lose my job and worse if they find out you have this file."

Derek continued scanning the pages. "Wait. This says Alex was identified as being alone north of Jalalabad on the Konar Jalalabad Road."

"It's an unconfirmed report," Eric said.

"But it's possible he wasn't taken as soon as he crossed into Afghanistan."

"It's possible," Eric agreed.

Evidently, every email, text, phone call, and search Alex made was listed. Documents detailed his movements from Kolkata to Afghanistan with dates and times.

Angrily, Derek continued flipping pages until he stopped abruptly. He picked up the next piece of paper. "What's this?" he asked Eric.

"It's an unsent email. It was in the draft folder of his email server. He may have been writing it just before he ditched the phone. But it doesn't make sense."

"No," Derek said, "it doesn't." Derek handed the paper to Bradley.

Eric started to protest as Derek glared at him.

"It's an email addressed to Max," Derek said.

Bradley read aloud. "'When you visit, say hello to my sister in Union City, CA.' I assume CA is California."

"I didn't know they had a sister," Zayt said.

"They don't," Derek replied.

"Right," Eric said. "We've looked for any contacts he may have in Union City and haven't come up with anything. I thought maybe you might be able to help."

Derek sent another glare Eric's way. Then he picked up his cell phone and called Cate.

"Hey, let me talk to Max," Derek told Cate.

"Yeah?" Max answered.

"Max, do you or Alex know anyone in Union City, California?"

"Alameda County? San Francisco area?" Max asked.

Derek put his hand over the phone and asked Eric if Union City is in Alameda County. He nodded.

"Yes, Alameda County," Derek said into the phone.

Bradley pulled the laptop from his briefcase and searched for Union City, California.

"I don't know anyone there. And as far as I know, neither does Alex. The only time we went north was to see my grandparents in Sacramento."

"Can you call them and see if they know if Alex has contact with anyone there?"

"Yeah, sure. Have you got something?" Max asked.

"Not sure. Call me back." Derek disconnected the call.

"Bradley, let me see that again," Derek said.

Bradley slid the paper from under the laptop and handed it to Derek. Derek stared at it intently.

The only sound in the room was Bradley tapping on his keyboard. Zayt had gotten off the couch and stood over Bradley's shoulder.

The size of Zayt at full stance caught Eric off guard. "I'm going to need that file back, Derek."

"Not until I make some copies." Derek didn't look up from the file.

Eric was horrified. "Those are classified documents. I can't let you copy them."

Derek met Eric's eyes. "I guess you would know the dangers of copying other people's work."

Eric stiffened as Derek used his personal printer to start copying the file.

The swish of pages shooting from the laser printer into its tray soon fell into the background when Bradley exclaimed, "I know where he is!"

Derek snapped his head around. "What?"

"I know where Alex is," he repeated.

"Where?"

"He's not in Nangarhar Province. He's in Kunar Province. He's in Asadabad!" Bradley announced confidently.

"How do you know that?" Derek asked.

"He's a smart guy, Derek. The unsent email. 'When you visit . . . sister . . . Union City, CA.' He's telling us where he was going. I searched Union City. It took some reading, but there it was. Union City is a sister city of Asadabad, Afghanistan. It also has sister cities in the Philippines, Thailand, India, China, and Mexico. But Asadabad is Ali al-Haqani's childhood home. That's where he is!"

"Son-of-a-bitch!" Derek said.

"How sure are you about that?" Eric asked.

"I'd bet my life on it!" Bradley said without thinking.

"Think about it," Derek said. "If Alex suspected he was being followed and might be in danger, he would have left word, if possible, as to where he was going in case he disappeared. As long as he kept in touch with his family, everything was fine. But when they stopped receiving his weekly postcards, we went looking."

"And found his phone," Eric said.

Derek continued, "I still don't understand what would bring him to Afghanistan. Especially if he thought he was in danger."

"What about the phone?" Eric asked. "Wouldn't he assume his brother was tracking it? Didn't you say it was common for them to do that? Max got worried when he saw that the phone hadn't moved."

"As long as Alex stayed in touch, I don't think Max would have worried. Alex could have easily lost his phone, and Max might first figure that."

Derek's cell phone rang. It was Max. "My grandparents said they don't know if Alex knew anyone in Union City."

"It's alright. We've figured it out. Thanks, Max. I'll call you later," Derek said.

"Wait . . . ," Max was saying when Derek disconnected.

"We need a map of Asadabad!" Bradley said.

Zayt pulled a map from his pocket and laid it open on the desk.

Perplexed, Eric turned to Derek and asked, "Who is this guy?"

Derek's phone rang again. Max was at the other end. "You hung up too quick. We found something that might explain why Alex went to Afghanistan. He met a professor when he was in Bangladesh. He was completely impressed with this guy. He wrote that he wished he could sit with him for days to learn what he knew of the region, but he couldn't, because the professor was leaving for Afghanistan and planned to be there for three months."

"What's the professor's name?" Derek asked.

"He didn't say," Max replied.

"Text me a picture of the letter. Have you found anything else?"

"No, not yet, but we're still going through everything."

"Okay, keep me posted. Good job, Max," Derek said before he ended the call.

"What is it?" Bradley asked.

"Alex may have been going to visit a professor he met in Bangladesh. The professor was in Afghanistan, but we don't have a name or location." Derek hit his hand on his desk. "What the hell was he thinking?"

"Easy, Derek. We've all made bad decisions before. He's young. Maybe this professor made him feel safe. Maybe that's why he sought him out," Bradley said.

"Maybe, maybe, maybe. I don't like dealing in maybes," Derek said. "Alright, let's deal with what we think we know. Zayt? How much do you know about Asadabad?"

The four huddled around the map.

"This is the Kunar River running along the east side of the city. The Pech river breaks off here and runs northwest, cutting through the middle of the city. Like most of Afghanistan, it's surrounded by mountains, but inside the city there are many farms and agricultural areas." Zayt moved his finger around the map as he spoke.

"See these red circles? Those are all mosques. Most of the markets are in this area." He drew a circle with his finger. "And the new schools are over here. There are others scattered about, but the concentration of shops and schools are in those two areas. This, right here, is where the ammunition warehouse was. There's nothing left but a big hole in the ground."

"Wait a minute. Slow down. The new schools?" Derek asked.

Zayt frowned. "Yeah. Unfortunately, there was a lot of collateral damage during the war. Several schools, hospitals, and mosques were destroyed."

"Al-Haqani's school was destroyed," Bradley said. "Farhad School. Do you know where that was?"

"Yeah, right here." Zayt pointed. "The new school was built a few miles away. The shell of the school was still standing when I was there."

"Do these buildings have basements? Or underground structures?" Bradley asked.

"The country has dealt with major wars since the nineteenth century. And since the Russians invaded in the late 1970s, war has been almost constant, so, yes. It was common for buildings to include underground bunkers for safety. The Taliban used burned-out buildings as attack positions. One of the worst battles we were in was at the old hospital, right here." Zayt stabbed the map. "They had stocked up enough weapons to . . ."

"Hold on," Bradley interrupted. "Which hospital?"

"It used to be the Kunar Provincial Hospital. All that's left of it is what's underground."

"That might be it," Bradley said. "Al-Haqani lost his whole family the day that hospital was blown up. And he was visibly angry when I brought it up. It was the first time I saw raw emotion from him. I think that's what pushed him over the edge. That's when he told me about Alex."

"What do you mean 'pushed him over the edge?'" Eric asked.

Bradley started to answer, but Derek cut him off. "He got angry and lost control. He said some things that I'm sure he regrets telling us."

Bradley glanced at Derek, then at Eric. "Yeah."

"Do you think he could be holding Alex there?" Derek asked.

"It's a good possibility. Both the hospital and the school are plausible," Bradley answered.

"Hold on," Eric said. "How can you be certain? Why not a mountain cave or an abandoned warehouse?"

"Because al-Haqani had . . . has a reason for everything he does," Bradley said. "Every detail meant something to him. What better place to kill a member of my family than at the hospital where his family perished?"

Derek flinched when Bradley used the word kill. "Eric, how soon can you get a team to surveille the old hospital?"

"I think we can have one there in a few hours, but I'll have to run this up the ladder."

"I'll go talk to Mendez now. I'm sure he can convince Director Rhoades to place a call to the CIA director," Derek said.

"No mention of these files, Derek," Eric said.

"No mention," Derek agreed.

"If this pans out, I want access to Ali al-Haqani. The CIA has a lot of questions."

"If this pans out," Derek said, "I'll make sure you get full access to him."

Eric smiled. "I'll call you when the surveillance team is in place." Eric turned and left the room.

Once the door was closed behind him, Bradley turned to Derek and said, "You just promised him full access to a dead man."

Derek smiled. "Serves him right for withholding information from me."

Bradley and Derek shifted their attention to Zayt when he burst into laughter. Zayt approached Derek and held out his hand. "I gained a whole lot of respect for you today, dude."

Derek grasped his hand and shook. "Let's go see Mike."

"I'll be right here when you get back," Zayt said.

"No. You're coming with us. Bring the map," Derek replied.

Aside from their having involved Zayt in the process, Mike was pleased with Derek and Bradley's developments and agreed to take their suppositions to Director Rhoades.

When they returned to Derek's office, Bradley asked Derek, "Are you going to tell them?"

"David, Sheila, and Max?"

"And Cate, yeah."

"Not yet. We might be wrong."

"I think it's a good idea to give them some hope," Bradley replied. "Why not tell them we may have a viable lead? Think about what they're going through."

"Bradley Whitman talking about hope!" Derek forced a grin. "Alright. I'll call David."

"Let's get a coffee, Zayt," Bradley said, motioning to the door.

Derek's private break room sat adjacent to the outer office where Madelyn worked. As they passed, Bradley asked if he could get Madelyn anything from the break room.

"You are sweet to ask, but I'm fine, thank you," she replied.

"Sweet to ask," Zayt repeated with intent to tease.

"You should be so sweet," Bradley replied. "Speaking of, how is Tasha?"

Zayt's girlfriend was a Boston police officer. She and Bradley had not seen eye to eye when they first met but had since developed mutual respect.

"She's doing great. She's thinking of taking the sergeants exam."

"Good for her. She's got the right temperament."

"So what are you saying?"

"She's scary," Bradley laughed.

"That she is! What about you?"

As much as Bradley disliked that question, he welcomed the respite from obsessing over what might be happening to Alex. And he always found it easy to talk with Zayt.

"As a matter of fact, I asked a woman to dinner. But I think she said no."

"You think?"

"Yeah. I was on a helicopter at the time, and the phone signal wasn't very good. But I'm pretty sure she said no."

"That's too bad, dude."

"Yeah, it is."

Zayt caught Bradley up on REACH community business. The Revere Enhancement and Community Housing project had been Zayt's idea. The abandoned sandpit behind Bradley's Massachusetts home proved to be the perfect place for it. The two had joined forces to make it a reality, and since then, the community had grown to house more than eighty people and feed hundreds daily.

"Have you thought any more about moving into my house?" Bradley asked.

"Tasha wants something a little less industrial," Zayt chuckled. "Besides, where would you stay when you come to visit? I don't see you in a hotel."

Bradley's Revere home consisted of a large metal building with the only interior walls providing privacy for the bathroom. The old commercial laundry facility had worked well for Bradley for many years, and he hadn't been able to let go of it.

Derek walked into the break room and went straight to the coffee machine.

"How are they doing?" Bradley asked.

"I think you were right. They needed some good news. I just hope I didn't get their hopes up for nothing. I told them it would be some time before we had anything further. I urged them to be patient." Derek sat in a chair with his coffee mug in both hands and his elbows resting on his knees. He gazed at the floor.

"Patience is not our strong suit, is it?" Bradley grinned.

"No."

Derek stood. "I'm going to call Sam and fill him in. Mike finally got him to go home. Are you going to stick around, Zayt?"

"If it's alright with you, I'd like to."

"Sure. No problem."

"Why don't you come with me, Zayt?" Bradley asked. "I wouldn't mind looking more closely at those maps."

Zayt glanced at Derek, and Derek nodded in return.

"Okay."

In his weakened state, Alex found it difficult to remain alert. He wasn't sure if he'd dozed off or passed out, but sounds of men yelling in the distance brought him back to the present. He strained to hear what they said.

The hood over his head, throbbing from his head wound, and the fact they spoke in Farsi made it difficult for Alex to understand the fast-moving conversation. He could garner only bits and pieces. No contact, kill him tomorrow, instructions from Ali.

He didn't know how much longer he would live. For the first time since his capture, he allowed himself to think about his family. His father, a man who had grown up in a privileged home but understood the meaning of integrity and hard work. His beautiful mother who shared her doubts, dreams, and successes with love and grace. And his best friend and brother. Max is the reason to my whimsy, the planner to my impulsiveness, and the intellect to my emotions. "I love you, Max."

Alex could feel himself slipping into unconsciousness. Before his lids fell heavy over his eyes, he made peace with his death.

SEALED IN SILENCE

Word reached Audrey by midafternoon that patients with the most desperate need had received the initial batch of vaccination and were recovering.

She felt as if she would burst if she didn't share the news with someone. The first person who came to mind was Bradley. But she couldn't do that. She didn't want to give him the wrong impression.

Reflexively, she thought back to the world literature course she took in college and possibly the only fact she remembered from that class. Published in 1578, Euphues: The Anatomy of Wit written by John Lyly suggested, "the rules of fair play do not apply in love and war."

It is unfortunate that I could never adopt Lyly's principal, Audrey thought, because I have a feeling Bradley Whitman might be worth it.

Instead, Audrey called her daughter Allison.

"Hi, sweetheart. What are you doing?" Audrey asked Allison.

"Watching TV with dad."

"Oh. I thought your teachers assigned online homework while the schools are closed."

"Mom, I finished that hours ago."

"Good job, honey. What are you watching?"

"The news. They have video of some really big ships. The lady said they're full of food. That's a lot of food!"

"It sure is. Can I talk to your dad, honey?"

"Okay."

"Hello," Kevin said.

"Do you really think Allison should be watching the news? They'll probably show things that aren't suitable for an eight-year-old, Kevin."

"She was asking questions, Aud. I think it's good that she has an idea what's going on. I've got the remote in my hand. If anything bad pops up, I'll change the channel. Give me some credit, will you?"

"Okay. I'm sorry. I just worry about the effect this could have on her. I don't want her living her life in fear."

"I don't, either. Besides, this is a good thing. How often does the world join forces for a common cause? History is being made today."

"You're right, I know. I've got more good news. The vaccine is working. Hundreds of thousands of lives will be saved."

"I knew you would do it, Aud."

"Not just me, Kev. We all owe an FBI analyst a huge thank you. I'll be by to see Allison tonight."

"Okay. Congratulations."

Audrey took a moment to reflect on the historical aspect of the day. Then she got back to work.

"There's activity where you thought it would be," Eric told Derek.

"What kind of activity?"

"Two vehicles. One of them has come and gone twice during surveillance. The other hasn't moved."

"Do you know who they belong to?"

"We're working on that."

"What's next?"

"Not over the telephone. Can you come to my office?"

"We'll be right there."

"Derek?"

"Yeah."

"Don't bring the big guy."

"Understood."

They had waited seven hours for Eric to call. But it was worth the wait. If Alex was being held at the old hospital, he was most likely still alive. Otherwise, the second vehicle would not have stayed put. But, Derek thought, it could still be a false alarm. Drug dealers or teenagers could be using the burned-out building for their own purpose.

Derek decided to wait until they received confirmation that Alex was in the building before telling his family.

Derek called Bradley. "Meet me downstairs" was all he said.

Derek watched Bradley and Zayt get off the lobby elevator. When they approached, Derek handed Zayt his car keys. "Take my car and go back to the house. Bradley and I are going to CIA headquarters. For obvious reasons, we can't bring a civilian with us. But don't tell the others yet. As far as you know, there are no new developments. Tell them you weren't allowed to stay in the building anymore, so I gave you my car to go home."

"He's there, isn't he?" Zayt asked.

"Maybe. We don't know. But there is activity." Derek looked at Zayt and raised his brows.

"Not a word," Zayt responded.

Bradley's truck was parked in a handicap space close to the door. Before Zayt continued to Derek's SUV, he said, "Good luck."

Once Derek and Bradley had gotten into Bradley's truck, Bradley asked, "What did Eric tell you?"

Derek repeated what Eric had said, then voiced his own concerns about the possibility of being wrong.

Bradley said, "All I know is if al-Haqani was writing the perfect script, this is what and how he would do it."

"I've never needed to believe in you more than I do right now!" Derek sighed deeply.

Derek's remark did not produce a lump in Bradley's throat, nor did it cause a pit in his stomach. That's when Bradley became certain that he was right about al-Haqani.

They all met in Eric's office.

"Our two bosses have been in contact multiple times to work out details," Eric said. "But let there be no mistake. This is a CIA operation. You can watch and feed us any information that might be useful, but we run this op our way. Agreed?"

"Agreed," Both Derek and Bradley responded.

"We ID'd the guy in the vehicle that comes and goes. His name is Abdul-Maalek al-Ahmadi."

"I know that name," Bradley said. "He and al-Haqani were childhood friends. After al-Haqani's father killed himself, he stayed with the al-Ahmadi family. He and Abdul-Maalek are as close as brothers."

"That's right," Eric said. "We've got a rescue team on the way. They should be in place in two hours. It will be 3 a.m. in Asadabad. We've also kept our surveillance team in place in case anything changes."

"Who's going in?"

"Seal Team 7."

"This should be easy for them, right?" Derek asked. "I mean, there's only one car. There can't be too many people watching him."

"Our guys have only seen two captors. But that doesn't mean there aren't others. And the place could be wired. But it's not just

229

the rescue at the hospital we have to worry about. It's getting the helicopter in and out without getting shot down."

"Jesus!" Derek put his hand on his chest. "I assumed it would be a land team."

"There's no time for that. But these guys are the best. And this isn't their first rodeo."

"Yeah, okay," Derek said.

"Hey," Bradley asked Derek. "Are you alright?"

"I'll be alright when this is over and Alex is back on friendly soil."

"Are you ready to go downstairs?" Eric asked.

"Yeah."

"Don't expect to see the director or any top brass. They'll be watching at the White House."

"The president will be watching?" Derek asked.

"Yes. We've been keeping the president apprised of the situation."

The room looked much the same as the FBI situation room except monitors on the walls showed maps of Afghanistan, inflight observation of Seal Team 7, and outlying areas of concern instead of current FBI focus.

Eric pointed out the large, blank monitor at the head of the room. "That's the monitor we'll be able to follow them on once they get boots on the ground. Because this is a classified operation, you won't hear any audio."

A clock on the wall counted down from 1:52:29.

"Make yourselves comfortable. We've got some time," Eric said. "I'll be back shortly." Then he left the room.

"There's no cell service in here," Bradley said.

"Good. I won't have to lie to Cate when I tell her I couldn't call."

"Things are moving very fast," Bradley said.

"Yeah. I'm not sure how I feel about that."

"Is this normal?" Bradley asked.

"I don't know. But I've never known any bureaucracy to move this fast. I guess we're not meant to know, are we?"

"I guess not. But I suddenly feel like a small fish in a big ocean."

"I know what you mean."

When the clock on the wall read 00:10:07, several people entered the room and took a seat. Eric was one of them. He sat next to Derek. Everyday conversations whirled around them, and it angered Derek.

How could these people be so oblivious as to what is about to happen, Derek thought.

Bradley noticed Derek's white-knuckled grip on the chair and placed his hand on Derek's shoulder. They shared a look of concern.

Several minutes later, the large screen in the front of the room flickered. When the picture came into focus, it displayed a fluorescent green image.

"Night vision camera," Eric explained. "That's the target," he said as he pointed to a building on the screen.

The target quickly grew in size as the helicopter got closer.

The wall clock counted—00:01:34.

"Here we go," Eric said.

Derek sat on the edge of his seat, Bradley gripped his chair, and the room went quiet.

The camera jolted as the clock struck 00:00:00. The barrel of a machine gun came into focus, and they could see a pair of boots at the bottom of the screen. On both sides of the picture, soldiers wearing night-vision goggles and carrying guns came into view and ran past a parked car. The camera followed them into the building. Then, for a moment, the screen went dark.

Derek stiffened and held his breath. Green outlines of soldiers soon reappeared and filled the screen. Derek exhaled.

"No shots fired yet. It could mean the captors didn't hear the helicopter or just didn't pay attention to it." Eric said. "Or . . . ?"

"Or what?" Derek asked.

"Nothing."

"Or they're doing what they were told to do. If infiltrated, kill the prisoner," Derek choked.

Soldiers from Seal Team 7 moved from room to room without incident. The camera showed them descending a stairway and gathering at the bottom. Once they had all assembled, the group took a left into a dark hallway.

Within seconds, the monitor showed a barrage of green flashes. Incoming and outgoing rounds filled the screen. Derek recalled using tracer rounds during a mock nighttime raid at the Quantico FBI academy. It looked much like that, only the tracers were red in color and not live rounds. He couldn't tell if the onscreen bullets hit any targets.

It lasted less than twenty seconds. The cloud obstructing the view of the camera slowly dissipated, and Derek saw a man with his arms draped around two soldiers being carried toward the camera. The wounded man was not one of the soldiers. Derek concentrated on the man's face and saw fear. He took satisfaction in the image.

The soldier wearing the camera made way for the injured man to pass him. He then walked forward and focused the camera on another man who lay motionless on the floor.

Derek smiled.

When the camera moved away from the dead man, Derek could see one of the soldiers motioning, directing the others. They moved quicker then down another hallway, through an empty room and then another.

Derek noticed Eric glancing at his watch.

"What is it?" Derek asked.

"They only have ten minutes on the ground. They're running out of time."

"But they won't leave until they find him, right?" Bradley asked.

"They have their orders. If they don't leave on schedule, the chance that any of them leave alive is thin." Eric said.

"How much time is left?" Derek asked.

Eric glanced back at his watch. "Three and a half minutes."

They watched the soldiers disperse. The camera took them through another hallway and another empty room.

"Two minutes, twenty seconds," Eric said.

Derek and Bradley made eye contact and exchanged a fearful look.

The camera suddenly jerked and whipped around. They watched boots run quickly through a series of rooms. Finally, the camera focused on a hole in the floor of one of the rooms. A hinged door lay open.

Not a breath could be heard in the CIA situation room.

A soldier climbed up through the hole. He held only his gun.

Derek dropped his head and covered his face with his hands.

A moment later, Bradley said, "Derek."

Derek looked up. The soldier had rid himself of his firearm and reached down into the hole. Two arms stretched upward."

"Forty-five seconds," Eric said.

A man appeared from the hole.

Derek stood and moved to the monitor. He couldn't see the man's face. Derek's heart pounded.

The soldier helped the man, thin and obviously weak, through the hole. He sat him down. Another soldier emerged from the hole in the floor. He handed the thin man a book.

Tears leaked from Derek's eyes.

The soldiers hoisted the man by his shoulders and carried him out of the room.

Derek could no longer see the man.

"Zero plus ten," Eric said.

Derek looked back at Bradley, who had his head in his hands as his body lurched. Derek went to him, bent down, and whispered, "He's going to make it!"

Bradley wiped his eyes, and they both looked back at the monitor.

The camera showed the man they presumed to be Alex emerge with soldiers from the building. They could see the helicopter in the distance.

"Zero plus forty," Eric said.

The soldiers lifted the man into the helicopter, then waited for the cameraman to get in. When the camera turned toward the rescued prisoner seated in the helicopter, Derek clearly saw the face of his nephew."

"Alex," Derek exhaled.

"Zero plus one minute," Eric said.

The helicopter quickly rose, and soon green flashes reappeared, this time coming from the ground.

"Anti-aircraft fire," Eric said.

The monitor went dark.

Derek jumped to his feet. "What happened?"

"Night vision isn't useful anymore. Without access to sound, all we have now is the tracking map." Eric pointed to the monitor on the side wall.

Derek and Bradley didn't take their eyes off the red triangle that moved on the tracking map to designate the position of the helicopter as it continued away from the captors.

"How long before they get to friendly airspace?" Derek asked.

"About an hour. But friendly is a relative term. This is a covert flight. Put it this way. The longer they are in the air, the better their chances. It gets safer as they go."

"It's gone," Bradley panicked. "The triangle is gone."

"It's alright. The pilot may be flying under radar. If he is, that could mean they made it through the initial attack."

"Jesus, Eric. How the hell do you deal with this?" Derek asked.

"The same way you deal with homeland threats. You get used to them."

The comment hit Derek hard. But he couldn't go there just then. He couldn't think of anything other than Alex making it home safe."

"Goddammit! Why doesn't he answer his phone, Cate?" David yelled.

"Easy, dude. He'll let us know something as soon as he can," Zayt said.

"Don't fucking dude me. Something's going on, and Derek is keeping us in the dark. I can feel it."

"David, please," Sheila sobbed.

"Dad, you're upsetting Mom," Max said.

"I'm fucking upset!" David paced in the living room. "I'm calling the airport." He reached for his cell phone.

"Whoa, David. What for?" Zayt asked.

"I'm getting on that jet and flying to fucking Afghanistan."

"And what will you do when you get there?" Zayt asked.

"I'll search every single place on that map of yours. Every fucking one."

David dialed a number on his phone. "Jackson, get the plane ready for overseas. I'll be there in thirty minutes." He placed his cell phone back in his pocket. "I'm going to pack." He stormed up the stairs.

"You can't let him leave, Sheila," Zayt said.

"Sheila, honey, Zayt's right," Cate added.

"I don't think I can stop him. And I'm not sure I want to," Sheila replied.

"Max, please?" Zayt pleaded.

"I don't know. Dad might have the right idea. We're getting nothing accomplished here. And the longer Alex is missing . . . " He couldn't finish saying what he was thinking.

"It's reckless and stupid and he's going to get himself killed," Zayt said. "Is that what you want?"

"No, but . . . "

"Don't listen to him, Max. I'm going, and he can't stop me," David said as he bounded down the stairs with a hastily packed suitcase.

Rusty became visibly upset. The dog paced the room and walked in circles. Cate tried to calm him to no avail.

David stood face-to-face with Zayt. "I want the map, Zayt."

"No."

"Give me the goddam map!"

"I won't."

David's eyes shone red as the devil. "I remember most of it anyway." He turned and walked out the door.

Zayt called his name once, twice, then yelled, "Alex isn't in Nangarhar Province!"

David stopped, set his suitcase on the walkway, and turned to face Zayt. He slowly walked toward him. Zayt met him halfway. David took Zayt's shirt collar in his hands and pulled. Zayt outweighed David by nearly sixty pounds, so he didn't budge. He could have shooed him off like a fly. But he didn't.

"You know something!" David said. "All this time you sat with us and watched us worry and wonder if my son is dead, and you know something."

"I don't know much, but I know he's not in Nangarhar Province. The map wouldn't help you."

"Where is he?"

"North. Somewhere in Kunar Province."

"Where?"

"I don't know."

"Then I'll go to Kunar Province and find him."

Zayt sighed. "You don't have to."

"Yes, I do."

"No. You don't. I think they've already gone in after him."

David's eyes widened. "Who's gone in after him?"

"Probably a Seal team."

"How do you know that?"

"I don't know it. I think it."

"Alright, then. Why do you think it?"

"Would you mind letting go of my shirt?"

David released his shirt collar and stepped back. "Well?"

"Derek and Bradley were heading to CIA headquarters when I left. I wasn't allowed to accompany them, and I wasn't supposed to say anything."

"Why?"

"Because entering a country illegally, especially an adversarial country, is frowned upon. Not to mention extremely dangerous. And, oh, yeah. Highly classified."

"You say you don't know for sure they sent a team in to get him. Why do you think they did?"

"Because if they didn't, Derek and Bradley would have already hijacked your jet and gone themselves."

"So, your job was to keep us under your thumb?"

"My job was to sit and wait just like the rest of you."

David started pacing on the sidewalk. At first, Zayt couldn't understand the mumbling that came from his lips. When he finally did, he grinned.

He picked up David's suitcase and turned toward the door. "You can beat the shit out of me later."

Zayt stopped short when he saw Sheila, Max, and Cate standing on the front stoop. He shook his head. Derek isn't going to like this, he thought.

The room had cleared except for Derek, Bradley, and Eric. It had been forty-three minutes since the red triangle on the monitor disappeared and fifty minutes since the helicopter left the ground in Asadabad. Derek had spent the time pacing. Bradley rocked in his chair.

After everything Derek had gone through in his life—every case, every tragedy, he could think only of one that matched the torture he felt right then. When he, Cate, and others were victims of a limousine bombing, Cate fell into a coma that lasted days. It was the hardest time in his life. And it took a lot of time for Derek to come to terms with what happened.

At minute fifty-two of the Seal Team 7 operation, Derek didn't know if he could ever recover from what he'd just seen on the screen.

Derek again looked up at the monitor and saw the triangle. Then, just as quickly, it was gone. Had he been mistaken? Had it really been there, or was his mind playing tricks on him?

"What happened?" Derek mumbled.

Eric glanced up. A flash of red again, then gone.

Again! Derek stood and watched.

Bradley's eyes never left the screen. Suddenly, a red triangle popped up big and bright.

Eric moved closer. "They made it to India! Son-of-a-bitch! They made it!"

A muffled voice came through the speakers. "Seal Team 7 confirms extraction."

His legs outstretched, Derek collapsed in a chair and covered his face with his hands.

Bradley wiped tears, rolled his chair over to Eric, and stuck out his hand. "Thank you!"

"Thank you," Eric replied as he shook Bradley's hand. "This was a team effort."

When Derek stood, dizziness overtook him, and he wobbled. Bradley reached out to steady him.

"Are you alright?" Bradley asked.

"I don't know if I'll ever be alright again," Derek answered. "Eric, I need to make a phone call."

Eric walked to the front of the room and flipped a switch. "Go ahead. Call your family."

Derek tapped Cate's cell phone number.

"Derek?" she asked hurriedly.

"Is everyone there with you, Cate?"

"Yes."

"Put me on speaker."

"Okay, Derek. You're on speaker."

"We've got Alex. He's on his way to India, and it looks like he's okay. I don't have any details yet, and I haven't talked to him, but I'm going to stay here until I do."

Derek almost couldn't hear himself finish his sentence over Sheila and Cate's screams.

"Derek?" David yelled.

"Yeah, David?"

Zayt braced himself for what might come out of David's mouth.

"Thank you!" David said.

"There'll be a lot of people to thank, David. I'm not one of them."

"Just the same, thank you."

"I'll call as soon as I have an update."

Sheila and Max remained in a tight hug for several moments. Cate held Rusty in a full embrace, and David slunk onto the couch with his head resting on the back.

Zayt knew David was physically and emotionally drained. He sat beside him and lightly slapped his thigh.

Without lifting his head, David turned to face Zayt. "I'm sorry."

"No need, dude? Can I call you dude?" Zayt smiled.

"Yeah, anytime!" David rolled his head back and shut his eyes.

THE SECRET IS OUT

Eric emerged from his office, then led Derek and Bradley to the CIA lobby. Two hours had passed since the helicopter landed safely in India.

"Have they identified the two guys who were guarding Alex?" Derek asked Eric.

"Yeah." Eric checked his notebook. "Naadir Mahmoudi and Obaid Hasan. We're looking into their backgrounds now."

"What about Abdul-Maalek al-Ahmadi? Any news?"

"Nothing yet, but it's still early in the morning there. The surveillance team is still in place in case he shows up at the hospital. Maybe we'll get lucky, and he doesn't know what happened."

"Well, I guess that's it. You'll call me, right?" Derek asked.

"Yes," Eric replied.

An awkward pause fell between them.

"I'll wait for you in the truck," Bradley said. "Take your time."

"I won't be long," Derek replied.

Derek watched as Bradley maneuvered his chair through the front doors. The sun had set hours before, and Bradley's form quickly melded with the darkness.

Derek turned back to Eric. "I'm serious. I want to know the minute I can talk to Alex."

"I know. I told you. His doctor said he needs a few days of rest before he can talk to anyone. My guys can't even get in to see him. Like I said before, he's extremely dehydrated, and he's lost a lot of weight. As soon as they give me the okay, I'll call you. I promise. But the doctors in India are no pushovers, trust me."

"How can I trust you? You lied to me. You kept information from me."

"Do you really want to play the trust card, Derek?" Eric raised one brow.

Derek glanced at him questioningly.

Eric continued. "I've got my sources too. I know about Agent Maestro, AKA Agent Whitman," he gestured toward the door where Bradley had exited. "So I know al-Haqani is dead. And you knew that when you promised me full access to him."

Derek grinned. "You can have full access to him. You'll just need to go to the morgue."

"We're even now! No more games. We both have jobs to do."

Eric paused, then stuck out his hand. "I'm happy your nephew is safe."

Derek shook his hand. "Thank you. I mean it. And, for what it's worth, I would never have used your college transgression against you. It was just the heat of the battle that made me bring it up."

"Goddam calculus!" Eric grinned.

Derek chuckled, turned, and left the building.

When Derek climbed into Bradley's truck, Bradley asked, "Do you believe that he'll call as soon as the doctor gives the okay?"

"Not for a minute. They're going to put him through the wringer—hope that he saw or heard something they can use. But I'll deal with that tomorrow. Right now, I just want to go home."

Bradley shifted the truck into gear.

The interior of the house was lit up from top to bottom. Derek and Bradley could see movement through the curtained front windows.

Bradley placed the truck in park and pushed the button on his dashboard to activate the driver's side door opening. The large panel first pushed out, then slid to the rear of the truck.

Bradley unbuckled his seatbelt and pushed another button. The metal panel his wheelchair sat on shifted him out of the truck and then down to the ground. Bradley moved his chair forward off the ramp and pushed a key fob button. The ramp lifted and slid back into place behind the wheel of the truck. He closed the door with another push of a button.

By then, Derek stood by his side.

"It looks like they're having a party," Derek said sullenly.

"Two hours ago, they thought Alex could be dead. I think they deserve to celebrate," Bradley said.

"Of course, you're right. I just wonder what long term effect it will have on him."

"I don't know," Bradley said. "But I know one thing." He pointed to the windows. "He's going to have a lot of love and support to help him."

As hard as he tried, Derek couldn't force a smile.

"Hey," Bradley said, "it's okay. Alex is going to be alright. We'll make sure of that."

Derek nodded, then headed toward the house.

The door flew open, and Cate ran to meet Derek. They wrapped their arms around each other. They still embraced as Bradley made it up the ramp and to the front door.

Rusty bounded onto Bradley's lap, and the others gathered around. No one spoke. They silently watched Derek and Cate cling to each other.

Finally, Bradley broke the silence. "Can I come in?"

Sheila laughed, then demanded a hug from Bradley.

Derek and Cate separated from their embrace, but Cate clung tightly to Derek's arm as if she needed him for stability to enter the house. Bradley, however, recognized it was the other way around. He had felt the same thing hours before. Something about Derek had changed, and Bradley wasn't sure what to make of it.

Sheila hugged and thanked Derek, as did Max. David, who'd been standing alone in the corner of the living room, approached Derek.

"I'm sorry I was such a pain in the ass, Derek. I should have trusted you from the start."

"It took everything I had not to jump on that plane myself," Derek replied. "No apologies necessary. You did what any father would do. You were willing to sacrifice your life to save your son's. I can't find any fault in that."

The two embraced.

Zayt breathed a sigh of relief.

Derek excused himself and walked upstairs. Cate followed. Neither came back down that evening.

Coffee had just finished brewing when Derek walked into the kitchen. "Good morning, Bradley. Are you the only one awake?"

"Not anymore," he grinned.

Derek didn't smile. He glanced at Rusty lapping water from his bowl. "Listen. I'm sorry I left you down here last night. I'm sure you had to answer a lot of questions. I didn't mean to put that all on you."

"No problem. I could tell you were exhausted. So was everyone else. I filled them in on the basics, then we all turned in."

"I appreciate it."

Bradley emptied the filter from the coffeepot, then said. "I was wondering. Is Sahani still in town?"

"I think so." Derek paused. "Why?" He glared at Bradley.

Unless he deserved it, Bradley generally did not find himself on the receiving end of Derek's glares, so it confirmed his suspicion that something wasn't right. Derek wasn't himself, and that put Bradley on high alert.

"When I met her in the hall the other day, we promised to catch up. I still feel bad about the way I treated her after Laney died."

Derek poured a cup of coffee, then turned on the television already set to a news station.

"I'm sure she understood."

"Well, I'd like to talk to her anyway," Bradley said.

Derek gave the newscast his entire attention. When Zayt walked into the kitchen, Derek didn't acknowledge him.

Looking at Bradley, Zayt twitched his head toward Derek. Bradley shrugged.

"Coffee?" Bradley asked Zayt.

"Please."

"What are your plans, Zayt? Are you going home right away?" Bradley asked.

"I hadn't given it much thought yet."

"It's Friday. You could stay with me for the weekend. It will be like old times."

Without looking away from the television, Derek huffed.

His gaze squarely on Derek's back, Bradley cinched his brows, then glanced at Zayt.

Watching Derek for a reaction, Bradley continued, "It will be nice to get things back to normal."

Derek placed his coffee mug down hard on the breakfast bar, then retreated to his den without a word.

"What the fuck, dude?" Zayt whispered.

In a soft voice, Bradley replied, "I've only ever seen him like this once before—when Cate was in a coma. I'm hoping he just needs a couple days to himself."

"I don't know. I'm sensing a lot of rage from him."

"From whom?" Cate asked as she turned the corner into the kitchen.

"Jeez, you're quiet," Zayt said.

Rusty trotted to Cate's side.

"Were you talking about Derek?" Cate asked.

"Yes, Cate. But we're just worried about him," Bradley said.

"Where is he?" Cate asked.

"In the den," Bradley replied.

Cate turned off the television just as the news focused its cameras on one of the station's political reporters standing in front of the White House.

She poured herself a mug of coffee, then sat at the kitchen table.

Bradley placed himself directly across from her.

She stared into her mug for several seconds before she said, "I don't want him doing this anymore."

Bradley sat back in his chair. "Shit. Did you tell him that?"

"No. But I'm going to. I can't watch him get eaten up by this job. It's destroying him." Tears formed in Cate's eyes. "It's changing him."

Bradley reached his hand across the table and placed it on hers. "This has been a bad one, Cate, I know. But . . ."

"No, Bradley. It's not just this case. It's every case he's had since we moved to this godforsaken place."

"I thought you loved it here?"

"I love being with my husband. But Derek isn't Derek anymore. He's developed ulcers, he doesn't sleep . . ."

"Wait, what?" Bradley asked.

"No, of course he hasn't told you. He puts on a good show around you and at the office."

"But not at home," Bradley said.

"He tries. He just can't find a way to enjoy life anymore."

"Why didn't you tell me, Cate?"

"He loves you so much. It would destroy him if he thought you thought of him as weak or unable to cope."

Bradley exhaled while slowly shaking his head. "He'll boost my ego all day but won't allow himself to be human."

"Something like that," Cate said.

"When are you going to tell him?"

"This weekend. I've decided."

"You can't do it with company here."

"I can't wait any longer. You must see it now?"

"Talk to Sheila. Ask them to stay at my house while they're here. I've got plenty of room. Make any excuse you want."

They heard the den door open. Derek walked down the hall and up the stairs.

"He's going up to get ready for work," Cate said.

Zayt, who had been listening quietly, said, "I'm going to head home today. I've got a lot of work to do, and you guys are going to have your hands full."

"Zayt . . ." Bradley started.

"Really, dude. I dropped some shit to come here. I've got to get back to it."

"We couldn't have done it without you. I can't thank you enough."

"It's what we do for each other, right?"

"It is," Bradley agreed. "I'd better get ready for work myself. Cate, if David or Sheila have any questions, have them call me, okay?"

"Thank you." Cate smiled.

Bradley rolled from the kitchen to the hall then to his bedroom. Rusty followed.

As he wiped excess shaving cream from his face, Bradley's cell phone rang. Caller ID said Audrey.

"Hello," Bradley answered.

"My God, Bradley. Is everyone alright?"

Surprised and confused, Bradley asked, "Everyone who?"

"It's all over the news about your godson. The White House made a statement about the hostage rescue during the night. The reporter identified the man as one of the FBI director's nephews and your godson."

"What?" When?" Bradley asked.

"About ten minutes ago. I was driving to work and heard it on the radio."

"Audrey, I've got to go. I'll call you back," Bradley said, panicking.

When he rolled into the kitchen, Cate sat at the kitchen table with Sheila, David, and Max.

"We've got a problem," Bradley said. "The White House released a statement about Alex's rescue. They used his name, Derek's name, and my name. It's just a matter of time before news trucks arrive."

"What should we do?" Cate asked.

"Go to my house. I'm unlisted. There's no way they could know where I live. But you and Derek are a different story."

"I'll go pack," Cate said.

"There's no time. Go now. Derek and I will bring whatever you need later. Please take Rusty with you. You have a key, right Cate?"

"Yes."

"Go!"

"What the hell is going on?" Derek asked as he came down the stairs.

"Go!" Bradley yelled again. "We've got this."

Cate, Sheila, David, and Max took Rusty and darted to Cate's SUV. Derek watched as they piled into the vehicle, backed out of the driveway, and drove away.

Zayt came out from the bathroom, saw Bradley and Derek by the door, and asked, "What's all the ruckus?"

The first news truck pulled up to the curb and a reporter, seeing them in the doorway, jumped out of the van with her microphone and ran towards the house. Derek and Bradley ducked back inside and locked the door.

"Shut the curtains," Bradley said to Zayt.

"What the fuck is going on, Bradley?" Derek asked, angrily.

Bradley explained what he knew.

"Why would they do that?" Zayt asked.

"Political capital," Derek spat. "The president will get a big bump in his ratings. And after this epidemic, he must figure he needs it. Dammit! Where are Cate and the others going?"

"To my house. I'm unlisted. They'll be left alone there."

"Thank you."

"But we're not getting out of here without at least getting on camera," Bradley said as he peeked out the window. "There are three of them already. What do you want to do?"

Derek thought for a moment. "Okay, here's what we'll do. I'll distract them with a short statement while Zayt paves the way for you to get into your truck. Once you're in, I'll wrap up my statement and go straight to the office."

"What are you going to tell them?" Bradley asked.

"A lot of nothing."

"I'm going to get my bag. I'll drive in with you and then head to the airport from J. Edgar." Zayt said.

By the time they finished getting ready, several more news vans appeared and blocked their vehicles.

Derek called the police department and voiced a complaint. When the patrol officers arrived, Derek, Bradley and Zayt made their move.

With Zayt by his side, Bradley traveled down the ramp while Derek stepped down onto the front lawn and moved away from the walkway. The horde of reporters followed Derek with microphones held high.

Derek spoke slowly and deliberately. "Good morning. First . . . let me say . . . that I haven't seen or heard . . . the report you seem to be . . . interested in . . . so I cannot answer any . . . direct questions . . . about it."

Bradley and Zayt reached the truck. Operating the door with the ramp took several moments, so Derek stalled as much as he could.

"I would ask . . . that you . . . respect . . . our privacy," Derek cleared his throat multiple times, "and . . . the privacy of the . . . young man's family."

Bradley's chair rode up to truck level on the lift.

Derek let the reporters scream questions all at once. He placed his hand behind his ear as if trying to hear one single question out of the bunch. He shook his head as if he had been unsuccessful.

Bradley's chair then slid into the driver's seat and his door began to slide closed. Zayt walked to the passenger side and got in.

"I'm sorry . . . that's all I have to say . . . at this time." Derek, with the protection of a police officer, made it into his vehicle and locked the door.

It took several minutes for the officers to get news crews to move their vans so Derek and Bradley could move their vehicles. Zayt laughed the whole time.

"I never knew how good Derek was at his job," Zayt said. "I always thought he was strait-laced as could be, but he's a real bullshit artist."

"Nobody can do what he does better," Bradley said—and meant it.

The vans followed them to the J. Edgar Hoover Building but could not get through the manned gate.

Bradley parked near the door not far from Derek's assigned parking spot and he and Zayt waited for Derek to join them.

"That was smooth. You might have a career in politics," Bradley smiled.

"Let's find out why the fuck this happened," Derek said, storming past them and into the building.

"Hey," Zayt said to Bradley. "I'm going to call a cab and head to the airport. Tell Derek I said goodbye, alright?"

Bradley held out his hand. "Thanks for everything. I'll call you later."

They shook hands, and Zayt pulled out his phone as he walked back toward the gated entrance.

Bradley went straight to his office and called Sahani Kumar.

"Derek really needs to talk to someone, and he won't talk to me," Bradley began.

"I saw the report. Is Alex alright?"

"We think so, yeah. He's in a hospital in India. Derek hasn't been able to talk to him yet. But it's more than Alex being kidnapped. I think there's something deeper going on with him. But he's resisting."

"I'll see what I can do. And how about you, Bradley? How are you holding up?"

"I've been hanging by a thread."

"Would you like to talk?"

"I would. But after Derek. He's about to explode."

It wasn't until Bradley hung up with Sahani that he remembered how quickly he had hung up on Audrey earlier. He tapped her contact information on his cell phone, then hit call.

"Hi," she answered.

"I'm so sorry I rushed you off the phone this morning. Is now a good time?"

"Yes, perfect. I'm taking a coffee break."

"Your call set off a series of unexpected events. We hadn't seen the report and definitely didn't expect it."

"I'm sorry. I hope I didn't cause a problem."

"You didn't cause a problem. The president caused a problem. As far as we knew last night's actions were classified. It shouldn't have made the press."

"But your godson. He's alright?"

"He's safe. I don't know how well he is. The doctors won't let us talk to him yet."

"Not even FBI Director Richards?"

"Not even Derek. It's been a tough few days."

"I won't pry," Audrey said, then paused. "I wanted you to know that the information you gave me about single strand RNA made the difference. The vaccine is working. A lot of people owe you their lives."

"Why does everyone keep saying that? All I did was pass on a message."

"I have a feeling it was more than that." Bradley could tell Audrey was smiling. And he really liked her smile.

"Audrey. When I was on the helicopter, I couldn't hear very well. Did I mishear your answer to my question about having dinner together? Did you say you can't?"

Audrey paused. "Yes, I did."

"Oh, okay. I just wanted to make sure."

"I'm sorry. I just couldn't do that to Cate."

"I don't understand? Do what?" Bradley asked.

"I wouldn't be comfortable doing that to another woman."

"Another woman? Do you mean Cate? My Cate?"

"Yes, your Cate."

"Cate. Mrs. Catherine Richards? Wife of my best friend Derek Richards?"

"Cate is your . . . your very good friend Cate is your best friend's wife?"

Bradley hadn't laughed in days, and it all burst out then. "You thought Cate and I . . .?"

"The way you talk about her, yes, I thought you were in love with her."

"I do love her. Next to her husband, she's my best friend." Bradley continued to laugh.

"Well, you should be more clear about that when you speak about her," Audrey began to laugh. "Especially if you plan on asking another woman to dinner."

"That's the best part," Bradley said. "I didn't plan it. I just asked. And you shot me down." He chuckled.

"Bradley?"

"Yes, Audrey?"

"Would you like to go out to dinner with me some night soon?"

"No." Bradley paused. "But I would love to cook you dinner some night soon."

"He cooks!"

"I do."

"I would love that."

"It's a date," Bradley said. "But Alex's family is staying with me until we can get him home. I'm afraid dinner will have to wait until then."

"The anticipation is part of the fun."

"You've just made my very difficult day much brighter. Can I call you tonight?"

"I was hoping you would."

"Until later." Bradley smiled as he disconnected the call.

"What the hell, Mike?" Derek exclaimed.

"The director can't control what the president does any more than you or I can. The CIA isn't happy about this either. We're all facing a lot of unwanted questions," Mike replied.

Derek tried to calm himself. "We managed to move my family out before the news crews arrived. But I had to give a statement."

"I saw." Mike smiled. "It was brilliant. Especially when you put your hand to your ear."

"There's nothing about this that's funny."

"I know. Look. You've got a lot on your plate right now. Take a few days to be with your family. I'll keep you updated on Alex, I promise. As soon as we get word from his doctor, I'll let you know."

"I can't take time off. And the CIA is going to grill Alex, Mike. You know that."

"That's why the doctor has been ordered to only talk to his family."

"You're not family."

Mike smiled. "Just call me Uncle Mike. I told the hospital that I am the spokesperson for the family, and we didn't want Alex to have any unwanted visitors."

"You're a good friend."

"Go home or wherever to your family. I'll be in touch."

"I'll leave in a while. I've got some things to do. But I need one more favor from you."

Derek had just returned to his office when Madelyn buzzed him.

"Dr. Sahani Kumar is here to see you," she said over the intercom.

Derek paused, then sighed. "Please send her in."

"Hello, Sahani."

"Hello, Derek," she said as she sat on the couch. "I see your days haven't gotten any easier."

"Who sent you? My wife?"

"I saw the report this morning. I wanted to see how you're doing. Can we talk?"

Sahani had a way of making a question sound like a pleasant command.

Derek stood from behind his desk and moved to a chair next to the couch.

"How's Alex?" Sahani asked.

"I don't really know. I haven't been able to talk to him."

There was a knock on the door.

"Come in," Derek said.

Madelyn entered with two cups of coffee, one black. She handed it to Sahani and the other to Derek. Without a word, she left the room.

"Does she always read minds?" Sahani asked.

"She's very good at what she does."

"So you haven't been able to talk to Alex. That must be hard."

"It is."

Sahani waited for Derek to expand on his answer, but he didn't. To her, that spoke volumes.

"How are Cate and her family?"

Derek shifted in his chair. "My wife and family had to leave our home this morning rather than be harassed by the media."

"You're angry."

"You're damn right I'm angry."

"Who are you angry at?"

"How much time do you have?"

"All the time you need."

"The president. That's who."

"Because he held a press conference?"

"Yes!"

"Has he ever done that before? Jumped the gun and used one of your cases to his political advantage?"

"Many times."

"And did you get this angry?"

"Of course not. It wasn't my family."

"Okay, fair enough. But there's always a family. Somebody's family is always affected. Sometimes many families."

"What's your point?"

"I don't think it's the president that's making you this angry."

Derek sat back in his chair. He turned his head to the ceiling and sighed. When he lowered his gaze to meet Sahani's, he said, "I don't think I can do this anymore."

Sahani leaned toward Derek. "Okay. Let's talk about that."

Derek went quiet. But this time Sahani could see that he was thinking deeply—and personally. She waited for him to speak.

"When we were watching the rescue on the monitor, there was a gunfight. We only saw green flashes because of the night vision camera, but they filled the screen. It only lasted seconds. It was intense. When it was over, the camera focused on one of Alex's captors lying dead on the floor and I . . . I smiled."

"You were relieved." Sahani said.

"No. It wasn't that kind of smile. I had my revenge."

"And you think that makes you . . . what?"

"Unfit to do my job! Unfit for humanity! I smiled at a dead man! I was happy he was dead. Not just because he couldn't hurt Alex anymore. Because I wanted him to pay."

"And how do you feel about it now?"

"I couldn't look my wife in the eyes last night. Or this morning. And I don't like what I see when I look in the mirror."

"How long, Derek?"

"How long what?"

"How long have you felt this way? This is too deep-seated to be from one moment of human fallibility."

Derek didn't respond.

Sahani decided to push. "Why didn't you tell me about the ulcers?"

Derek paused, then asked, "You read my medical file?"

"Your duodenal ulcer was diagnosed not long after the limousine bombing. Your stomach ulcer was diagnosed last year. You've got a prescription for eight-hundred-milligram ibuprofen that you seem to eat like candy. And who knows what else? You're not sleeping at night, so you may be using some sort of sleep aid, and we've already established the vomiting, which I'm guessing you underestimated when I last asked. You're taking medication for high blood pressure, and your cholesterol is off the charts.

"So, I'll ask again. How long have you felt this way?"

"Those files are personal."

"So I guess I nailed it." Sahani waited for a denial. "I didn't read your medical files. I did read your fitness-for-duty reports. The ulcers figure prominently in them. I've actually watched you gobble ibuprofen, and ulcers frequently keep people awake at night. I guessed at the sleep aid and, as I said, the vomiting is well established. You're a man in his fifties who has a stressful job and eats at his desk. Hence, high blood pressure and bad cholesterol. So, are you going to answer my question or not?"

"I can't answer your question."

"Why not?"

"Because I don't really know. It's been a . . . gradual thing, I guess."

"I'm going to ask you a very important question, and I don't want you to answer right away. I want you to think about it. Really think about it before you answer."

Derek felt uneasy but nodded his head.

"Are you happy in your life?"

Derek jerked his head and made direct eye contact with Sahani. It wasn't the question he expected to hear. He was about to speak but remembered Sahani's instructions and stopped himself.

Myriad thoughts darted through his mind like green flashes in a nighttime firefight. He loved his life with Cate, his family, and his friends, none of whom he got to see very often, except for Bradley, due to his demanding job. Lately it seemed he only saw the worst in people—strangers, not those close to him. Those close to him could do no wrong. They were barometers of himself. None of them would have smiled at a dead man.

Derek flinched at the thought.

"What just happened?" Sahani asked.

"Nothing, I don't know."

"This isn't going to help if you're not honest with me."

He hesitated before he answered. "I don't like the person I've become."

"And therein lies the rub."

"What?"

"It's from Shakespeare."

"Godammit, Sahani, I know it's Shakespeare!" Derek barked. He jumped from his chair and paced, taking deep breaths as he crossed the room. After his third lap he stopped and sheepishly glanced at Sahani. "I'm sorry."

"We go back a long way," Sahani said. "I think I know you pretty well. So, let me take a stab at this, alright?"

Derek nodded.

"Why don't you sit back down."

Derek did as she suggested.

"There are few things in this world that you deeply love. Obviously, your wife is top of the list. You're devoted to your family and friends. And your sense of duty is what makes you so good at a job you have always been passionate about. You gave up that job once to take care of your wife. But when given the opportunity, you jumped back in with vigor. So, the quandary, or Shakespeare's rub, seems to be whether your happiness matters. And, if you decide it does, the route that will bring you happiness."

"That's a little selfish, isn't it? Thinking only of my happiness?"

"I believe the opposite is true. I believe life is precious, and it's selfish not to live every moment to its fullest. But we've been societally conditioned to think it is selfish to put one's own happiness above all. We don't spend a lot of time focusing on how happy we are. But the happiest societies are healthiest and, dare I say, safest."

Sahani paused. "I didn't mean to go into speech mode. The point is, it's okay to want to be happy. In fact, I'd say it's the most important thing you could do for those around you. So, Derek, what route will bring you happiness?"

Derek sat with his elbows on his knees, his hands cupped, and his eyes focused on his future.

They sat on Bradley's screened-in back porch overlooking his perfectly manicured lawn and watched as David and Max walked toward the majestic black walnut tree in the distance. Rusty lay on the porch in his bed, one of multiple dog beds scattered throughout the house.

"This place fits Bradley so well," Sheila said. She sipped iced tea and cast her nervous energy into the rocking chair.

"I knew it as soon as I saw it," Cate said.

"I should have known you found it for him," Sheila chuckled. "Bradley probably would have looked in the nearest industrial park."

"The house fits him, but I'm not sure DC does. All he does is work."

"Isn't that what they both do? Him and Derek?"

Cate frowned. "I suppose so. I just thought this job would be different for Derek. I thought . . . well, I don't know what I thought."

Cate's cell phone pinged—a message from Derek.

"Oh, Sheila!" Cate exclaimed, then handed her the phone.

Sheila glanced at the screen then placed a hand to her open mouth. Tears streamed down her face. Through them she focused on the picture Derek had forwarded. It was of Alex smiling in a hospital bed. He looked thin and drawn, and an IV line ran from his arm, but he was smiling.

"David! Max!" she yelled. "Come here!

Sheila jumped from the rocker and ran to meet them. Cate watched as they formed a triangle, examined the photo, then joined in a hug. She couldn't help but cry.

When they returned to the porch, they looked at each other and laughed.

"It's like a redeye epidemic," Max said.

"Please, no more epidemics," Cate replied.

Sheila didn't want to give up the phone, but Cate wished to text Derek.

"I'll forward the picture to you so you can look at it all day," Cate smiled.

Reluctantly, Sheila forked over the phone.

Cate texted,

Thank you! I wish you could see how happy you just made them!
Derek replied,

Good, I'm glad. Still no word when we can talk to him. This will have to do for now.

"You know, Cate, sometimes I wonder if Derek knows how truly special he is," Sheila said.

"I can assure you, he doesn't."

He read the text while sitting on the bed in his and Cate's bedroom. He had managed to leave the office without being detected by a waiting news van. When he arrived at the house, he was relieved to see that all the media vans had vacated.

After reading Cate's text, he glanced at the framed photo on the night table next to their bed. It was a picture of him and Cate on the cruise ship where they met twenty-three years earlier. It had been formal dress at dinner that night, but Derek didn't have a tuxedo. Derek was thirty years old and Cate, twenty-six. They were laughing with each other. As hard as he tried, he couldn't remember a recent moment when he and Cate were that happy.

He gathered the suitcases belonging to Sheila, David, and Max. He packed clothes for him and Cate, added bathroom items and a cooler full of food from their stocked freezer, then loaded everything into the SUV. It took twenty minutes for him to reach Bradley's house in East Riverdale, Maryland.

The house seemed empty until, coming from the porch, Derek heard Sheila giggle. He startled Cate by stepping through the sliding glass door, and she nearly jumped out of her skin.

"What are you doing here?" she asked as she stood.

Derek smiled, took her in his arms, and kissed her. Cate's eyes were as wide as melons. "I brought supplies," he said as he let her go. "I need help bringing them in."

He turned and walked with a spring in his step. Cate stared as he walked away.

David and Max followed Derek, and soon had placed suitcases in bedrooms and packed the food in Bradley's freezer. Derek reached into the refrigerator and withdrew a bottle of beer. "David? Max? How about it?"

"Derek, it's two o'clock in the afternoon," Cate said.

"I'll take one," Max replied.

"Me, too," David said.

Derek smiled at Cate and winked.

After distributing the beer, he opened one of Cate's favorite bottles of wine. Bradley always kept some on hand. Without asking, he poured Sheila and Cate a glass.

With drinks distributed, Derek raised his beer and said, "To Alex being safe and home soon!"

They each raised their drinks, cheered "To Alex," then drank.

Cate put her wineglass on a side table and asked, "Why are you home so early? What's going on?"

Sheila signaled to David and Max that they should give Derek and Cate some privacy. As they started to leave, Derek motioned them to sit. "Relax, enjoy your drinks. Cate, let's go for a walk."

"A walk?"

"Yes, a walk. It's a beautiful day." Derek reached for Cate's hand and took it in his.

"Okay," Cate said warily.

They left the porch through the door with a ramp to the backyard. When they were out of earshot of the others, Cate stopped and said, "You've never asked me to go for a walk before, Derek. What's going on?"

Sheila, David, and Max watched Derek and Cate walk away.

"He's in a good mood," Max said as he and David tapped the longnecks of their bottles together.

They watched as, nearly forty yards away, Cate stopped abruptly and turned to Derek. Derek leaned in and kissed her. Cate seemed upset by the action. Derek seemed amused.

Derek then reached for Cate's other hand, holding them both in his as they faced off. He said something to Cate that made her smile. Then he released one of her hands, and they continued walking toward the black walnut tree.

"What do you think is happening," David asked Sheila.

"I don't know."

"You don't think it's about Alex, do you?"

"No. It's definitely not about Alex." Sheila's sideways glance told David he asked a dumb question. "Maybe he got a promotion?"

"That's got to be it. That's another reason he wanted to celebrate," David said.

Suddenly, Cate stopped walking and jumped into Derek's arms. Derek caught her, then steadied himself. She wrapped her legs around his body and her arms around his neck.

"Whoa! How the hell didn't he fall over?" Max asked.

"He's a better man than I," David said, smiling at Sheila.

Sheila giggled.

"Wait a minute. Don't tell me you . . . " Max said to David. "Have you . . . ? Never mind, I don't want to know."

David laughed. "Your mother happens to be a very excitable woman."

"No!" Max said, "That's enough!" He held his palm out in front of him.

Sheila and David laughed. Then Sheila said, "I don't think it's a promotion."

"Why not?" David asked.

"I don't think Cate would be that excited," she responded.

"Huh!"

The three watched Derek and Cate as if they were in the top billed movie of the year.

"A raise?" Max asked.

"No," Sheila responded.

Derek and Cate reached the walnut tree and sat at the base, backs against the trunk.

"Okay! I'm definitely going to add this scene to my next movie," David said.

"What if it's a thriller?" Max asked.

David thought. "The knife-wielding murderer will jump out from behind the tree."

"David! Stop!" Sheila said. "You're ruining this moment."

Max chuckled, "Good one, Dad."

Sheila sighed. "How come we never go for walks?"

"Because you hate them," David said.

"Oh. That's right. I do!"

The smells in the kitchen kept Max and Rusty glued to their positions. Max sat at the center island, while Rusty lay by the oven door.

Derek and Cate moved in harmony as they prepared the meal. It had been a long time since they cooked together. It used to be one of their favorite activities.

Cate frowned when Derek's phone rang.

"It's Bradley," Derek said after checking caller ID.

"Oh, he's okay," Cate nodded.

Derek smiled and answered the phone. "Hey, what's up?"

"I'm here with Madelyn. She said you're not in your office."

"That's right."

"Where are you? I've got some information on al-Ahmadi."

"I'm standing in your kitchen."

"You're in my kitchen?"

"Yes. Say hi to Cate."

Derek moved the phone to Cate's ear.

"Hi, Bradley. When are you coming home?"

Bradley paused, "Ah, I'm not sure."

"Well, we'll save you some dinner."

"Okay," Bradley responded with suspicion.

"Here's Derek."

Derek put the phone to his ear.

"Cate is outdoing herself. Don't be too late," Derek said.

"What . . .? Why are you at my house? It's only five o'clock."

"I left early."

"You left early?"

"Why do you keep repeating what I say?" Derek smiled.

"I guess I'm just surprised."

"Well, dinner is in about an hour. You should come. Oh! And pick up some beer and wine on your way home. See you later."

Derek placed the phone in his pocket and continued peeling shrimp.

Bradley met Sahani in the cafeteria.

"So, I just talked to Derek," Bradley said.

Sahani didn't respond.

"He's at my house," Bradley continued.

Sahani still didn't respond.

"It's only 5:10."

Sahani displayed a pleasant smile. "So, how are you, Bradley? It's been some time since we've talked."

Bradley understood that there would be no discussion of Derek's odd behavior.

"It's been a struggle this last week, but we survived. I survived."

"I'm glad to know your godson is safe."

"Thank you."

"The last time I saw you, you were wound pretty tight."

"Yeah, there were a lot of things happening at once."

"And now?"

"It's better."

"What about outside of work?" Sahani asked.

"Not much has changed," Bradley quickly responded, then shifted his eyes to the floor.

"What is it?"

"What's what?"

"You almost said something. What were you going to say?"

Bradley smiled. "You are very good at your job, Sahani. How I ever fell for that phony Predator profile I'll never know." Bradley referred to a ruse Sahani had used several years before to jolt him out of his depression.

"You weren't at your best. It happens to all of us at one time or another. And you're evading the question."

"I met someone," Bradley grinned.

Sahani sat back in her chair and smiled. "Tell me about this person."

"She's brilliant! And she's very easy to talk to. It's not like I planned it or anything."

"Have you gone on a date?"

"I've been a little busy. And so has she. She works for the CDC."

Sahani nodded, "Yes, I imagine she's been swamped."

"But," Bradley smiled, "we have made plans."

"That's wonderful."

"There's just one thing I'm worried about."

"Only one?" Sahani joked.

Bradley chuckled. "She has an eight-year-old daughter."

"And?"

"And what? Isn't that enough to scare anyone?"

"You have a point," she grinned. "But, seriously, why would that bother you. You've talked about wanting a family of your own."

"I know. But, for some reason, I always pictured my family as young boys."

Sahani released a full-scale, face-brightening laugh. Bradley couldn't help but follow her lead.

When laughter subsided, Sahani said, "Sometimes, Bradley, I can see things so clearly in my head. And I can clearly see how wonderful you would be at helping to raise an eight-year-old girl."

A wave of emotion swept through him. His misty eyes concentrated on Sahani, and he replied, "That's just about the nicest thing anyone has ever said to me. Thank you."

"You're welcome. But try not to get ahead of yourself. Just enjoy her company, why don't you? You don't have to jump right into planning your investment portfolios. I think my work here is done. I'm going home in the morning. But you know you can call me anytime."

"Well," Bradley said, "if you're leaving in the morning, then you're going to spend your last night in DC with friends and a home-cooked meal. That is, unless you have a better option."

"My only other option is pre-packaged tuna fish. I gratefully accept your invitation."

Bradley texted Cate when he and Sahani were on their way.

Don't forget wine and beer!!! Cate texted back.

"I don't understand. I have wine and beer at home, but her text sounds adamant. She used three exclamation points."

Sahani laughed. "We'd better stop then."

Sahani insisted on paying for the alcohol. She suggested it was the least she could do for his rescuing her from cold tuna fish from a foil pack.

When they arrived, the atmosphere was party-like. Someone had figured out Bradley's music system—Bradley guessed it was Max. From the speakers bellowed 1980s soft rock. It didn't take long for him to figure out why he and Sahani had needed to stop at the liquor store.

The house smelled of Cajun spices and fresh lemon. The large dining room table that Cate insisted Bradley buy was set for eight.

"Are we expecting someone else for dinner?" Bradley shouted over the music.

"The eighth setting is for Alex," Sheila said, pointing to the cell phone lying on a plate. The phone displayed Alex's photo.

Bradley hadn't seen the picture. A sweet calmness overtook him, and he smiled, then nodded.

He restocked the refrigerator with beer.

Sahani glanced over to the stove where Derek stood behind Cate with his arms wrapped around her. They swayed in unison to a popular 1987 hit. Sahani could not take her eyes off them. She watched as Derek kissed the back of Cate's neck, then belted out the song's line, "I want to be with you everywhere."

Bradley returned to Sahani's side and watched with her. He hadn't seen Cate and Derek engaged so completely with each other in a long time, and his heart filled. It was as if they had no idea there was anyone else in the room.

David and Sheila moved into the living room, wrapped their arms around each other, and danced. Max grinned as he sat cuddled with Rusty on the couch and watched.

"Should we join them?" Bradley asked loudly, holding up a bottle of wine. "I promise I will only have one so I can get you back to the hotel safely."

"I think this calls for one," Sahani said, still gazing at Derek and Cate.

The selection of music turned to quiet classical for the meal. Dinner consisted of blackened salmon and seafood bisque topped with roasted gulf shrimp. In Bradley's cabinet, Cate had found a bag of white corn Masa Harina, imported from Mexico. She had used it to make chili-lime tortillas to serve with the soup.

"Aunt Cate and Uncle Derek, this is an amazing dinner," Max said.

"Thank you, Max," Cate replied. "But, I've got to tell you. I look forward to the day of grilling a nice steak or chicken breast again."

Bradley said, "I've been doing some research on the components of the virus and I . . . "

"Of course, you have!" Derek cut him off.

Everyone but Bradley laughed, but he did roll his eyes. "As I was saying, I read that the contaminated fields just need to be deep ploughed to kill the harmful bacteria. It can't survive if it's buried more than an inch."

"How long before they can plant again?" David asked.

"Relatively soon. Most cereal-type crops aren't tilled these days, so once the soil is turned, it might be ready. But I plan to ask Dr. Howe about that tomorrow." Bradley said.

Derek, who had switched from beer to wine, asked, "When are you going to ask that woman to go to dinner with you?"

Bradley nearly choked on the tortilla he was about to swallow.

A slight titter escaped Sahani's lips, but the rest of the group looked questioningly toward Bradley.

Cate asked, "Wait a minute! Who is this Dr. Howe, and why haven't I heard about her?"

"Yes, Bradley. Who is she? Where did you meet her?" Sheila asked.

"What kind of doctor is she?" Max added.

Bradley lowered his gaze. Then he slowly raised his head and peered from the top of his eye sockets at Derek who sported a wide grin.

"You're enjoying yourself with my wine and beer, aren't you?" Bradley asked him.

"Absolutely!" Derek raised his wine glass.

Bradley debated within himself the next words he would speak. Under normal circumstances, he might not have said anything in response. But that night seemed to be the night for honesty.

"As a matter of fact, I already have," he said.

Derek's face grew serious, and he placed his wine glass on the table. The others did the same. All eyes were on Bradley.

"You asked her out?" Derek asked.

"I did."

"When?"

"This morning."

"What did she say?"

"Well, the first time I asked her she said no. But that was when she thought Cate was my girlfriend. Once she found out that wasn't the case, she changed her mind."

"She thought what?" Derek asked.

"She thought Cate was my girlfriend." Bradley felt a twinge of satisfaction after seeing Derek's reaction.

"Why would she think that?"

Bradley laughed. "It's a long story. Let's save it for dessert, shall we?"

"Not on your life, Bradley Whitman. I want to hear everything about this woman right now," Cate said before asking, "And, how does she know me?"

For the remainder of the evening, they bombarded Bradley with questions about Audrey Howe. He kept trying to change the subject, but Cate or Sheila would steer back to it.

Derek sat back and enjoyed the interrogation.

At 9 p.m., Sahani announced it was time for her to leave.

"I'll get my keys," Bradley said.

"No, I've already called for a car. It's due any minute. But thank you. Stay here and enjoy your guests. And thank you all for a wonderful evening," Sahani said.

After saying goodbye to the others, Derek walked Sahani to the front curb where her driver waited.

Bradley watched from inside as the two had a conversation, then hugged. Derek then opened the car door and watched as the sedan drove away.

Derek stood outside alone for a few more moments. When he turned to go back to the house, Bradley moved back into the living room.

By 10:30, Cate had already slipped into bed, Sheila and David were about to, and Max enjoyed the comfort of Bradley's home office couch.

Bradley had just finished turning out most of the lights when he noticed movement on the porch.

"I thought you had gone to bed?" Bradley said to Derek, who sat looking out into the night.

"Soon," Derek replied.

"Can I get you something?" Bradley asked.

Derek looked at his glass filled with water and replied, "No, thanks. I'm good."

"This was quite a night. It felt like old times."

Derek chuckled. "It's funny. When you used that phrase this morning it really pissed me off."

"I noticed. What changed?"

"That's what I wanted to talk to you about. I've made a decision, one that may or may not impact you."

"What is it?"

"I'm leaving the bureau. I'm going to talk to Mike on Monday and let him know he needs to start looking for my replacement. I just can't do it anymore. It's time."

Bradley sighed. "Cate told you how she felt."

Derek smiled. "Yes. But not until after I told her my plans. The fact that she wants the same thing confirmed without a doubt that this is what I need to do. What I want to do."

They allowed a long silence to express the weight of Derek's remarks.

Then Bradley said, "I enjoyed watching you with Cate tonight."

"I enjoyed being with her again. I haven't given her my full attention since I took this job. And the thing is, after the bombing, I swore I would always put Cate first." Derek shook his head. "I'm not sure how I lost sight of that."

"Sometimes life pulls us away from the people we need most." Bradley's thoughts went to Laney.

"I'm proud of you, Bradley."

"What for?"

"For taking that first step. I know how hard that was for you. And I look forward to meeting the woman who pierced that armor."

Bradley chuckled. "Well, let's see how the first date goes, shall we?"

Derek paused. "I'm going to recommend you as my replacement."

His eyes shot open. After feeling exhausted, Bradley was suddenly wide awake. "Me?"

"I can't think of anyone better."

"I don't know, Derek."

"It's what you've always wanted—to rise in the ranks. What's not to know?"

"What we want isn't always the best thing for us, is it?"

Derek nodded.

"Well, just because I recommend you doesn't mean they'll offer it to you. But they'd be crazy not to," Derek smiled. "Besides, you can always say no."

"Can I? You couldn't!"

"Touché! On that note, I'm going to go cuddle in bed with my wife. Goodnight."

"Goodnight."

A NEW BEGINNING

It was the first Saturday in months that Derek didn't go into the office. He took phone calls and responded to emails and texts but never left Bradley's home.

Because the White House press secretary kept the story alive, the news media persisted in trying to get access to the family. Neighbors had called the police when they noticed someone looking into Derek and Cate's windows. News vans parked near the gate of the J. Edgar Hoover Building hoping to capture images of Derek, Bradley, or any family member. From where the news vans sat to where Bradley parked his truck there was no clear vantage point.

Knowing what he knew about Derek's intentions, Bradley felt awkward going into the building. He reminded himself to be cautious of his remarks.

Only six other agents sat at their desks when Bradley entered the bullpen. He had been there for fifteen minutes when Sam rolled into the room struggling to turn the wheels of his manual wheelchair. When he entered, the six agents stood and clapped their hands. Bradley clapped as well.

"Enough!" Sam waved them off with a slight smile. Whitman, my office!"

Bradley followed Sam into his office with the push of his chair's joystick.

"Maybe you should get one of these," Bradley said as he slapped the arm of his electric chair.

"No offense, but I don't plan on being in this thing much longer," Sam replied.

Bradley chuckled.

"Mike has arranged a video call for later this morning for Alex Carson so he can speak with his family. He was going to have Derek set it up, but he's not coming in today. Can you take care of it?"

"Absolutely!"

"You'll need to establish a secure link."

"No problem. I'm set up for that in my home office."

"Can you get them there?"

"They're already there. The media doesn't know where I live so they're staying with me for now."

"Okay. Set it up for 10:30 our time."

"How are you doing, Sam?"

"Right as rain. I'll be working on my final report on the al-Haqani case. I might have some questions for you."

"No problem."

"In the meantime," Sam continued, "I'm going to forward some information to you. There was a train derailment during the night in southwestern Wisconsin. The train was carrying toxic chemicals. Three of the train's cars dropped into the Mississippi River. We don't think it was an accident. I want to hear your thoughts on what we've got so far."

"I'm on it," Bradley said, then turned his chair and headed back to his desk. And life moves on, he thought.

When Bradley called home and told the others about Alex's upcoming video call, he heard a roar of happiness.

"Use my office computer. I'll walk you through the security setup," Bradley said to Derek. "I'll call a half hour before so we have plenty of time to get ready."

"I'll be waiting," Derek replied.

Back at his desk, Bradley worked on a preliminary report of the train derailment based on known facts and speculation of why and how the railway had been sabotaged.

At 10 a.m., Bradley called Derek and Max and walked them through the security protocols on his home computer.

When finished, Bradley said, "Alright, you should be set. I'll be watching from here."

"Uncle Bradley?"

"Yeah, Max?"

"Is he going to be able to see us?"

"Yes. He's got a laptop, so he'll be able to see and hear you."

"I better warn Mom not to cry. It always upsets Alex when she cries."

"Yeah, good luck with that, Max," Bradley said. "We've got five minutes."

"I'll let Sheila, David, and Cate come into the room now. They're chomping at the bit," Derek said.

Bradley chuckled.

Derek opened Bradley's office door. The three stood waiting.

"Come on in. We're ready for him. Bradley's on the line, too." Derek directed Sheila to the desk chair right in front of the monitor. David sat to her right and Cate to her left. Derek and Max stood behind them.

At precisely 10:30, the computer screen flickered, then focused on Alex sitting up in his hospital bed.

"Alex? Can you hear me?" Sheila asked.

"Hey, Mom! Dad! Hey, everybody." Alex waved his hand at the screen.

Immediately, Sheila began to cry.

"Mom, please don't cry. I'm okay. See?" Alex spread his arms out from his sides.

"Honey, you look so thin."

"It didn't hurt to lose a few pounds," Alex joked.

"You look fine, son. When are you coming home?" David asked.

"The doctors wanted to keep me a few more days, but I think we've got it worked out so I can leave tomorrow. I'll be coming home on a military plane with medical personnel. They're going to bring me to George Washington University Hospital in DC."

"That's great news!" David replied.

"I can't wait to see you guys—in person, I mean," Alex said.

"Are you really alright, Alex? Really?" Sheila cried.

"Yes, Mom. Just a little dehydrated, and they're watching my kidney function, but other than that, I'm good."

"What happened, Alex?" Max asked.

Derek said, "Maybe we shouldn't get into that right now, Max."

"No, it's okay, Uncle Derek," Alex said. "I know it must have been hard on you guys. Besides, I don't know if I'd be able to get through the story if we were face-to-face."

"Only if you're sure! We don't want to push," David said.

"I'm sure. I'd rather get this over with and move on."

"Alright," David said.

Alex took a deep breath. "It started in Kolkata. I had just left Mother House of the Missionaries of Charity, the home of Mother Theresa."

Alex took a moment to reflect.

"It was an amazing experience, and I felt completely at peace. Anyway, I was heading to St. Theresa Church only a half mile away when I saw a man in the back of an alley get stabbed and fall to the ground. The guy who stabbed him looked up and saw me, then laughed. Then I saw the others. Three more. And they all had sticks or pipes or something like that."

"Oh!" Sheila put her hands to her face. Cate placed her hand on Sheila's shoulder.

"They started to walk toward me, so I backed away. I mean, it was broad daylight, and these guys walked around with bats or whatever. I wasn't too worried at first because there were people all around. But then, when the guys came out of the alley, all the people scattered. I could tell they were all scared of them.

"So I ran," he continued. "As fast as I could. I looked back once. They were running after me. All I could think about was getting to the church. I don't know why. It seemed like the thing to do. They were right behind me, but I made it into the church and hid behind one of the pews. They didn't come in.

"After a few minutes, I got off the floor and saw a priest standing at the end of the pew. He told me it was alright. That they wouldn't come in the church. He said as bad as they were, they would not challenge God.

"Then he told me they were part of India's organized crime group. Very bad people. When I told him what happened, he said they would probably be waiting for me outside. He said if I saw something they didn't want me to see, they were the type of people that would track me down until I was dead. And he said they had a broad reach."

"Oh, my God!" Sheila cried.

For a moment, Alex looked away from the computer screen. Then he continued. "The priest led me to a back passage. It was a tunnel that came out about two blocks away from the church. When I came out of the tunnel, I was close to a bus stop. There were people waiting there, so I figured I'd blend in. When the bus came, I got on. It took me to Howrah Station.

"That's when I decided to leave India, but I didn't know where to go. Then I remembered about the professor. I had been thinking about going to Afghanistan to see this professor I had met. I didn't think they would follow me there. So I bought a ticket to Jammu/Tawi station. And then I waited.

"I thought everything was going to be alright until I saw them on the train platform. Eight of them, all with construction pipes. People just moved and let them pass.

"The train was just coming into the station, and I didn't know how many more guys they had with them or if they had spotted me. Just before the train stopped, I typed a text message. I wanted someone to know where to look for me if something happened. But I didn't want these guys to know where I was going if they happened to find my phone. So I wrote the first thing I thought of from my research of the area, the sister city of Asadabad, where the professor was. Then I stashed the phone. Later, when I had time to think about it, I thought it was pretty stupid. Even if the authorities found the phone, who would figure that out, right?

"Anyway, I mingled with the crowd, then got on the train. I found the baggage compartment and hid behind a stack of luggage. I don't know if they got on the train or not, but I never saw those guys again. Once I got to Jammu/Tawi, I figured continuing on to see the professor was the best thing to do.

"When I was blind-sided waiting for a bus on the road to Asadabad, I knew they had caught up with me. I thought they'd kill me right there and then, but they didn't.

"The next thing I knew, I woke up tied to a chair in a dingy room with a dirt floor."

Sheila sobbed uncontrollably. She reached her hands to the monitor as if she could touch him, then buried her head in them.

"I'm sorry, Mom," Alex began to cry. "I'm sorry I put you through this." Alex covered his face with both hands, and his body shook.

From off screen, a doctor appeared, and said, "That's all. He needs to rest."

The laptop screen jolted and then faced a window.

"Let me tell them goodbye," they could hear Alex cry out.

Then the laptop went quiet and dark.

"What happened?" Sheila cried. "Is he okay? Is my baby alright?"

Cate hugged her sister. "He's fine. The doctor doesn't want him to exert himself, that's all." Cate rubbed Sheila's back as if comforting an infant.

David sat silently looking at the blank screen.

Max rubbed his eyes.

From the laptop, Bradley's voice said, "That's it. The transmission was terminated."

"Thanks, Bradley. We'll see you when you get home," Derek said, then turned off the computer.

Derek went to Sheila and knelt by her side. With his hands placed on her shoulders, he said, "The worst is over. Alex is safe, and he's coming home."

"He's coming home," Sheila repeated. Then she hugged him.

David and Sheila went straight to their bedroom. Max said he needed some time alone, so he took Rusty and went for a walk out to the old black walnut tree. Cate and Derek watched him sit at the base of the tree. With his elbows resting on his bent knees and hands grasping his forearms, he buried his head.

"My God, Derek. That was only half the story. God knows what they did to him in that room!"

Still bound by classified information, Derek could not tell Cate that Alex's captors were not Indian mafia but Ali al-Haqani's henchmen.

Derek held Cate close and told her the same thing he said to Sheila. "He's coming home, Cate. Let's concentrate on that."

Later that afternoon, Derek's cell phone rang. When Derek checked caller ID, he went into Bradley's office and shut the door.

"Hello, Eric."

"I know what your boss did with the Indian doctor. I just want you to know that I will personally be speaking with Alex tomorrow when he gets to the hospital. This is important, Derek. Don't try to stop me."

"I won't. On one condition."

"What's that?"

"I'll be in the room with you."

"No. I can't authorize that."

"Then it's not going to happen. I'm going to be outside his door all day screening visitors. And I'm sure the doctors will agree with me that he's not ready to be grilled by the CIA yet."

"Goddammit, Derek." Eric paused. "Alright, I'll get authorization for you to be in the room. But no interference."

"Okay."

"I mean it! Not an f'ing word!"

"I'll see you tomorrow."

They jumped out of their waiting room chairs when the ambulance pulled up to the emergency room door. A liaison for the medical staff who accompanied Alex on the airplane approached them.

"Okay, let's not overwhelm him," the liaison said. "Mom and Dad, you two can walk alongside while they bring him to his room. The rest of you will follow me."

They bobbed their heads in agreement. Derek, Cate, Max, and Bradley followed the liaison, a woman named Maria, to a private hospital room. As they walked, Maria explained that because Alex suffered dehydration, his kidneys were not functioning properly. She assured them the effects could be treated and, in most cases, reversed.

When they arrived at his fifth-floor room, they watched from the hallway as two orderlies lifted Alex using the sheet from the gurney and transferred him to the bed. Once he settled, a nurse transferred IV bags hung from the gurney to a stand next to Alex's bed. A few feet away, Sheila and David clung to each other and waited.

"It's best if you give them some time alone," Maria told the others.

When the orderlies and nurse left the room, Maria closed the door and followed them down the hall.

A few moments later, David opened the door and asked Max to join them. To the others, David said, "He wanted me to tell you how much he loves you."

"Tell him we love him to Pluto and back," Cate said.

David nodded.

Once David closed the door, Bradley asked Cate, "Pluto? I thought the saying was to the moon and back."

"For most people, it is. But when Alex was a little boy, he didn't think the moon was far enough away," Cate sniffled.

"That's Alex! Always looking to stretch the parameters," Bradley grinned.

"Damn!" Derek exclaimed as he gazed toward the elevator. "Eric is here."

"Who's Eric," Cate asked.

"Today, he's a nuisance," Derek answered.

Derek walked toward Eric and met him halfway down the hall.

"He just got here. Give him some time with his family," Derek demanded.

"This is time sensitive. We need to see what he knows about al-Ahmadi. He may have heard something to help us find him."

"He's exhausted. Wouldn't it be better to wait until he's rested?"

"You know it's not. The longer we wait, the less he'll recall. You know all this, Derek." Eric tilted his head and sighed. "I promise to go easy."

Derek exhaled loudly to show his displeasure, then turned around and walked to Alex's room. Eric followed.

"Hello, Whitman," Eric said.

"Hey, Sampson," Bradley replied.

"Eric," Derek said, "this is my wife, Cate."

Eric shifted his eyes from Derek to Cate, back to Derek, then back to Cate. "It's a pleasure to meet you, Cate. Derek never mentioned how stunning you are."

"Thank you, Eric. And how do you two know each other?" Cate asked.

"Old college friends. Occasionally, our paths still cross."

"I see," Cate said.

"Shall we?" Eric said, turning to Derek.

"Give me a minute," Derek replied.

Derek knocked lightly on the door. When David opened it, Derek whispered in his ear. David nodded and shut the door.

"It will be just a minute," Derek told Eric.

Moments later, Sheila, David, and Max exited the room.

"I don't like this, Derek," David said.

"We don't have a lot of choice, David. I'll be in there with him. I promise we'll make this as quick as possible, right Eric?"

"Certainly." Eric nodded to David who gave him the stink eye.

When Derek entered the room, Alex's face lit up. "Uncle Derek! Man, it's good to see you!"

Derek moved bedside and grasped Alex's hand as if about to arm wrestle. Then, Derek sat on the edge of the bed. "How are you feeling?"

"Tired. It was a long flight."

"It's great to have you home."

"It's great to be here." Alex shifted his eyes to Eric standing at the end of the bed.

"Alex Carson, this is Eric Sampson. Eric is with the Central Intelligence Agency. He needs to ask you a few questions. But I want you to tell me when you've had enough. We don't want to wear you out. Alright?"

"Okay," Alex replied.

Derek moved away from the bed and stood by the window.

"I'm sorry for what you've been through, Mr. Carson," Eric said.

"Call me Alex."

"Well, Alex, I've read the report about the men that were after you in India. But I need you to tell me everything you can remember about your captivity in Afghanistan. From the moment you were taken, until the rescue mission."

"I'll try."

"Where were you when you were abducted?"

"At a bus station on the road heading to Asadabad. I don't remember the name of the road."

"What happened?"

"I don't really know. One minute I was standing there. The next I knew, I was lying in the dirt with a massive headache. Then I must have blacked out."

"Were there other people at the bus station?"

"Yes. About eight, I think."

"But you didn't see who assaulted you?"

"No."

"What's the next thing you remember?"

"I remember waking up and not being able to see anything. I panicked. I wanted to run, but my hands were behind my back, and I couldn't move my legs."

"Why is that?"

"I could feel the ropes on my wrists. My hands were tied behind me. When I tried to move my legs, I realized they were tied to the legs of the chair."

"You were sitting in a chair?"

"Yeah. When I moved, I got a shooting pain in my head. I remember telling myself not to do that again. That's also when I realized I had something like a hood over my head."

"Was anyone else in the room?"

"I don't know. I don't think so. It was quiet. And damp."

"How long was it before someone came into the room?"

"I don't know. It seemed like a long time. And I think I kept blacking out. I just remember every time I woke, I panicked and tried to move before I could stop myself. Then the pain would come back."

"You were hit on the head?"

"That's what they said, yeah."

"They who?"

"The doctors."

"Oh."

"I didn't know what had happened. I just knew it hurt."

Alex told how for the first part of his capture, he only saw the woman in a hijab who brought him food and a man who would untie him so he could eat, then tie him back up afterwards.

He continued, "Then one day, three guys came in, but only one talked."

"Did you see them?"

"Yes. Well, one of them. They took my hood off when they came in. Two of them stayed in the shadows. But I saw the one who asked the questions."

"Do you think you would recognize him."

"Yeah." Alex looked angry. "I'd know him."

Eric pulled a photo from his pocket, moved to Alex's bedside, and showed him the picture.

"Is this him?"

Alex's nostrils flared and his face turned crimson. "Yes. That's him! Did you get him?"

"What did he say to you?"

"He kept asking me who I was bringing. That's all he ever wanted to know. Who I was bringing. I kept telling him I wasn't bringing anybody and that they are the ones who brought me there.

"It went on for what seemed like weeks. Sometimes he spoke in Farsi, sometimes in broken English. I think it must have been once a day when they'd come in and ask me who I was bringing.

The way I figured it was they had a rival gang and they thought I was part of it. But they wouldn't believe me that I wasn't."

"Rival gang?" Eric squinted. "What do you mean?"

"Yeah. You know, like the Italian family versus the Irish family."

Eric paused. "Alex, are you talking about the Indian crime organization?"

"Yeah. You wanted to know what they asked me. That's what they kept asking me."

Eric shared a glance with Derek.

"Did he ever ask you anything else besides who you were bringing?"

"I don't think so." Alex placed his palm on his forehead and groaned. "Not that I can remember. But he did keep saying that I was lying."

"Are you alright, Alex?" Derek asked.

"Headache. It's pounding."

Derek pushed the call button to bring a nurse.

"We're not done yet," Eric said.

"Yes, I think we are."

"Did the man ever mention going anywhere or coming from somewhere?" Eric persisted.

"I . . . no, I don't . . . ahhh!" Alex moaned.

"Enough, Eric." Derek moved and stood between Eric and Alex.

A nurse came into the room, looked at Alex's monitor, and said, "You'll have to go now. He needs to rest."

Derek took Eric by the arm, directed him out of the room past the others waiting outside, and down the hallway toward the elevator.

"Alright!" Eric said as he released Derek's loose grip from his arm. After a brief moment, he asked, "Does he really think it was the Indian mafia who held him?"

"It sounds that way." Derek paused. "When you think about it, why wouldn't he? If that's the case, I don't think you're going to get any useful information from him."

"Dammit!" Eric pounded one fist into another.

"Relax, Eric. You got a positive ID of one of his captors. I have faith that you'll get these guys."

Eric grunted, "Oh, we'll get them. I'm going to have a few more questions for Alex before he goes home."

"Yeah. About that. Listen. Maybe it's not a bad idea to let Alex think it was the Indian mafia that abducted him. I think he's traumatized enough. There's no reason to mention al-Haqani's involvement. What good would it do?"

"I can't make any promises, but if I don't need to tell him, I won't." Eric held out his hand to shake. "I hope the kid's going to be okay."

Derek took Eric's hand. "See you around."

Eric walked to the stairwell.

Bradley met Derek before he reached the others.

"How did it go?" Bradley asked.

"He ID'd his captor. Eric said he might have more questions, but I'm going to do my best to shield Alex from any more. Alex doesn't know about al-Haqani. He thinks the Indian mafia held him captive. I think we should keep it that way."

"Are you sure you want to lie to him?" Bradley asked.

"I'm not lying. I'm just not divulging classified information. I think he's been through enough."

"Well played. Is Eric on board with that?"

"He says he is, but I'll make certain he sticks to it."

The two rejoined Sheila, David, and Max.

David said to Derek and Bradley, "I don't think I like that guy."

"Well, we need to give him a little credit. He helped arrange for the Navy Seal team who rescued Alex," Bradley said.

"Those are the guys we should be thanking. The Seal team," said David.

"I agree. But it's doubtful we'll ever know their names," Derek responded.

Arm in arm, Sheila and David, then Derek and Cate walked toward the elevator.

Bradley held Max back. "You deserve credit, too, Max. It was your information that led us to your brother. You saved his life. And I'm proud of you!"

"Thanks, Uncle Bradley."

DANCING AROUND THE ISSUE

"Are you sure he doesn't know?" Cate asked Bradley over the phone.

"The man is one of the best FBI agents I've ever known, so, no. I'm not sure Derek doesn't know. I'll tell you one thing. If he does, it's going to be hell trying to get him there."

"I know he said he didn't want a party, but he deserves this. And I know he'll have a good time once the initial shock wears off."

"And if he won't come?"

"That's not an option. So, you'll have him at the club at five o'clock, right?"

"I'll do everything that I possibly can to get him there on time. I told him we're meeting you and Audrey for dinner."

"Okay. I'm trusting you."

"Has Sheila and the family arrived yet?"

"They just called. They're on their way from the airport now."

"And what about Holly, John, Mike, and Olivia?"

"Mike and Olivia flew in yesterday. So, yes, the whole cruise ship gang will be accounted for."

"My parents mentioned showing up early to help you decorate."

"I already talked to Lynn. She and your Dad have already left your house and are on their way here. They'll follow us to the country club."

"Alright then. Everything is in place. Enjoy the morning with everyone. Try to relax."

Bradley no sooner hung up with Cate when his phone rang. Caller ID told him it was Cassie. He hadn't talked to Cassie since she last visited more than five months before, but that wasn't unusual. Their routine had been to see each other every four to six months, depending on how lonely or depressed one of them had been. He hadn't thought to call her about Audrey, and he suddenly felt extremely guilty.

"Hey, Cassie. How are you?"

"I'm going to get right to the point."

Bradley chuckled. "Okay."

"I'm getting married."

Bradley paused. "Married?"

"Yeah."

"To who? I mean, that's great news! But, who are you marrying?"

"Tom."

"Tom, the lawyer?"

"Have you ever heard me talk about another Tom? Yes, Tom the lawyer."

"You just surprised me, that's all." Bradley said.

"Well, I surprised me, too. I . . . I'm . . .," Cassie stuttered. "I'm sorry."

"For what?"

"Well, I can't see you anymore."

Bradley laughed. "Of course, you can, just not in . . . that way. You're getting married. Wow! I'm so happy for you, Cassie."

"I just feel terrible. Like I'm abandoning you or something."

"Hey. We had a deal, right? No strings."

"I know, but . . ."

Bradley interrupted. "No buts. You deserve to be happy. Does he make you happy?"

Cassie's simple response implied a smile behind it. "Yes, he does."

"When's the wedding?"

"In fifteen minutes."

"Fifteen . . . ? I guess I'm not invited then," he chuckled.

"We're at city hall. Just the two of us. And Damien. He's our witness."

"I wish you all the happiness in the world."

Cassie paused. "I wanted to thank you. I was a mess for a long time. You helped me through it."

"That goes both ways, Cassie. I love you. Be happy and stay in touch."

"I love you, too, Bradley. Take care of yourself."

He couldn't help but smile as he hung up the phone. He took a moment to reflect on the paths he and Cassie had traveled. Different but similar, each path had led to depression, mistrust, and loneliness. But both had emerged stronger from their experiences—Cassie from a world of physical and verbal abuse, Bradley from his paralysis and deep grief. Things were changing. And this time, Bradley embraced the change.

He watched the clock closely. He had a plan. He knew getting Derek to the club would be a difficult sell. His only hope would be to guilt Derek into leaving work early. Derek had been working less on weekends because of the commitment he made to Cate, which meant his weekdays had gotten longer. With his remaining number of workdays dwindling, Derek would resist shortening any of them. Knowing that, Bradley called Derek's office at noon.

"Director Richards's office," Madelyn answered.

"It's Bradley. Is his schedule cleared?"

"Yes. Once his three o'clock is finished, he's got nothing until Monday," Madelyn replied.

"Thank you. You're coming tonight, right?"

"I wouldn't miss it. I'll be right behind you."

"Great. Can I talk to him?"

"I'll put you through."

Madelyn put Bradley on hold. Seconds later, Derek answered.

"Yeah, Bradley."

"I just wanted to make sure you remembered that we're meeting the girls at five."

"Ah, yeah. Can we move that back to six, maybe seven? I've got a lot of paperwork to wade through before the weekend."

"I knew you would do this. No, we can't push it back. Audrey needs to pick up Allison at seven o'clock. Besides, you have all next week to finish up paperwork."

"I don't know if I can . . ."

"You promised."

"Whose idea was this anyway? Five o'clock."

"Cate's. And if you mess this up, she won't be happy."

Derek sighed. "I know. Alright."

"Call me when you're ready to leave," Bradley said, then chuckled after he hung up.

He knew he should be happy for Derek, but a sense of sadness suddenly struck him. He thought back to when they first met. Bradley was only twelve years old when he and his parents, Lynn and Doug, took a weeklong cruise. Derek was an ambitious FBI agent who, on short notice, had been assigned to a case involving passengers on the cruise ship. Bradley and Derek's lives became entangled and had been ever since. And although Bradley knew they would remain close, the thought of not working together anymore unsettled him.

Bradley calculated it would take twenty-five minutes with traffic to get to the Arlington Country Club. He hadn't yet heard from Derek, and his watch showed 4:15. He shut down his computer and headed to Derek's office. Madelyn announced his arrival via intercom.

"Please tell him I'm not ready yet," Bradley heard Derek's voice.

Madelyn raised her brows and glanced at Bradley.

Rather than put Madelyn in an awkward position, Bradley rolled to Derek's door and opened it.

Derek looked up. "I said I'm not ready."

"Too bad. I'm saving you from yourself. And I'm covering my own ass. If we're late, we're both in trouble."

"Just give me a couple more minutes."

"Nope. Get up now, or I call Cate."

Derek glared at Bradley, sighed, then dropped his pen on the desk. He stood and swung his suit coat around his back as he slid his arms into the sleeves.

"You're a pain in the ass, you know that?"

"I do. But you'll thank me as soon as you see how happy your wife is to see you on time. I'll follow you to the club."

"Was it Cate's idea to have dinner at the club?"

"Yup. Who else?" Bradley answered as they left Derek's office.

It was 4:55 when they pulled into the Arlington's nearly full parking lot. Bradley found a handicap space up front as Derek circled the lot to find an open spot. While waiting, Bradley texted Cate they had arrived.

He got out of his truck and waited for Derek to make the long walk from the back of the lot. The clubhouse had previously been a stately mansion on a private plantation, but since its use as a country club, several additions had been constructed. White with burgundy trim and black shutters beside pane windows, the building stood at the edge of a championship golf course.

"This place is a bit pretentious, wouldn't you say?" Derek said to Bradley as they reached the entrance.

Bradley just chuckled.

The large foyer painted white with gold trim led to rooms on either side. Straight ahead with gold railings were two curved stairways—one on the left, the other on the right—meeting at the top on the second floor. A small, private vestibule sat between the staircases. A man dressed in a tuxedo stood just ahead of them at a podium under a massive crystal chandelier.

"May I help you?" he asked.

"Yes," Bradley said. "We have a reservation under the name, Richards."

"Ah, yes," the man replied. "If you'll follow me."

The man briskly walked to the large double doors on the right side of the foyer and waited for them to catch up to him before sliding the doors open.

"SURPRISE!" came the shout.

Derek jumped and nearly tripped over Bradley's wheelchair. Bradley reached out to keep him from falling, smiling at the expression on Derek's face.

His mouth open, Derek stood motionless and staring into the large ballroom filled with more than a hundred people holding their drinks high and staring back at him. Near the door hung a banner that read, "Happy Retirement, Derek." Bundles of blue and white balloons were evenly spaced from the front of the room back to the stage where a live band began to play, "For He's a Jolly Good Fellow." The crowd joined in the singing.

Derek still hadn't moved.

Bradley tapped his arm and said, "I think you're supposed to go inside the room."

Cate came forward and slinked her arm through Derek's. He finally closed his mouth and peered at her. Bradley thought he seemed less than thrilled.

"Smile, Derek. It'll only hurt for a minute," Cate said, one brow raised. She stood on her toes and kissed his cheek. Derek manufactured a smile.

Bradley watched from the doorway as Derek shook hands, gave hugs, and accepted congratulations from the guests. The band continued to play, and the room surged with camaraderie. He watched as a genuine smile replaced Derek's pasted one.

Bradley glanced to his right and spotted Audrey seated at a table with Holly and her husband, John. Holly was the first of the group Bradley met when on the cruise ship twenty-three years before. She had been taking photos of the sunset as they pulled out of port when twelve-year-old Bradley's wheelchair inadvertently ran over her foot. A dubious but opportune beginning. Audrey seemed to be enjoying their company.

" . . . and then Bradley rammed right into him," Bradley heard Holly say as he rolled up to the table.

"Please tell me you're not telling that story again," Bradley said as he stopped his chair next to Holly.

"Are you kidding? I'll be telling that story until there is no one left on this planet who hasn't heard it."

Holly smiled and jumped from her chair to hug Bradley. "God, I've missed you."

"Same here, darlin'. You look as stunning as ever." Once Holly sat back down, Bradley reached for John's hand and shook. "I know I've said this before, but you are an awfully lucky guy, John."

"It seems you're lucky yourself, Bradley," John said as he nodded his head toward Audrey.

With a wide smile, Bradley moved to Audrey's side and gave her a soft kiss. "Where's Allison?"

"She's already made some friends. They're out on the dance floor," she said, pointing to three young girls laughing and moving in circles. An amused look on her face, Audrey then glanced at Bradley.

"What?" Bradley asked.

"I didn't know you were a hero at such a young age," she replied.

"Don't listen to any of them," Bradley said. "They were all of drinking age at the time, so their memories can't be trusted," he laughed.

"Bradley. Are you ever going to accept the fact that you are an exceptional man?" Holly smiled.

"I'll tell you what. I'll accept the fact that I'm an exceptionally lucky man if that will make you happy."

"It's a start," Derek said as he walked up from behind Bradley. "You're definitely a lucky man that I don't knock your block off for not warning me about this thing."

"I'm more afraid of Cate than you."

"I guess I can't fault you there," Derek chuckled.

Holly got up and hugged Derek as she extended her congratulations. John shook Derek's hand and told him how envious he was about his retirement.

Derek leaned down and kissed Audrey on the cheek. "It's nice to see you again, Audrey. Make him pay for this, will you?"

Audrey laughed, "I promise, I will."

Then Derek moved to the next table to thank some colleagues for being there.

Bradley noticed Eric Sampson walk into the ballroom. When Cate had asked for Eric's contact information to invite him to the party, Bradley wasn't sure how to respond. He decided not to make a big deal about it, because Eric probably wouldn't show. But there he was. He wasn't sure how Derek would feel about Eric's presence.

Bradley then spotted Max and Alex standing by the bar and realized that Eric most likely meant to use the opportunity to question Alex about his abduction. Over the past five months, Derek had gone to great lengths to keep the two apart. Alex had been through enough, and since he didn't seem to have any helpful information, Derek thought the CIA should leave Alex alone.

Bradley was determined not to allow Eric access to Alex, so he excused himself from the table and made his way over to the bar where Alex was recounting his abduction story to some people Bradley didn't know. Knowing Alex was tired of talking about it, Bradley interrupted. "Alex, Max! It's great to see you two. Listen, I need to talk to you about something." Bradley politely acknowledged the couple Alex had been speaking with, then added, "In private."

"Sure, Uncle Bradley," Alex replied.

The disappointed couple nodded, then walked away.

"What's up?" Alex asked.

"Oh, nothing. I just thought you could use a break. You've told that story so often it's like you're reading it off a script," Bradley answered.

Alex grinned. "Thanks, I appreciate it."

"So do I," Max said. "I've heard it so often, I can recite it by heart."

The band began to play "The Time of My Life."

"Uh, oh!" Bradley said.

"What?" Max and Alex asked together.

"Just watch," Bradley said as he turned to face the dance floor.

Cate, Sheila, Lynn, and Holly hurriedly escorted Derek, David, Doug, and John onto the dance floor.

Sensing something was about to happen, the rest of the partygoers stepped aside.

"I've got to see what this is all about," Max said as he got closer to the dance floor.

Alex knelt beside Bradley and said, "I really do appreciate you looking out for me. I just want you to know that I'm doing okay. You don't need to worry about me."

"I know I don't need to. But that doesn't mean that I won't."

Alex stood and stretched his neck to watch the four couples spin in unison around the dance floor, singing as they twirled.

Bradley smiled. "It's not their first rodeo."

Alex shook his head in disbelief. "I've never seen them do this before. That is one heck of a maestro move."

As if all the air in the room had just evaporated, Bradley choked. He then forced a cough to regain his breath.

"Are you alright?" Alex asked.

"Yeah," Bradley replied. "What did you just say?"

"I said I've never seen them do this."

"No, the other thing."

"Oh!" Alex replied unconvincingly. "I said they're pretty good."

"No. You said it was one heck of a maestro move."

"Oh, yeah. It's . . . just . . . an expression I picked up somewhere." Alex seemed awkward with his response.

Bradley's head swirled.

He pictured Ali al-Haqani's handwriting on the back of the college paper contained in the classified report. Then he spoke the words in his head, 'You've told that story so often it's like you're reading it off a script'. Bradley realized then that Alex's story hadn't changed a word since the first time he told it. Nobody retells a story word for word unless they've . . . memorized it.

Questions continued to explode in his head. Why would you leave your cell phone at the train station when you knew you might need help? Unless you knew someone would be looking for it. Why leave a coded text? Why go into Afghanistan at all?

Bradley looked into Alex's eyes and saw a hint of panic. He was about to confront Alex with a barrage of questions when Eric Sampson made his way over to them.

"Hello, Alex. Remember me? My name is Eric Sampson." He held out his hand to shake. "I'm a friend of your Uncle Derek. We met in the hospital."

"Um . . . yes, Mr. Sampson," Alex replied.

"Could we go into the foyer for a moment?" Eric asked. "I have a couple of questions."

"No way, Eric," Bradley replied. "You shouldn't even be here."

"I was invited to be here," Eric smiled.

"It's alright, Uncle Bradley. I don't mind," Alex said.

"I'm coming with you," said Bradley.

"That's not necessary, Agent Whitman," Eric responded.

"I'm not asking."

Followed by Eric then Bradley, Alex went through the double doors to the semi-private vestibule.

Bradley said, "You don't need to talk to him, Alex."

Alex shifted his eyes from Eric to Bradley and back to Eric. It was subtle, but it didn't escape Bradley's notice. Suddenly it all fell into place.

Bradley placed his elbows on the wheelchair's arms. With his hands cupped, he rested his forehead on them. "No, no, no! Godammit!" He lifted his head and glared at Eric. "He's one of yours, isn't he?"

"What are you talking about?" Eric asked.

"Don't fuck with me!" Bradley yelled.

The gentleman in the tuxedo turned from his podium near the front door and glared.

"Easy. The whole damned room will hear you," Eric said.

Alex said, "I fucked up, Eric."

"Maestro move?" Bradley scowled at Eric.

Eric dipped his head and sighed. "Alright. Calm down, Bradley."

To Eric, Bradley railed, "Calm down? You piece of shit. This whole time? The whole goddamn time you knew exactly what happened to him and where he was. And you let his family twist in the wind."

"That's not completely accurate," Eric replied.

"How long?" Bradley glared at Alex. "How long have you worked for the . . . " and then in a clenched whisper " . . . CIA?"

"Since college," Alex answered. "They recruited me my junior year. I started training right after graduation."

"How? You were traveling. We got postcards from Argentina, Peru, fucking Africa." Bradley found it hard to control his anger.

Alex looked at Eric who nodded. "I wrote the postcards, others mailed them."

"And Derek. He knows?" Bradley asked.

"NO!" Alex yelled, thrusting his hands out in front of him as if to stop an onslaught. "He doesn't. And he can't."

"You're telling me that this was all a ruse? You insisting on seeing Alex in the hospital for what? A fake interrogation? Alex lying about the Indian mafia abducting him? All of it? Was there even a rescue or was that fake too?"

"That was real. But I had to cut off communication as soon as we had him in the air. Just in case someone slipped and said something. And Alex may have lied, but he was protecting his cover," Eric replied.

"Bullshit! Alex, how could you do this to Derek? To your family?"

Alex sheepishly shook his head.

"Who else knows?" Bradley asked.

"Just you." Eric replied.

"What about Max? He tracks your phone."

"He tracks one of my phones. It gives me another level of deniability if I can prove I wasn't in a place I shouldn't be. Sometimes someone else travels with the tracked phone," Alex said.

"So, you have people who mail your postcards and someone to travel with your phone." Bradley shook his head. "Jesus, Alex."

Alex replied, "Not always. Just sometimes. Unfortunately, I was abducted before I could pass the rest of my postcards to a handler. I could've saved my family the worry."

"This can't go any further than you, Bradley," Eric said with authority. "You can't breathe a word of this to anyone. Especially Derek."

"You're out of your mind. I can't keep this from him."

"For chrissake, you're going to be the new executive assistant director of criminal, cyber, and response. There are a lot of things you won't be able to tell Derek once he's retired."

Eric caught Bradley by surprise. "How did you know that? We haven't made the announcement yet."

Eric shrugged.

Alex smiled. "Really? Congratulations, Uncle Bradley. I didn't know. That's great!"

Bradley's angry reaction caused Alex to look away.

"Bradley?" Eric asked.

"He's not retired yet," Bradley said, then turned his chair and went back into the ballroom.

He sat just inside the double doors and scanned the room. The sound of music, conversations, laughter, and silverware clinking on china all lumped into one loud and chaotic heap. Chaos into cohesion, Bradley thought.

He moved to the bar and ordered a bourbon. When he turned back toward the party, he watched Eric enter the room without Alex. Eric searched the ballroom, then walked directly over to Derek and shook his hand. Bradley detected a smile on Derek's face.

Eric, you son of a bitch, he thought. Bradley wove through the people until he reached them. Eric shot him a warning stare.

"Bradley, where've you been? You missed the group dance," Derek said.

Concentrating on Eric, Bradley's knuckles turned white as he gripped his glass. He paused. Then he turned to Derek and said, "I . . . got called away for a few minutes. How did it go?"

"I was as clumsy as ever. But I don't think anyone was looking at me." Derek smiled as he nodded toward Cate standing a few feet away.

Cate caught Derek's smile and joined them. "I'm happy you could make it, Eric. Are you having a good time?"

"Yes, thank you, Cate. Bradley and I were just saying what a great party this is, weren't we?"

With a pasted smile, Bradley raised his glass and replied, "Absolutely."

"I'm ready to dance again, Derek." Cate snaked her arm through Derek's. "Audrey looks a little lonely over there, Bradley. I'm sure she would rather be dancing with you than chatting with Derek's colleagues."

Bradley glimpsed Audrey and Allison, Mara, Nick, Zayt, and Tasha amidst the crowded room. He watched them laugh in response to something Zayt said.

Behind them against the wall, stood Alex and Max. Alex fixed on Bradley with pleading eyes. And with that quick plea, Bradley knew he would keep Alex's secret.

Oh, hell. It's not like I haven't kept secrets from Derek before. Bradley nodded to Eric, a subtle acknowledgement that he would keep the man he considered to be his brother in the dark.

With a slight nod in return, the unspoken deal was sealed. "I'm afraid I have to go now," Eric told Derek and Cate. "I snuck out for a bit, but I have to get back to work. Congratulations, Derek."

"Thank you, Eric," Derek replied as they shook hands.

Bradley noted that Eric and Alex never looked at each other as Eric left the room. The kid's good! Bradley thought.

A sense of cohesion returned to Bradley as he watched Derek and Cate together. He thought of them spending their days devoted only to each other. He thought about Cassie having found love and the way that his cruise ship family continued to lift him in ways he never could have imagined. Zayt and Tasha had moved in together. But mostly, he felt gratitude for finding happiness with Audrey amidst the recent chaos. And his parents could not have been happier to consider Audrey as family and to have eight-year-old Allison to spoil.

With his new job on the horizon and a new relationship to explore, Bradley looked forward to an exciting and challenging future.

He tilted his head toward the ceiling and quietly whispered, "Thank you for everything, Laney. I love you. I'll take it from here."

He wheeled his chair over to Audrey and Allison, then reached a hand to each and said, "Ladies, I believe this is my dance."

Looking confused, eight-year-old Allison asked, "But, Bradley, how can you dance when you're in a wheelchair?"

A warm smile spread across Bradley's face as he took hold of her hand. He replied, "Allison, it's the best way to dance!"

photo by Paula Francis

ABOUT THE AUTHOR

You can't always plan where life will take you. That certainly proved true for Christine Noyes.

Without a clear vision of what her life should be, she went where she felt most comfortable: to the kitchen. At the age of eleven, she began her work life in her grandfather's restaurant. She spent the next several decades reinventing herself, becoming an accomplished chef, sales representative, entrepreneur, and eventually a writer and illustrator.

Chris never chose her professions. They chose her.

When not at her keyboard, she can be found in her kitchen: back to her roots and love of cooking.

COLOPHON

MVB Verdigris is a Garalde text family for the digital age. Inspired by work of sixteenth-century punchcutters Robert Granjon, Hendrik van den Keere, and Pierre Haultin, MVB Verdigris celebrates tradition but is not beholden to it. Created to deliver good typographic color, Mark van Bronkhorst's design meets the needs of today's designer using today's paper and press. A full-featured OpenType release with an added titling companion, it's optimized for the latest typesetting technologies, too.

Garalde: the word itself sounds antique and arcane to anyone who isn't fresh out of design school, but the sort of typeface it describes is actually quite familiar to all of us. Despite its age—born fairly early in printing's history—the style has fared well. Garaldes are the typefaces of choice for books and other long reading.